Last Boy

HANNAH GRAY

playlist

"I Had Some Help" by Post Malone, featuring Morgan Wallen

"Where the Wild Things Are" by Luke Combs

"Beautiful Things" by Benson Boone

"A Symptom of Being Human" by Shinedown

"Simple Man (Rock Version)" by Shinedown

"What Was I Made For?" by Billie Eilish

"The Freshman" by Verve Pipe

"Jaded" by Miley Cyrus

"No Matter What" By Papa Roach

"Nightmare" by Halsey

"Eastside" by Benny Blanco, Halsey, and Khalid

"Just Pretend" by Bad Omens

"WYD Now?" by Sadie Jean

"hate myself" by Tate McRae

"Say You Won't Let Go" by James Arthur

"Over" by Jimmy Eat World

prologue

POPPY

With my knees pulled to my chest, I sit on the worn steps to my house. I watch Walker walk out onto his front lawn with the ratty duffel bag slung over his shoulder. He moves like a zombie, never looking my way. Not even once. Unlike his older sister, Briar, who gives me a sad look and a pathetic, tiny wave.

Despite how Walker might feel right now, I'm not naive enough to believe that what is happening to them is completely my fault. It's not. But can I blame him for being upset with me right now? No, I suppose I can't. After all, my father sold his parents the drugs that ended their lives, leaving their children orphans. So, now, he and Briar have to move away and live with their estranged uncle.

But that wasn't the straw that broke the camel's back and made him not want to look at me. That is my fault. Because when it came time for me to tell the police that it was my father who had sold them the lethal drugs, I lied and said I knew nothing. I had to. It was the only way to keep my brother Jake safe.

Jake is my hero. And even as unfair as this is, as a kid with Down syndrome, he's already dealt with enough shit from society treating him differently.

If I had told the truth, my father would have gone to jail, forcing me and my brothers into foster care. If we're separated, that means I won't be around for Jake to be his advocate and help him the way he always helps me.

In Walker's mind, I betrayed him out of loyalty to my father. That can't be further from the truth. As far as I'm concerned, Ron Wilson could keel over and die tomorrow, and I'd be fine. But Jake deserves more. And us being split apart isn't going to get him that.

But protecting my oldest brother means losing Walker and Briar as friends. It doesn't matter that Van—my twin brother—Jake, and I consider Walker and Briar to be our best friends, practically family since we were young kids. We were all out roaming the neighborhood while other kids our age weren't allowed outside without supervision.

It didn't even matter that we had all vowed to always have each other's back. When something as catastrophic as this happens ... all that shit goes out the window because there's always someone to blame. And as far as Walker is concerned, that someone is me. I think he thought, between Van and me, I'd never go against him. I never planned to either.

He and his sister are being ripped away from all they've ever known, and now that they are going to live with their rich uncle, they will no longer be referred to as kids from the wrong side of the tracks. Will my brothers and I go on to carry that title? Of course we will. We'll never get out of this hellhole. But the five of us—the poor kids of Sunset Drive—are no longer each other's family.

And despite having my brothers still, I've never felt more alone in my entire life.

Briar is a year older than Walker. And she's the sweetest human being I have ever met. She thinks everything has a silver lining. Her whole life, she's brightened up this shithole street with just her smile and enchanting personality. She began taking homemade cards from door to door when she was eight, and then her cards became baked goods. But she's also fiercely protective of her loved ones. And she's got to be one of the smartest people I've ever known. Not just book smart, but street smart too.

Me? Well, I've been in love with Walker James since the first time he snuck in through my window at age ten because he couldn't sleep. He was too worried that some of the rough characters my father had at our house would hurt me. That was five years ago now, but it seems like ages ago because we've been through so much since that night.

His parents were drug addicts, but they would never let anyone hurt their children—unlike our dad, who only cares about himself and his drugs.

Though I can't see who's inside the car because of the deeply tinted windows, I watch as Walker opens the door to the SUV, and for a moment, he stands still, staring straight ahead, like he's rooted in place. I hold my breath.

Maybe, just maybe … he'll look my way. Just one last time, telling me that he still cares despite what he said last night when he told me I was dead to him.

Any hope I have is taken away from me when he climbs into the seat and slams the door shut behind him. My heart hurts more. I never thought that was possible.

When the car starts to drive away, I consider leaping up and chasing it. It isn't who I am as a person. I've never been one to wear my heart on my sleeve; instead, I keep it hidden from the world. When you keep your heart locked away, it's safe from injury. At least, that's what I've always thought.

Today … I'm learning that my heart can be hurt either way.

My foot bounces as the car pulls away from the curb and inches farther down Sunset Drive. Soon, he'll be gone forever. He will move on with his life with his rich uncle—whoever this mystery uncle is. He'll forget about me. So will Briar.

My feet push my body from the ground, and before my brain can tell me to stop, I'm running on the sidewalk behind the car. When I finally get next to the car, I reach out and slap the dark window, and the car stops abruptly.

Walker swings his door open, his eyes angry as he leaps from the backseat.

"What the hell are you doing, Poppy? Are you trying to get run over?" He stops a mere inch in front of my feet, glaring. "Huh?"

There are so many things I want to say to him. Briar too. After all, she's one of my best friends. But Walker? I'm in love with him. Desperately, wholly, unendingly … in love. And as cheesy as it sounds … he's my soulmate. I've known that since the second we locked eyes.

Because when you can look at someone and exchange words without ever opening your mouth … you know that your souls are intertwined.

"I'm sorry," I cry out. "I'm so sorry, Walker."

"I will never forgive you for what you did." His voice is low, and his blue eyes darken. He looks at me in a way he never has before. "You could have given my parents justice by telling the truth about your old man. Instead, you chose to stand with your own blood even though he's a murderer." He inhales, his nostrils flaring. "Go to hell, Poppy. You're dead to me."

He begins to turn away, but I grab his hand.

"Don't go! Please," I sob. "You don't understand! I had no—"

Spinning toward me, he grabs my wrist and squeezes. "You what? Had no choice?" he hisses. "I don't want to fucking hear it. Go. Go back to your fucking trailer. Amount to nothing, just like the man you stuck up for. You are not the girl I thought you were. And now, you're no one to me. You will always be *no one.*"

When he releases his hold with force, I stumble backward a few steps. And then he finishes me off with the worst words ever.

"I've protected you for most of my life. And now, I'm leaving. I'm leaving, and you're on your own." His eyes cut through me, chilling me to the bone because I know he's right. "And the only person you have to blame for the wrath you face without my protection … is yourself."

He turns away from me, climbing into the backseat of the car and slamming the door shut. My entire world spins as a sharp pain shoots through my chest, taking the breath out of me and making me squeak as I try to pull in a breath desperately.

I don't have to watch the car drive away as it takes Walker and Briar from me forever.

Instead, I crumple into a pile on the sidewalk, asking myself … *Am I going to die right here?*

WALKER
THREE YEARS LATER

I pull my helmet from my head and trudge into the locker room. Preparing myself to listen to my teammates critique me on how I'm not their old center.

"That was sloppy today, James," Link Sterns calls out, not surprising me in the least. "Hardy would be fucking pissed to see that shit on his ice."

Setting my helmet down, I sit on the bench, unlacing my skates. I shouldn't say a goddamn thing. I'm the new guy—the freshman who walked in here and was chosen to be the starting center.

I shouldn't, but I can't fucking help myself.

"Well, good thing it's not his ice anymore," I mutter quietly.

I respect our captain, Link, so much. But the dude is intense. Plain and simple. And he also needs to get over the fact that Cam Hardy is gone. In the pros. In Boston. Not Brooks. See ya later.

"What was that?" Link snaps.

"Nothing," I grumble. "Absolutely nothing."

I look up to meet Sterns's harsh glare, assaulting me. He huffs in and out, clearly mad.

"Sorry." I shrug. "But I wasn't the only one looking sloppy out there today, and you know it."

"Nah, your dormmates looked sloppy as fuck too. But guess what. You're the only one who's supposed to start this season who can't keep up."

Elias and Nixon look at each other and frown.

"How the hell did we get brought into this?" Elias pouts, shaking his head.

My dormmates are both freshmen and very good players, but are second string. Elias is a defenseman, and Nixon is a goalie.

"Your boy brought you into it," Link says, giving me an amused look.

Elias is guaranteed to get more playing time than Nixon will this season because the Wolves already have a goalie, Watson Gentry. And unless he gets injured this season, Nixon's chance of being pushed to goalie one isn't likely. Nixon is good, but he has a lot to learn. Gentry is an absolute beast in front of the net.

Cade Huff sits next to me on the bench and starts unlacing his skates. "Don't be worried about Sterns. He and Hardy have some sort of special relationship. Now that he is gone, Linky here is a Grumpy Gus." He grins before nodding his chin up toward Sterns. "It's okay, Linky Winky. I'm here for you through this troubling time, not having Cam Hardy to jerk off to."

"Fuck off." Link shakes his head. "Babying him isn't going to do this team any good. Kid needs to be ready for the opening game. If he's not, how's an L to start the season going to feel?"

"Don't be a Negative Nancy. He'll be ready," Cade chimes. "Won't you, James?"

"Oh, I'll be ready." I nod, keeping my eyes fixed on Sterns. "I'm always ready."

"Guess we'll see," Link says before shutting his locker and heading toward the showers.

Pulling my gear off, I head toward the shower farthest away from him and turn it on. I climb in once it gets hot enough to burn my skin off.

Cam. Hardy.

A name I've heard over. And over. And over. And motherfucking over again since I arrived at Brooks this summer to start training. One would think now that I earned a full scholarship to Brooks University—a D1 college in Georgia—and was chosen to be the Wolves starting center, my teammates would stop talking about their old center.

Fuck no, they haven't. In fact, I get the luxury of living in his shadow *constantly*. And I get it. I really do. He is a great player. A weapon on the ice and a huge asset to any team he's on. He left behind big shoes to fill. But the thing is, I don't want to be the next Cam Hardy. I'm Walker James. And just like Hardy, I'm going to the NHL too.

I've played hockey since I was six years old. Back then, it was an escape from my shitty reality. And the older I got, the more I was noticed. When I was fifteen, my parents died of a drug overdose, and I was dragged out of my shithole neighborhood to live with my loaded uncle, who was a bit of a celebrity star. Some would say it was probably the best thing to happen to me.

And those people … haven't met my uncle.

The only reason why his greedy ass brought me to live with him was so that he could get even more famous. One day hoping that I'd make it to the pros and acknowledge that he saved me. That shit couldn't be further from the truth because when I make it pro, I'm going to hide it from him until it becomes public knowledge.

Despite the fancy hockey clinics he got me into when I was a teenager, I've made it this far because of me. Because of the hunger to be more than the shitty place I came from. Not because of him or his money and connections.

Being here, at Brooks U, I feel like I've escaped him in a way—much more than my sister has. Last I talked to Briar, she was traveling to different countries with my uncle Beckett and his wife, Natasha. They've brainwashed her into thinking that's the lifestyle she should want. And now, the sister I grew up with is someone completely different.

But when I got away from him by coming to Brooks, I sort of just came back to my past. This place was far from my first choice. It's a great program with one of the nation's best college hockey coaches. But it's also close to my childhood home. The street I grew up on and where my parents died are just a few miles away.

It was easier to block out the memories when I was hours away. But having it a hop, skip, and jump away, passing by the same stores I did before I left … well, it's fucking with me.

But what's making it worse is wondering if *she* still lives on that street. Or worse, if she attends school here. At Brooks.

Poppy Wilson has haunted my dreams since the moment I left her crying on that sidewalk. That was over three years ago.

Now that I'm at Brooks though, I can almost *feel* her presence.

And that only makes me resent her more.

Poppy

"I love it." I grin, looking around my brother Jake's new apartment from a counter stool. "This place is amazing, J. I'm so happy for you."

"Thank you." He can't stop the smile from spreading over his face.

It's obvious how happy and excited he is right now. And my heart warms. "I like it too."

When good things happen to the best people, that's what makes my day. And my brother is one of the kindest, most deserving souls I know.

Everyone seems to have a different opinion about what someone with Down syndrome can or can't do. What their goals should be and what will never happen. My brother's mission has always been to prove to the world, as well as himself, that he could do anything he set his mind to. And after holding a steady job and getting his own place after always dreaming of it, it's safe to say he's doing just that.

"Maybe Van will come to see my new home," he says thoughtfully.

I don't have the heart to tell him Van won't be over because I instructed him not to. If Van showed up here, he'd ask Jake for money. And Jake is too nice and would give it to him. And the money would simply be for Van to get high. Again.

"Maybe. You never know." I shrug. "Even if he doesn't, you should be so happy. This is huge for you! You've talked about this for years!" I jump up from my stool. "I gotta run. Dance starts in a bit, and I still have to take the bus home to get my stuff." Throwing my arms around him, I give him a squeeze. "Proud of you, dude!"

As I release him and head toward the door, he calls from behind me, "Nice to see you. Next time ... bring Ryann."

I turn to find my brother wiggling his brows at me.

Shaking my head, I pull the door open. "Not going to happen, man. She's too wild for my brother!" I blow him a cheesy kiss. "Love ya! Don't throw any parties at your sweet new pad!"

"I will make no promises," he tosses back just before I close the door behind me.

Jake has the biggest crush on Ryann. Then again, every guy does. Bringing new people around him always makes me nervous. Not for them, but because I'm always afraid they will disrespect my brother in some way. Not every human being is like me and has been brought up around someone who has Down syndrome, and people can be just plain ignorant in understanding that my brother is not dumb and isn't a baby. So, when I hear people's voices change when they speak to him, it makes me go on the defense. With Ryann, she always treats him like he's a normal person.

Because he is. Only way cooler.

As I walk out of his apartment building, I pass one of his neighbors, a girl who seems to stop in and visit him quite a bit since he moved in.

"Hi, Poppy," she says, holding her hand up.

"Hi, Bonnie!" I wave but keep moving.

Bonnie is a sweetheart, but my Lord, she loves to chat. Most days, I stop and talk for as long as she wants to. Today, I'm too short on time.

Bonnie and my brother actually both started off in the same housing situation shortly after my father was taken to prison. Jake's plan was always to gain enough independence to live alone. But he wasn't ready for that until recently. So, a few years ago, he ended up living in a house with other men and women who, like him, had Down syndrome. Not everyone in the home had the ability or wanted to leave there, but Bonnie and my brother wanted help getting ready to live on their own. Now, someone from the home visits them once a day to make sure all is good, but aside from that, they have their freedom. And they both have jobs.

Jake started working as a janitor at a local health clinic a year ago and absolutely loves it. He gets to see people and be social, and most of all, he's a very hard worker.

Walking along until I reach the bus stop, I sit on the bench next to an older man and wait for the bus.

"Beautiful day, isn't it?" He smiles.

"It sure is," I say back.

And it really is. The sun is shining, and it's in the seventies, the absolute perfect temperature.

But now, I have to go to dance and listen to Jolene, my dance coach, fawn all over our newest dancer, Sutton Savage.

Her father is the senator of Tennessee. She left Juilliard to come here. *Juilliard.* My freaking dream school that I couldn't even bother to apply to because I knew it was so out of reach.

So, even though the girl hasn't personally done anything to me, she rubs me the wrong way.

And that right there is enough to cloud this gorgeous day.

"Gorgeous, Sutton," Jolene gushes, watching my new nemesis dance across the floor. "Way to extend those legs and point those feet." Looking around the room, Jolene gives us a less enthused look. "Good work today, everyone. Cool down a bit, and then you're free to go."

Sutton's a good dancer. It's true. I mean, for the love of God, she transferred here from Juilliard. She *should* be good. No, great.

Which she is. Even though I want to roll my eyes, even thinking it, she is extremely talented and has an amazing technique.

But for the months before she arrived here, the other dancers and I had been working hard. I was deemed Jolene's number one dancer from week one. And as a freshman, I felt pretty great. But then she showed up and dimmed my shine with all of her damn blinding, annoying sparkle.

What's worse is that we're stuck being roommates too. Thank God Ryann and Lana live there with us. There's no way I could live alone with Sutton without feeling the urge to put a laxative in her coffee.

A part of me wishes I hadn't been offered to skip the mandatory freshman year in a dorm because then I wouldn't have to go home to my rival every night of my life and watch her gloat that she's the top dog.

All right, fine. She doesn't really gloat, but I still find her infuriating. With her perfect bun when my hair always has random frizzy pieces everywhere. And her extremely straight legs, like it's just second nature to stretch them like that.

Sutton Savage is everything I'm not. Nor will I ever be. She comes from a rich family. And I'm sure she's always gotten everything she wanted. I grew up with charity dance lessons and hand-me-down ballet slippers. There were no fancy dance camps or incredible choreographers for me. But I've always made do with what I was given. But I still wonder, if I had more opportunities or if my upbringing were different than it was … would I be at Juilliard right now?

What irks me most about her is that she walked away from Juilliard to be here. At Brooks. While our school is Division 1, our dance program certainly isn't the best in the country—unlike our football and hockey programs.

She gave that up. Something that I've wanted my entire life, but knew I could never have. Not just because I don't have the proper training, but also because I've never wanted to leave Jake or Van behind. After all, we're all each other has.

Whenever my dancer friends bitch and complain that their parents push them to be perfect, I usually go along with it, too, saying that my parents have been the force behind my hunger to be the best. Truthfully, they have been part of my reasoning for trying so hard. But it's not because they've pushed me, but because I want more for my life than what I saw while growing up.

I finish my cooldown and head toward my bag in the corner of the room. As I start to pull my ballet slippers off, I look up to see Jolene and Sutton chatting. Jolene's entire face lights up as she hangs on every word that flows from Sutton's lips.

"Bitch, your ears are smoking," Ryann mutters, appearing next to me. "She's not a bad person, you know."

"Yeah, all right." I shove my shoes in my bag, slide my knockoff Birkenstocks onto my feet, and stand. "Sorry, Ry. Princesses just aren't my type of friends."

She tosses her head back and laughs. "She is so not a princess. In fact, I'm much more princess status than that chick." She steps closer, sighing. "She's way nicer than you think. And her life isn't perfect either."

"What? Did Daddy not buy her the latest sports car model?" I snort. "Please, Ryann. Let it go. Some people just aren't meant to be friends."

Spinning her body completely toward me, she sets her hands on my shoulders and drops her gaze. "I love you. You know this. Bitchiness and all, you're my friend. But come on, Pop. Don't assume the worst of someone just because it looks like their life is perfect." She tilts her head to the side. "Because *no one's* life is perfect, babe. I promise you that."

I shrug away from her. "For months, I've been here. And to be here, I had to physically *live* here. You know what that meant. It meant I had to scramble to find Jake somewhere to move into last spring to make sure he was situated before I could move from the trailer to here."

I exhale. "Don't get me wrong; it all worked out. I got away from Van and his ... business. And Jake ended up living at The Birches for four months, where they got him ready to be on his own. But either way, for a few weeks leading up to that ... it was pure chaos, and I was sick, thinking I had to physically leave my brother or risk Brooks pulling my scholarship if I didn't move in and start training this summer."

I nod toward Sutton, who is now getting her shoes on by the door. "She decides Juilliard—my *dream* school—isn't good enough. Strolls in here two freaking weeks into the school year when we've all been training since August, yet she's the one who Jolene is acting like is the lead girl." I shrug. "It's bullshit. And unlike the rest of y'all, I'm not kissing her left asscheek."

"Well, first of all, you should know by now that the only asscheek I'd kiss was if Chris Pratt walked in here right now. Because ... yum." Her expression softens. "And I get it. I get all of that. But she's here for a reason, Poppy. She didn't just walk away from there because she decided she was bored one day. Trust me on that."

"Yeah, okay," I huff out, annoyed that my closest friend drank the Kool-Aid and is now one of Sutton's minions. "Whatever you say."

"It is whatever I say, biotch." She winks. "And one more thing: don't be killing her in her sleep. I'm a ride-or-die sort of girl, but I don't want to help bury a body. That shit grosses me out, and I'd never survive jail." She pulls her lips to the side, widening her eyes. "Annnnd ... I like her. I think, someday, you will too."

With that, she practically skips away, calling, "I'll be in the car," over her shoulder.

Trudging behind her, I wave good-bye to Jolene and watch Sutton and Ryann pile into her car.

When Sutton sees me approaching, she shuts the door, and her eyes widen. "Do you want to sit in the front? I didn't mean to just jump in the front seat."

"Well, you're a princess. And princesses get what they want." I smirk before yanking the back door open and sliding into the car.

If I didn't have to be at work in an hour, I probably would have just walked my grouchy ass home. But like every day of my life, I have no idle time. And walking and catching a bus everywhere is time-consuming as hell.

I know that my attitude toward Sutton isn't warranted. I understand that I'm acting like a toddler whose mother just brought home a new baby who's sucking the attention away from everyone else. But Sutton Savage could have any opportunity she wants in life. Brooks is my only opportunity. I have to prove to the dance world that I'm good enough to work for a company on Broadway.

I might be acting like a mean girl, but she's in my way.

WALKER

"I stand by what I said. Coach is losing his mind," Link huffs out as we walk out of the dance studio. "We're getting ready for the opening game. I mean, what the fuck happens if one of us gets injured, doing this shit?"

At the beginning of the week, we learned that we would be participating in a fundraiser. The team is always up for helping to support a good cause, but this time is a bit different.

We literally have to dance with ballerinas at some fancy event. Aside from Cade, we're all pretty irritated with the whole ordeal. Balancing our class load and grueling hockey schedule is already a lot. Add in dance practice? I'm tired from just thinking about it.

"Check it out," Elias says, nodding his head toward the side of the building. "I sense all sorts of sexy tension going on between those two."

Following his gaze, I see one of our wingers, Hunter Thompson, in a heated conversation with one of the ballerinas, Sutton Savage. Usually, I'm not good with names, but it's not every day that you meet the senator of Tennessee's daughter.

Sutton's beautiful and sassy. And I sense some sort of history between Thompson and her. No one was as pissed off as him when we all learned about this fundraiser pairing. And now, I see why when I can feel the tension between him and his partner from twenty feet away.

My dance partner's name is Lana. She seems nice enough. And she's absolutely gorgeous too. But ballerinas are a sore subject for me. To be honest, even the sight of ballet slippers pisses me off and reminds me of *her*. All Poppy did growing up was dance down every sidewalk and into every room.

"You're awfully quiet, James," Cade says, bumping his fist into my shoulder. "Don't tell me you're a salty bitch over this arrangement too. I mean, fuck, you guys … it's dancers!"

Cade's the type of guy who takes nothing seriously at all. Everything is a joke, and I'm not sure if he can stand silence or anything deep. He seems to mask everything with drinking, and there's even been some chatter that he also likes to dabble in other things despite the fact that he's already been to rehab. But out of all the guys on the team, he's one of my favorites because he's got a heart of gold.

"I'm good," I mutter, not wanting to dive into the very fact that I fucking hate anything to do with dance and ballet.

"Are you though?" Nixon asks, pulling his hat down on his head further, making a few brown pieces curl from under it. "You seem grumpier than normal."

"Wanna talk about it?" Cade pops into the conversation … yet again. "Because I'm here. And I'm a good listener, just FYI. I'm not afraid to light a candle or put on a chick flick with you either. I'm confident in my manhood enough for that type of shit." He nods toward Watson Gentry. "Gentry's mama keeps our closet stocked with candles. I'll light one up any day, buddy."

"The kid is here to take Hardy's spot. He probably just doesn't want to risk getting an injury before his first season as a Wolf begins, you clowns," Link says. "I know I don't want to get hurt right now."

Sterns already has a position waiting for him in the pros once he graduates. So, I'm sure he doesn't want to risk getting hurt from doing something like dancing right now. But I'm also betting his girlfriend isn't too happy with this whole dance-partner arrangement—probably because she's not a ballerina, but a space nerd or something.

"Well, aren't you a ray of sunshine?" Cade grins at him before pinching Link's nipples. "Turn that frown upside down!"

Link eventually fights a chuckle but rubs his chest where Cade pinched him. "Dick," he mutters.

As we pile into our trucks, I remind myself of the one good thing that happened today. When I first learned about this fundraiser, I was scared as fuck that there was a chance Poppy was attending Brooks and was a ballerina. I'm not ready to see her yet. I never want to see her again. Now that I know she's not here, I can breathe easier. Because if that girl did attend Brooks, there's no way she wouldn't be a dancer here.

But annoyingly enough, even though I'm relieved she isn't here, I also can't help but wonder … *Where the fuck is she?*

POPPY

Bailing Van out of jail wasn't on the list of things I planned to do today. Yet here I am, waiting outside of the jail for his dumbass to walk out of the doors.

Every time this happens, I lose all the money I've saved from working at the coffee shop. And that makes me only resent my brother more each time. But he's my family. And my brothers and I need to always have each other's back.

One good thing about the timing of his arrest is that it got me out of the mandatory pair-up between the hockey players and dancers chosen to participate in the fundraiser. Because I couldn't be at today's meeting, I'll get out of the fundraiser altogether, which works out well for me because there's a certain someone that I'd like to stay hidden from.

Walker James. My childhood best friend and first love. Someone I never really thought I'd see again because I never imagined he'd come to Brooks for college. But a few months ago, the buzz began, and I knew that I'd have to deal with sharing a campus with someone who'd exited my life and never looked back.

Walker is now the big hotshot center for the Wolves. Everywhere I go, I hear people talking about him. My teammates chat about how hot he is. And now, he will be paired with one of my fellow dancers, and I'll have to listen to that too.

I hear the doors open, and out struts Van. Every time I see him, he gets a little skinnier, his skin looks worse, and his eyes grow darker and more sunken into his head. He loses that sparkle he always had, and that charming grin all the girls used to gush over at school while we were growing up is nowhere to be seen.

I never thought he'd follow in Ron's footsteps and deal drugs, but I guess I was wrong.

Growing up, he loved anything to do with cooking. He was kind, and people loved him.

In fact, he and Walker could get away with being the poor kids in the ratty clothes. Me? I didn't fare out as well. Girls thought I was a bitch. And the guys weren't all that nice either. That was, until Walker deemed me untouchable. Threatening anyone who dared to breathe a mean word about me. But people didn't have to say what they were thinking. When their noses turned up or they looked me up and down like I was a piece of trash, that was just as bad.

But Walker tried to protect me—really, really tried. When he left, Van stepped in and made sure the bullying was kept to a minimum. But by age sixteen, he was getting high more than he was attending school. And shortly after, he dropped out. That left Jake and me both wide open to the ugliness of the world—the ugliness that makes people say and do things to hurt people like us.

I push myself from the bench and walk toward Van. I'm fuming right now. After watching our father throw his entire life away for drugs, I thought all of us kids would know better than to go down that road. Now, here Van is, addicted to heroin, dealing drugs from our childhood home, and getting arrested for stealing. Guess I was wrong because he clearly didn't learn from our father's mistakes.

I've never been so disappointed in someone my entire life.

Okay, maybe that's not true. But to be fair, my list of people who have disappointed me is abnormally long.

"Say what you need to say and get it over with," Van grumbles before lighting a cigarette. "I don't have all day."

"Oh. Okay." I snort out an annoyed laugh. "*You* don't have all day?" I shake my head. "Why, Van? Do you have customers showing up?"

Quickly looking around, he shoots me a glare. "Shut up. You can't just say that type of shit outside of a police station, you know. Are you trying to get me locked up?"

"Maybe." I shrug my shoulders. "If that'll get you clean, maybe I should let your ass sit in there next time."

"Whatever," he utters, taking a drag on his cigarette and blowing the thick white smoke out through his nose slowly. "You think you're so much better than me just because you started college. Well, guess what. You forget that you came from that trailer, Poppy. You can't erase where you're from. The place that made you."

He takes another long puff from the cigarette, narrowing his eyes at me. Once he starts to walk toward the bus stop, I follow close behind.

"It's not about where we came from, asshole. It's about where we end up."

He looks at me before laughing. "Jesus Christ. Who are you, and where's my sister? When you find her, tell her she's welcome to come visit me. That is, if she's not too good for Sunset Drive these days."

"Don't mock me just because I'm not doing and dealing drugs while ruining people's lives out of a mold-infested trailer," I hiss.

And the words that come from my mouth next are ones I know I'll regret for the rest of my life. But I can't stop them because I'm so tired of being everybody's lifesaver and giving pieces of myself for the sake of everyone else.

"You're a loser, Van. Just like Ron," I say through gritted teeth. "Don't call me next time to bail you out. Rot your ass behind bars, just like he did. I don't care anymore. I'm done with you."

There's no mistaking the shock, followed by the hurt on his face. But within seconds, his eyes grow angry, and I know he will spew some words in the hope that I'll feel bad about what I said. Because something I've learned about Van, the drug addict … he's a master manipulator.

The opposite of Van was my brother and friend, who was clean and sober.

Tired and sick of his shit, I don't wait around for him to answer.

I simply walk away, starting my long walk back to campus and knowing that every step will be filled with regret for the words I said.

Because you can't take words back once you put them into the universe. A lesson I learned years ago from none other than Walker James.

3

POPPY

"Yeah, like that, except faster. Also, for the love of all things, stop thrusting your freaking hips," I say, pointing to Cade. "We're not making a porno here."

"Or are we?" he throws back, moving his eyebrows up and down. "Because if you're into it, we totally can. It wouldn't be my first rodeo." He makes some insanely weird face, like he's trying to be sexy, but it's just … not. "Ballerina meets hockey player. And he shows her his … *huge* stick."

I've never felt the urge to laugh while also being disgusted at the same time. "Dude … no." I shake my head. "Never going to happen. Never. Ever." I drive my finger into his chest. "Ever."

He pretends to pout, but I know he's just joking. This is our second time practicing in two days, and I'm already starting to see how little he takes seriously. But it could have been worse. I could have been paired with someone else.

Someone like the traitorous asshole Walker James.

But instead, my roommate Lana is working with him. Which actually sucks equally as much.

The bliss of not having to partake in the fundraiser originally was quickly demolished a few days ago when Jolene called me. Apparently, Cade Huff's partner injured herself, and now, I'm stuck working with debatably the biggest man-whore of puck boys, who also has the mind of a freaking child. Cade spends ninety-nine percent of our practice cracking jokes. Which is great and all, but I need him to learn this routine in the next few weeks.

On the bright side, he's a pretty good dancer. But no way am I telling him that. If I did, his head wouldn't even fit through the door to get in and out of the studio.

"From that move, we're going to go to this." I show him the next move, and once I'm done, I glance at him, nodding to the side. "Ready?"

"Babe, I was born ready." He winks, and I restart the music.

Together, we run through the first thirty seconds of our routine, which is all I've choreographed so far. Going into this yesterday, I had no idea what sort of music we should dance to. But because I got thrown into dancing with Cade a week after practice began, Jolene was kind enough to let me choose our music—unlike the other couples, whom she chose for. And after spending an hour and a half with the infamous playboy, I realized it had to be something fun and carefree. And when I was walking home from work last night, listening to music, "What a Night" by Flo Rida came on, and I knew I had found our song.

Cade has this charismatic energy about him that you can't really help but smile about. He might flirt or joke about sex, but he's harmless. And considering how dark and dramatic my life has been lately, it's sort of nice to spend time with someone who's all … light and shiny.

"I think that's good for today," I tell him. Walking toward my bag, I grab a water from it and take a drink. "I'll text you with some possible times to get together again and see what works for both of our schedules."

Pulling his sneakers on, he nods. "Sounds good, Princess Poppy." He stands. "Hey, need a ride?"

My cheeks heat. When he saw me walking into the parking lot yesterday, he asked me if I didn't have a car. Then, he offered me a ride home yesterday and picked me up today. I don't want to be his charity case.

"That's okay." I wave my hand toward him. "I don't mind walking."

He rubs his chin with his fingers for a moment before shaking his head. "Nah, wrong answer. No one likes walking that much." He nods his head toward the door. "Let's go."

Giving him a shy smile, I trudge behind him as we head for the door. But before I get there, my eyes find those of a man who is staring at me through the studio window. My heart lurches into my throat, and I feel like someone just sucker-punched me in the chest.

Walker freaking James.

I might have been aware he was on campus, but nothing could have prepared me for this moment—seeing him for the first time in over three years.

And, yeah ... he's grown up—a lot.

WALKER

If there's background noise, I can't hear it. Hell, if the room was filled with smoke and someone yelled fire ... I wouldn't know it. Because the second I walked into this hallway and saw her dancing through the window, the entire world melted away. And all that's left is me and the girl I haven't seen in over three years.

The girl I'm supposed to hate.

But she's not a girl anymore. She's a fucking woman. A beautiful, sexy, enchanting woman. Who is still scrawny but has filled out in the right places enough to make me notice. I can't tear my eyes from her even though I know I need to. Especially when her eyes find mine, snapping me back to reality. And then it hits me.

She's dancing with Cade Huff.

Moments ago, his hands were on her body. And now, after freezing for a second, she's following behind him, headed right toward me. As much as I like Huff, I want to fucking murder him right now for touching her. Because she's not his to touch.

Sadly, she isn't mine either.

"Walker?" Lana's voice is muffled, though I know it's just my brain making it that way.

I know I should look at her and acknowledge that I heard her. But as Poppy and Cade walk through the door, mere feet from me, I can only look at Poppy. Her green eyes do everything to avoid looking up at me, which is probably for the best because if she looked right at me, I might stop breathing.

"Sup, James?" Cade grins. "Got me a new dance partner."

He slings his arm around Poppy's neck, and I grind my back teeth together, swallowing hard. My entire body fills with rage, but I know I can't act on it. How would Cade know how fucking crazy that girl makes me?

"Sweet," I mutter, glaring down at Poppy, who looks straight ahead, avoiding eye contact with me at all costs.

"Hell yeah, it is," Cade says slyly before bumping my shoulder with his fist. "Later, my man."

As they walk outside, I watch them go to Huff's truck and get into it. I feel sick, imagining him taking her home.

Fucking A. This day blows.

"Are you going to stare at my roommate all day, or can we rehearse?" Lana snaps. "Seriously, Walker, what is your deal?"

When Cade's truck pulls out of the parking spot and drives away, I stand there, completely numb, for a few moments before finally turning back to Lana.

"Yeah. Let's, uh … let's go." I inhale. "Sorry about that."

As she walks into the studio, I follow close behind. She bends down, setting her things on the floor. Since we started rehearsing together, her every move has been intentional. She'll lean forward, giving me a perfect shot of cleavage, or move her ass against my crotch, or rub her tits against me every chance she gets. And I feel bad because I don't want any of it.

Lana is a gorgeous, attractive woman. And, yeah, I considered hooking up with her because she seems to want it so bad, and sometimes, I like to take my mind off the past by burying my cock in an eager chick. But now that I've seen Poppy, all thoughts of that are out the fucking window.

Tightening her ponytail, she gets positioned in the center of the floor. "You didn't answer my question." She raises an eyebrow. "What's your deal?" She looks down. "Do you have a history with her? With … Poppy?"

"No," is all I offer. Walking behind her, I plant my hands on her hips to begin practice. "Let's just get this over with."

"Fine," she huffs out, annoyed as hell.

I won't be worth a fuck this practice. Because now, the only thing on my mind is that dirty-blonde, green-eyed beauty with lost eyes and lips that curved down in a pouty frown.

Oh, and I'm feeling sick over Cade Huff and her being together right now.

POPPY

I stare out the window on the short ride home from dance practice with Cade. I knew I'd eventually run into Walker. I just didn't think it would be today. Then again, nothing could have ever prepared me for that moment.

He looked at me like he had seen a ghost, and I knew right away that he had no idea I was here, attending college at Brooks.

I couldn't bear to look his way when Cade and I walked by him. I was afraid of what would happen if I looked at him for too long. If I did, I'd probably be at his feet, begging him for forgiveness, even though I don't think I'm the only one who has fucked up.

He'd left. He chose to break the pact that we had made. Briar had only followed his lead because he called the shots.

In my eyes, he's just as much of a traitor as I am.

There has never been a day when I haven't thought about Walker James. That I haven't gone to bed, wearing his hoodie, closed my eyes, and pretended he was holding me. For so many years, he was my knight in shining armor. And then … he was gone.

Seeing him today felt like seeing a stranger. Because the last words we'd spoken made me realize that maybe I didn't know him as well as I'd thought.

No one is ever really who they say, I suppose.

"You're awfully quiet over there, Princess Poppy," Cade drawls from the driver's side of his truck. "I hope none of my jokes offended you. I was just playin' around."

I give him a small smile. "No, they didn't. I'm just tired, I guess."

Pulling in front of my house, he shifts the truck in park. "Is something going on between you and James?" He pauses. "He was staring at you like he might pass out. And then he looked at me like he wanted to put me through a window. Pretty sure that fucker's eyes were black. And normally, he's got some pretty fucking blue eyes." When he sees the look of surprise on my face, he shrugs. "What? Dudes can notice these things too, you know."

Wringing my hands together, I shift nervously in my seat. "No, definitely not." I shake my head. "I have no idea what you saw, but you're clearly delusional."

He gives me a suspicious look, but reaches over and pats my hand. "If you say so, lady. But just FYI, that dude is a fucking scrapper. There's been talk that even though he's been living with his rich uncle for the past few years, he was basically raised in an abandoned junkyard and is a stone-cold killer. I don't really want to be on his bad side." Pulling his hand back, he spins his hat backward. "And that's saying something because everyone knows I'm a complete fucking psychopath who loves fighting on the ice. And even I don't want none of the snacks he's packin' in his lunch box."

I snort at his weird analogy. I really can never predict what will come out of Cade Huff's mouth. But I'm not surprised by any of what he's saying. Walker is one of those guys who moves like he's ready to attack. My brothers weren't fighters, but Van always seemed to run his mouth to the wrong people and get into bad situations. Lucky for him, he had Walker James always willing and ready to back him up.

"Nothing is going on between me and Walker," I assure him before pushing the door open. "See ya next time. Stay out of trouble."

"I make no promises!" He cackles like a little kid who just got away with something. "Have a nice night, Princess Poppy."

Shutting the door, I wave good-bye as he pulls out of the driveway before heading toward the front door. When I walk inside, Sutton and Ryann are painting their nails at the counter, giggling like they are sixteen-year-olds at a slumber party. I mean, I've never been to a slumber party, but I imagine that's how it goes down.

"Hey, Pop," Ryann says, blowing on her nails. "Come. Sit. Let me make those stubby little nails of yours prettier."

Glancing down at my nails, I scowl. "What's wrong with my nails?"

She scrunches her nose up. "Well, I mean … you chew them so much that I'm surprised you even have any fingers left." Holding up a few bottles of polish, she widens her eyes and gives me a big smile. "If I put some paint on those bad boys, you will have no choice but to not bite them. Right?"

My eyes shift to Sutton as she twists the top onto the nail polish she chose. And when she glances up at me, she chews her bottom lip before standing. "I have some homework to do, Ry. Thanks for letting me use your nail stuff."

"Anytime," Ryann mutters, her eyes staying fixed on me. And once Sutton leaves the room, she gives me a pointed look. "Girl, do you always have to scare everyone out of the room every time you enter it? I mean, good gawd."

Happily taking the seat next to her, I hold my hand out now that Sutton is gone. "Just an effect I have." I shrug. "You're welcome. Now, you don't have to listen to her talk."

"I *like* listening to her talk." She shakes her head before twisting the cap off the polish and bringing it to my nail. "Good grief, girl. Why do you insist on being such a bitch?"

Ignoring the name-calling because this is just how Ryann and I talk to each other, I look down at the nail once she's swept the brush over it. "Black?" I scoff. "Am I emo now?"

Glancing up at me, she narrows her eyes. "Black … just like your heart."

I scowl at her, but don't protest for another color because to be honest, I like the black. It's edgy and dark, and it goes with everything. Not like I have a huge selection of clothing to choose from, but still.

"You act like you aren't the same way," I say, pressing my lips together. "I mean, just look at you with your poor dance partner, Watson Gentry— aka Brooks University's very own golden retriever. I have seen you guys during practice. He's so sweet to you, and you are straight-up rotten to that dude for no good reason." I tsk her, rolling my eyes. "But now, here you are, all pissy with me for not being shoved up Sutton Savage's asshole—which,

I'm sure, smells like flowers. However, I hate to break it to you, with you already shoulders deep there, it's too crowded!"

She doesn't stop painting my nails. And she doesn't look up at me either. She simply sighs. "You know that men are a trigger for me, Poppy. He might be known as the golden retriever, but to me, he's just the dude trying to get in my pants." She bobs her head from side to side like she's having an internal argument with herself. "Well, guess what. I'm not falling for it."

"You're protecting yourself," I say, thinking out loud. "From getting hurt by him."

"Someone has to," she utters. "Men are always sweet when they want something. But once they get it? Pfft ... see you later, nice guy. Hello, dickwad."

Ryann is the kindest, most down-to-earth girl I've ever met. She's always up for a fun time. But when it comes to men and dating, she becomes a monster. She's mean and downright terrifying to those who try to pursue her.

She's how I am with girls like Sutton Savage.

"Well, maybe I'm protecting myself too," I toss back. "Ever think about that?"

Her eyes move to mine, and she snorts. "From five-foot ... maybe three, Sutton Savage? Who might possibly weigh one hundred ten pounds soaking wet?" She laughs. "You're insane. I love you. But you're a nut."

"I mean, she did take my number one spot on the dance team. But ... yeah, no biggie, right?" I roll my eyes. "Don't worry about me. Make way for the princess of Tennessee."

"Dude, shut up. Jolene never even said that." She rolls her eyes.

"She didn't have to," I sass back.

"You get crazier by the second." Closing the polish, she looks proudly at her work. "And now, you have bitchin' nails to go with your bitchy self!"

I think I've always felt more comfortable with Ryann than the other girls in the house because it's so easy to talk to her. I guess that's because I know she's faced her own hardships in life, and maybe that somehow connects us. She works as a stripper and sends money to her little sister back in Canada because her own mother isn't the best parent. The moment Ryann told me that, I felt a deep connection to her. I felt the pain in her words as she talked about her sister and her mother. And weeks ago, we learned that we were going to be dancing in Brooks' annual *Nutcracker* show together. And I'm so glad it's her and not Sutton Savage. *Praise the Lord.*

Maybe it isn't fair to judge Sutton when I don't know her, but my brain has this picture painted of who she is, and it's hard to overlook that.

"Oh, hey," she says, sliding her polish back into the bag it came from. "How's working with Cade Huff? Is he, like, totally cray-cray? Everyone says he's the hot dude with some screws loose. Similar to the infamous Brody

O'Brien. Only Huff has apparently done time in rehab for drugs." She widens her eyes. "How insane is that?"

I frown. I had no idea he had a history of addiction. I'm glad he went to rehab though. And more than anything, I hope he can stay on the straight and narrow. He deserves that. He's a good person—that much I can tell.

"It's good," I answer softly. "He goofs off a lot of the time. I had no idea he had been to rehab, but I guess I shouldn't be surprised because I've heard he parties a lot."

"But, like, do you find him hot?" She pauses, shaking her head. "What am I saying? Obviously, you find him hot. Look at the guy. Yum. But, you know, do you guys have chemistry?"

I stare at her before scrunching my nose up. "No! Ew. Yes, he's attractive. But I don't think of him like that." I give her a curious look. "Do you and Watson Gentry have chemistry? Because last I saw him, he's also pretty freaking hot."

"No," she says quickly. "I mean, not really. He's … we're just dancing together! That's it."

Ryann isn't the type of person who gets flustered that often. And right now, she's flustered as hell.

Tapping my now-dry nails on the counter, I grin. "Ryann has a cruuushhh."

"I do not!" she belts out. "Don't ever say that again. Trust me, he's basically obsessed with me. I don't need him getting the wrong idea."

"Yeah, yeah." I nod slowly. "Whatever you say."

"Why don't you ask Lana about her partner when she gets back? She's literally in love with the dude after a week and a half of practicing together." She sighs. "That's Lana though. God love her, but the girl falls hard and fast. According to her, she's close to hooking up with him. She said she can *sense* he's getting more into her." She giggles. "She is pretty charming—I'll give her that."

Lana isn't just incredibly boy crazy. She is also recently single and is wasting no time jumping back into the dating … or sleeping-around pool. Not just *in* the pool, but in the deep end. I knew the moment I found out that she and Walker were paired up, she would be crushing on him—hard. But it still sucks to hear.

Standing up, I inhale and tell myself to fix my face. I don't want Ryann or anyone else to suspect that there's history between Walker and me by showing I'm a jealous bitch. Even though it's actually painful to attempt to smile and stop glowering.

"Good for her," I say, trying to sound like I don't care. "Hey, I have to go get ready for work." I hold my hands up, wiggling them. "Thanks for the new nails."

"Don't you dare chew them! It's black, so it'll look like you have bugs in your teeth!" she hollers behind me as I head toward my room.

"Yeah, okay! Maybe bugs will keep Cade Huff from hitting on me!" I laugh—or pretend to.

Going into my room, I close the door behind me and lean against it.

Lana and Walker. The thought of the two of them together ... right now ... it's enough to drive me insane. And make me incredibly grouchy. Or ... grouchier than normal.

Lana is beautiful. And when she wants something or someone ... she gets it. Walker is a catch by anyone's standards. Of course they are going to hook up. And I have no right to care either. He's practically a stranger to me now.

I swallow back the lump of emotion, knowing that I don't cry. I haven't in years, and I'm not going to start now just because I'm envious of Lana working with Walker.

Seeing someone who used to be such a big part of my life for so long has derailed everything. And the way my heart is aching, I feel like I'm right back on that sidewalk, watching him leave me. Feeling the same pain again.

I can't avoid him forever, especially with this fundraiser coming up. I just hope that I can avoid seeing him for a little while. Because when we run into each other ... that's bound to mean trouble.

POPPY

"I cannot believe I let you talk me into this," I complain to my brother as we get situated in our seats. "You do realize this is the first hockey game I've been to in over three years, right?"

Jake looks at me, a mischievous grin on his face. "You mean, since Walker moved away." He takes a long sip from his orange soda. "Walker James is the Wolves new center. I heard it on the radio."

I rear my head back. "So, that's why you begged me to bring you here?" I shake my head in disbelief. "Well played, traitor! You know he'll think we're here just for him, right?"

"I am here for him," he says thoughtfully. "He's still my best friend."

Jake adored Walker from the day they met. And I loved how well Walker always treated my brother. School wasn't always easy. Kids were cruel. A lot of people saw Jake as an easy target despite how incredibly smart he was. Walker didn't stand for that. And before the school ever had to step in, Walker took care of it. However, one thing about Jake is that he fixates on certain things. And when Briar and Walker left, he fixated on the fact that they were gone. It took months for him to think about anything else. And now that he's aware Walker is back, I'm afraid he'll get his hopes up for nothing.

After all, the new Walker James spent the last three years living with his rich uncle, probably having the nicest, most expensive things at his fingertips. He isn't the same boy we knew. The one with hunger pains in his stomach or worn-out secondhand clothes, like the rest of us. And I don't want to see my brother getting hurt because of it.

"You know, Bonnie could have come with us." I nudge him. "Don't think I haven't noticed that you seem a little sweet on her."

His cheeks redden, and he smiles so hard that his nose scrunches up. "She is very pretty."

His neighbor seems to stop in and check on him … a lot. And every time I'm around when she does, he can't wipe the grin off of his face.

All of a sudden, Jake stands in his seat and starts waving both hands like a maniac. And when I look down, there's Walker, skating toward us. He holds his stick up with one hand and waves with the other. As much as I want to be pissed at my brother for being so nice, I can't push my negative attitude about the situation onto him. Jake believes in the magic in life and the good inside of people.

Me? I think that's all a bunch of bullshit most days.

I just keep my eyes on my brother, who is living his best life right now. But once he sits down again, still grinning, I suddenly feel Walker's stare. I don't look at him. I'm afraid to.

Maybe the boy that I fell in love with as a kid is still in there somewhere. But I'm not willing to risk finding out.

WALKER

The ice has always been the one place I can count on for peace. Right now, peace is the furthest thing I feel. We're about to win this game, and that's great and all, but I know I didn't fully bring my A game tonight. And that's all because of the pretty distraction in the stands.

The distraction is named Poppy, and she makes me nervous as fuck.

I'm happy as hell that Jake is here. And I'm even happier that he waved to me and smiled. For years, I've worried about how his life ended up. Seeing him tonight shows me that he's more than okay. And I think a lot of that is thanks to the girl beside him. His sister is the most protective person of him ever to live.

While I'm glad they are here, having her here is distracting as hell. I can't focus on anything besides the fact that she's in the stands, watching my every move. And I feel her eyes despite her refusal to look at me when I waved to her brother. But now, if I looked their way, her gaze would be on me.

She's so fucking beautiful. Even with her resting bitch face, as she always called it, she makes it hard for me to take a breath.

I've scored a goal tonight and had a few assists. But I was sloppy, and I know it. Link Sterns is champing at the bit to tell me again that I'm no Cam Hardy. Maybe if I score in the last thirty-six seconds of this game, it'll make him a little less pissed. Maybe.

I push it out of my brain that the girl I'm supposed to hate and be completely resistant to is here. I don't think about the fact that all I want to do when the clock runs out is run up there and ask her how she's been and hug her. But that isn't going to fix anything. Too much shit has happened between us. She turned her back on me and didn't do the right thing, and I abandoned her.

I still get fucking sick when I imagine the horrors she could have gone through when I wasn't there to protect her.

Nothing will ever be the same, and I need to let her go. From my brain and my life. So, instead, I get the puck, and I fucking make it my mission to get it in the other team's goal. Out of my peripheral vision, I see a maroon jersey headed toward me. But before he can check his body into mine, I pull my stick back and slap the puck as hard as I can toward their goal.

Everything else turns to background noise as I watch the goalie attempt to stop it—a solid attempt, but still a fail for him and a victory for me.

We won the game, and I made a goal with seconds left on the clock. And the first person I look at ... is her.

And just like before, she won't fucking look at me. And every effort it just took to get that goal means nothing to me now. And it's all that she-devil's fault.

"It's public knowledge that you're referred to as Cam Hardy's replacement now that he's gone pro. How do you feel about that?" the female reporter says, her deep red lips pressed together for a split second. "And does that add more pressure, or is it something that fuels your fire?"

This is the same question I've been asked for weeks upon weeks, just worded slightly differently. To be honest, ever since I announced my spot as the Wolves new starting center, it's the main thing people want to talk about instead of the damn game I just played.

"You know, Hardy is one of the greatest players to ever play for Brooks. And hands down the best center. But I've worked hard to get to where I am.

And I'll continue to work hard too." I shrug, giving her a small grin. "I have that same hunger not just to make it to a Frozen Four, but to also win one. Just like Hardy."

I know I didn't answer her question, but I've given them basically the same answer every time, and I'll continue doing so. I'm not here to ruffle feathers. But I'm also not here to constantly talk about how great Hardy was.

Before she can ask me anything else, I pat her shoulder. "Thank you. Have a great night."

And then I get the hell out of there before another vulture finds me.

I don't bother worrying if I'm going to run into Poppy or not. If I know her, she hightailed it out of here the second the game ended. The last thing she'd want to risk was running into me. That's been clear since I haven't had a single run-in with her or Cade since last week when I saw her for the first time. Something tells me she's figured out my and Lana's practice schedule and made sure hers is the opposite.

As I walk through the half-empty stadium, making my way to the exit, I spot Hunter talking to his dance partner and wave but keep on trucking. As I head across the parking lot, I glance over at the football field. Shocked that there are two people standing in the center of it this late at night. Squinting a bit to focus my eyes more, I know it's Poppy and Jake right away.

Since Jake was a little kid, he's loved football. He's obsessed with the New England Patriots and even more so with Tom Brady.

The last thing I need to do right now is talk to either of them. Especially her. But Jake came and watched my game tonight. Hell, I bet he forced his sister to bring him. I want to thank him for showing up even if I don't want to see Poppy.

Opening my truck door, I toss my duffel in the back before heading toward them. Poppy's hands are stuffed in the front pocket of her hoodie as she looks at Jake, smiling. I think he's the only person who can make her smile like that.

When I walk between the bleachers, I consider turning around. She has this crazy power over me that makes me forget why I'm mad. She's had it since we were little kids. She'd do something to piss me off, like put herself in danger, and I'd get mad, but before long … we'd be laughing again.

She's harder now though. I can see that on her face. The world has made her tougher than she already was. And that's something I never thought was possible.

Jake spots me just as I come into the lights. He gives me one of his huge smiles and does some sort of salute. When she sees me, it's a much frostier gaze.

"Where's your ball, man?" I ask him as I get a few feet away. "We could have played pass."

"I … I left it at home. Next time, I'll bring it, and we can." He looks over at his sister. "Poppy and I came to watch you play tonight."

Aside from Jake, everything about this is awkward. She's visibly tense, just from my presence. And I can tell he's feeling her out, seeing how receptive she is to me. I know her well enough to know that she'd never do anything that might make her brother feel uncomfortable. So, maybe I'm saved for today.

But I also feel the anger and spite radiating from her body, telling me how pissed off she is that I'm standing here.

"I saw that." I hold my hand out, and he shakes it. "It's so good to see you, J. You look great."

"Thanks." He nods. "I moved into my own apartment. And … my girlfriend, she lives next door."

I don't miss the surprise on her face when he drops the word *girlfriend*. And he notices it, too, because he grins, tipping his chin up at her.

"She is my girlfriend."

"Way to drop that bomb, J," she mutters, widening her eyes at him.

"Holy shit, man. That's amazing." I can't help but pull him in for a hug. "I'll have to come check out your place sometime."

"Yeah. Yeah, you should." He nods again as I release him. "Poppy can bring you."

I don't even have to look at her to know she's likely rolling her eyes at the thought of bringing me anywhere. But because she doesn't want to make him feel bad, she says nothing.

"Sounds good." I glance back at where I came from before jerking my thumb. "Well, I need to get home. It was nice to see you, bud."

"You too," he agrees, glancing over at his sister like he wants her to say something.

Of course, she doesn't. She simply gives him a tiny, unnatural smile.

"We should get going too. I have to be up early," she tells him before she begins walking toward the sideline.

Once she gets far enough away from us, I shuffle slowly next to Jake.

"She'll forgive you," he says quietly. "Someday."

I don't have the heart to tell him there's far more to it than he knows. I'd have to forgive her too. For lying. For not taking my side. But he doesn't need to get caught up in all that.

So, I chuckle and hold my fist out once we reach the exit. "See you soon?"

Looking down, he bumps his fist into mine. "See you soon."

As they walk away, I notice they are heading toward the sign where the bus stops a few times an hour. And then it hits me—they must have been wasting time until the next bus comes. She doesn't have a car, and I don't know if he drives or not.

Having an internal battle with myself, I wish I could just give him a ride and leave her ass at the bus stop. *No, that's not fucking true. As much as I want to hate her, the thought of her on the bus drives me insane.*

"Do you guys need a lift?" I call behind them and watch her face contort into pure annoyance.

"No," she says at the same time her brother yells, "Yes, please."

As he heads toward me, she grabs his hand. "J, we planned to ride the bus. We like the bus. Right?"

"No one likes the bus," he says matter-of-factly. "I want to ride with Walker. He probably has a big truck."

I cringe because I do indeed have a big, very fancy truck now. And the thought of Poppy seeing it while she's been spending her days taking the bus places makes me feel like fucking shit.

He grins when she reluctantly releases his arm, and he heads toward me. "Which truck is yours?"

Grimacing inside, I point to the blacked-out Chevy on the end. "That black one right there."

Wasting no time, he heads toward it.

And slowly, she starts toward where I'm still standing. "Look, I don't know what you're trying to do here, but pick another person. Don't bring Jake into whatever fucked up game you're playing."

"What the hell are you even saying?" I scowl at her, holding my arms out. "It's a fucking ride home. If you don't like it, don't come with us."

She looks amused—and angry—by my words. "Oh … oh, wow. You really think I'd let your selfish ass be responsible for getting him home? You didn't seem to care much about him before tonight. So, no. I'll be riding with you tonight, asshole. But know this: Don't mess with my brother. Or you'll regret it."

I stand tall, and she finally looks at me. Though it's not the look I'm used to. Her eyes have always been filled with pain. But now … that pain is replaced with something worse.

Hate.

"Am I supposed to be scared of you, Poppyseed?" I toss my head back. "Funny. Nice to see you're still bitchy."

"Nice to see you're still a douche," she sasses back before pushing past me and heading toward my truck. "Oh, and glad to see your uncle gave you everything you ever wanted," she mutters. "Guess all of your dreams have come true."

As she climbs into the backseat, slamming the door shut behind her, I drag my hand over my face. Five minutes. Five fucking minutes, and she's already driving me insane.

Before I left Sunset Drive, she looked at me like I'd hung the moon and all the stars. Now … well, now, she looks at me like she does every other human being. With absolute loathing and disappointment.

I'm supposed to hate her. She's supposed to be dead to me. But right now, the way my heart is racing from her sweet cinnamon scent hitting my nose when she walked by or the way her plump lips just mouthed off, sending a jolt right to my cock … it doesn't feel like hate.

POPPY

Luckily, Walker says it's late, so he'll see Jake's place another day. I didn't want to have to go inside the apartment and visit any more tonight. This entire ride has been spent with Jake and him chatting and me staring out the window, reminding myself how much I love my big brother.

As we drop Jake off in front of his door, I push my door open and climb out, slamming it quickly. I wait for Jake to say his good-byes, and once he does, he exits the truck and comes and hugs me.

"Thanks for taking me," he says, slowly releasing me. "I'm sorry if tonight made you sad."

I give him a small smile and shake my head. "No, no. It was fun. We will do it again."

He and I went to a lot of Brooks football games, but never hockey, until tonight.

I'd rather go watch the golf team all day before attending another hockey game. But I'm not going to piss in his Cheerios and tell him that.

Once he heads inside, I awkwardly walk past Walker's truck and head toward the bus stop, unsure why he isn't leaving.

"Poppy, what the fuck are you doing?" Walker says from his now-open window.

Ignoring him, I pull my hood up and keep walking until I'm under the streetlight before sitting on the bench. Pulling my phone out, I see the next bus will arrive in about nine minutes. If Walker continues to sit in the parking lot across the way, staring at me, this will make for a really freaking awkward wait.

Suddenly, his door flies open, and he stalks toward me. I continue staring at my phone. However, because I have no social media, there isn't much to look at. So, I check my emails, which are also nonexistent.

"Get the hell in my truck. I'm taking you home," he growls next to me. With each second I stay seated, he grows more agitated. "I'm not fucking playing. I'm tired. I'm sore. And I want to go home."

"Poor baby," I say childishly before I continue to ignore him.

Because honestly, I don't know who the hell he thinks he is. Showing up here, pretending like he actually cares about any of us. *I'm not buying it.*

"You've got till the count of three to march your bitchy ass across the parking lot and climb into my truck." His voice is low and annoyed. "Or I'll throw you over my shoulder and take you there myself." He pauses. "And judging by how skinny you are these days, that shouldn't be a problem."

"I'll just scream for help." I shrug. "And then you'll look like a creep."

"I'll just cover your mouth."

The words come out so gritty. And because I'm clearly deranged, they send a shiver right down my spine ... and right between my legs.

Pull it together, girl.

Finally, I shove my phone in my pocket and glance up at him. For once, I really let myself look at him. His hair is a bit longer than I remember him ever having it. He looks like a true puck boy now. He seems to have shot up a foot in height since the day he left me crying on the sidewalk. And he's doubled in size. And from the way his Wolves shirt hugs his arms and chest ... he's all muscle now.

His eyes ... they are the same. But he doesn't smile. Not one bit. He just glares down at me, waiting for me to oblige him. Apparently, he's forgotten who I am.

I guess he needs some reminding.

"Why would I get a ride home with you, Walker James?" I shrug, a bored look on my face. "You're the last person I want to or should be riding with."

"And you're the last person I want in my truck. Spreading your lies all over it," he bites back. "But if you think for one fucking second that I'm leaving you at this bus stop this late at night, you have another thing coming."

When he leans down, I punch his stomach. "Touch me, and I'll fucking punch you in the dick next time. Try me," I hiss.

His hand flies to the spot where I hit him, and he grinds his teeth together. "What the *fuck*, Poppy?" He's mad. "Jesus fucking Christ, you're in-fucking-sane."

He stands there for a moment, breathing in and out and rubbing the spot where I hit him. But suddenly, when I glance up, his gaze relaxes. And slowly, he leans down, but this time, not so close.

"Let me take you home, Poppy," he says softly. "I know you hate me. I get it. But I just want to make sure you get home safe." His head tilts slightly. "Let me do that, please."

"No," I say, shaking my head, though I can't stop my hard exterior from melting the slightest bit. "I don't want to go anywhere with you."

"I can't just leave you here, Pop," he drawls so smoothly, and my heart races.

It's like I'm seeing the old Walker. My Walker.

My heart and my head are so confused. I know I should push him backward and not fall for his charm. But, God, he makes it so hard. And when his hand reaches for me and he brushes a strand of loose hair from my cheek, tucking it behind my ear, I'm completely frozen. I should get up and run away. Yet, instead, my breath hitches, and I wait to see what he'll do next.

He crouches down so that he's eye level with me, and his gaze flicks to my lips. If he kissed me right now … I'm not sure if I could resist it. I know it wouldn't be the right thing to do, but I've wanted him for so long.

Waited for him for so long.

His head dips closer, and on instinct, my eyes flutter a few times before closing. My heart pumps so hard that I hear it in my ears as I wait for his kiss.

My first kiss ever.

And just when I think he's going to kiss me, his hands slide to my waist, and he quickly throws me over his shoulder before standing up.

As he walks us toward his truck, it takes me a few seconds to realize what is happening. But when I do … I'm pissed off.

"You … you—" I start to growl through gritted teeth.

"Got you all fucking hot and bothered just so that I could get you in my truck without getting punched in the dick?" I can hear the smirk in his voice. "Yeah, Poppyseed, I sure did."

Pulling the door open, he acts like my body flailing as I fight him is nothing. Quickly, he drops me down in the seat.

"Poppy, Poppy, Poppy," he drawls slowly. "You should know better. You really think I'd kiss you after all you've done?"

"I don't want to kiss you, prick," I hiss. "You're the last person I'd ever want to kiss!"

His smirk only deepens. He's clearly amused, looking at me like I'm a joke. "When your lips parted and your eyes shut … that told me otherwise."

Pulling the seat belt around me, his hand brushes my thigh as he secures it. And dammit if I don't feel another lightning bolt shoot right between my legs.

"Nice gothic nails. Matches your soul."

"Fuck off," I hiss.

"Know this, Poppyseed: When it comes to me, you won't win. You won't win the battles, and you sure as hell won't be winning any wars." He pats my head and then taps his finger on my nose. "Remember that."

As he closes the door and walks around to the driver's side, I'm ashamed of myself for being so pathetic tonight. I gave him the power and let him see the effect he still has on me.

But he's wrong about one thing: I might have lost this battle. But I'm sure as hell going to win the war.

5

POPPY

I wash my hands and look at my reflection in the mirror. I look tired, but that's probably because I am tired. And, yeah, I guess I am skinny, just like Walker made sure to throw in my face the other night, but I'm always on the go. And it's not like I have endless cash to buy snacks either.

Taking my strawberry ChapStick out of my pocket, I smear some across my lips and rub them together before capping it and sliding it back in.

My hair is down in messy waves, and for once, I'm having a damn good hair day. Too bad it's wasted on this *not* date with Cade at Club 83. After dance practice, he asked if I wanted to get a bite to eat. I could tell he was down in the dumps about something, so here I am. I've grown a soft spot for that guy— and he's the last person I expected to say that about.

Swinging the door open, I head down the short hallway that leads back into the club.

"Huff, huh?" A deep voice comes from behind me, and I instantly know it's Walker.

My steps slow to a stop, but I don't turn around. I don't speak either. I just simply wait to see what the hell he's going to say to me that he thinks might hurt my feelings.

"Never took him for your type." This time, he coos the words in my ear. "But lucky for you, everyone is Huff's type."

"Some could say the same about you," I mutter, staring straight ahead.

His body doesn't touch my backside, though I know he's there. I feel everything about him. His body heat. His energy. All of it makes me want to back up a mere inch and physically *feel* him there. But I remain strong and don't give in to my desires.

"Careful, Poppyseed. You almost sound ... jealous." This time, his lips are closer to my ear.

"Jealous?" I let out a loud laugh. Surprising him, I spin my body to face him. "I'm here with Cade Huff, Walker. What the fuck do I have to be jealous of?" I shrug. "And of course, he's my type. Have you seen him?" I coo. "He's everyone's type, *babe*."

"Shut up," he growls. "Shut the fuck up."

Satisfied as I watch his jaw tense, I continue to stare up at him, batting my lashes innocently. "What, James? You don't want to think about me fucking your teammate?"

All at once, my back is pressed to the wall, and his hands are gripping my wrists at my sides. I have to stay strong. I can't give him the satisfaction of thinking I want him now. This battle is mine. Taking two losses to this asshole isn't an option.

"Now, who's jealous?" I say slowly, remaining cool as a cucumber on the outside. But on the inside, I'm in a puddle at his feet, begging for more.

"I'm not fucking jealous," he says through gritted teeth.

"Are you sure?" I roll my tongue over my lips. "So, it's okay with you if I bring Cade into the back room, drop to my knees, and suck his—"

His hand covers my mouth, his face barely hovering over mine. "Don't finish that fucking sentence, Poppy. I'll burn this entire fucking place down if you do. And I'll fucking kill Cade Huff, and it'll be your fucking fault that he's dead," he growls, his eyes floating to my lips, but I don't give in.

Through his pants, I feel his growing erection brushing against my stomach, making me physically ache. But I'm not letting him make a joke of me again. It was a joke to him the other night. Who's laughing now?

"Everything is fine and fun until the rabbit gets the gun, isn't it?" I taunt, pressing my chest to his. "Stay the hell away from me, James. Consider this a warning."

"Oh, I'm shaking in my sneakers from your empty threat," he snarls. His chest thrusts against mine with every breath he takes.

Finally, he drops my wrist down and steps back. And I keep myself composed, stepping around him and heading toward the door leading me back to where Cade sits.

"You should be. And I'm no soldier ... but I don't think you won this battle, big boy," I say calmly. "Guess that means we're all tied up." I wink before walking back into the club. Inside, I'm shaking from feeling his hardness on my body, knowing I did that to him.

On one hand, I'm proud that I got him worked up this time, just to let him down. On the other, I'm turned on as hell right now, and there's only one person who could help relieve this pressure. And hooking up with him isn't an option.

Everyone knows you don't sleep with the enemy. And Walker James has proven that's exactly what he is.

WALKER

My dick has been unbelievably hard since I saw Poppy in the hallway after she came out of the restroom. From the corner of the bar, I had watched her and Huff laughing and chatting it up since they had come in. Each passing second pissed me off more and more. And when she went to the restroom, I couldn't stop myself from following her. I knew I shouldn't, but my self-restraint had snapped.

The anger I felt while watching them talk was nothing compared to right now. Elias and Nixon continue their conversation, but I can't hear any of it. All I can do is fix my eyes on the bar, where Poppy flirts with Huff, never looking my way. Her hand slides up his arm, and before I know it … she's fucking kissing him.

She kisses *him*. Initiating the entire thing.

My teeth grind together so bad that it gives me an instant headache. And my jaw tenses to the point that it fucking hurts. The kiss doesn't last long, but it's long enough to ruin my entire night.

And it makes me want to murder Huff.

Right now, with A-fucking-1 timing, Lana chooses to strut her way toward me and plop her ass down onto my lap. Her dress is short. So short that I can almost see her pussy. She smells like vanilla. Absolutely delicious. But it doesn't matter because she doesn't smell like cinnamon, and that means she doesn't smell right to me. But if she wants me so bad, who the hell am I to push her away? Especially since on the other side of this fucking bar, Poppy's tongue was just down Huff's throat. She even threatened to suck his dick.

I ball my hands up at my sides, just thinking about my girl with anyone else's cock down her throat that isn't mine.

"Hi, handsome." Lana giggles, brushing some hair away from my face. "How's it going?"

"Fine now," I mutter just as I rest my palm on her thigh. Maybe being with her could make this ache in my soul lessen. Maybe it would make me forget, even if just for a moment. I'd give anything for a few measly seconds when Poppy wasn't the only thing on my fucking brain.

No, I know deep down that while I was balls deep in Lana, I'd squeeze my eyes shut and imagine I was buried inside Poppy's tight pussy. *Wishing* that I were. And that's not fair to Lana.

Lana kisses my neck, and then I feel her tongue drag across my jawline.

She's intoxicated—that's pretty clear. Then again, after all the shots I poured down my throat after my interaction with Poppy, I'm not in my right mind either.

"Come on," she whispers in my ear. "What's a girl got to do to get laid around here?" She pulls back, poking her bottom lip out. "I get that you don't do relationships. But I need a … release." She winks. "And I think you're a prime candidate to give me just that. Besides, it'll make us dance better, don't you think?"

"You're right about one thing: I don't do relationships," I tell her, glancing at Poppy and Cade as they laugh about something else. "Not sure about the other shit though."

"Come on. Don't be a party pooper," she whispers as she reaches down, placing a hand on my thigh, dangerously close to my cock.

I'm begging for it to harden the way it just did for Poppy a mere five minutes ago. But nothing happens. Lana's tan legs are fucking scrumptious. I should be rock hard right now, ready to fuck her.

"Lana, come dance with us!" a few of her friends yell from the dance floor, waving for her to join.

Smirking down at me, she hovers her lips above mine. "I'm going to dance with my friends, but just know, big boy … it's you I'm dancing for." Slowly moving off my lap, she slides her palms down my thighs. "Eyes on me, handsome."

As she saunters off to join her friends, Elias nudges my side. "She's rather … aggressive." He nods toward where she's dancing, rubbing her palms down her body. "But, wow … she's fucking hot. And willing. Really, really fucking willing."

"Then, you should go join her," I say, patting his shoulder and standing up. "I'm gonna pass."

"Yeah, I, uh … that's not really how I move." He looks nervously at her, and I swear the fucker doesn't even blink. "But she's beautiful. Really, really beautiful."

Elias is one of those players who is terrifying on the ice. Can probably bench the most on the team, yet is bashful with the ladies. Hell, Lana might be perfect for him. At least she'd get him out of his shell.

I walk toward Lana, and the hope in her eyes when she notices I'm approaching her makes me feel even worse than I already do. Seductively, she snakes her hands on my body, biting down on her bottom lip.

I waste no time dipping my lips to her ear when I reach her. "Hey, look, I'm going to talk to Huff for a minute. But just so you know, my friend over there, Elias … he's been checking you out all night."

When I pull back, her face falls, and her lips form into a frown. I can tell right away that her feelings are hurt.

She tilts her head to the side. "Who's got you too worked up to blow off some steam with me tonight?" She bites her bottom lip. "No one turns me down."

Cupping her cheek, I look her in the eyes. "You're fucking beautiful. And hot. And your body … sexy as hell. And trust me, I know I'm one crazy fucker for walking away from you tonight." Nodding toward the bar where Elias sits, talking to Nixon, I smile at her. "I promise you, he's a good guy. Much better than me. And he thinks you're gorgeous."

Nervously, she glances his way before she suddenly seems to sober up, tucking her hair behind her ear shyly. So not like the girl that was practically begging to ride my cock minutes ago.

Swallowing, she turns toward me. "And he's been checking me out?"

"You know it." I nod. "See you at practice, babe."

Walking toward the bar, I clasp my hand on Elias's shoulder. "She's waiting for you, big boy. Be good to her."

He looks like he might actually piss himself. And I don't wait to see if he heads toward her before I walk toward the other end of the bar, where Poppy and Cade still sit.

Knowing it'll piss her off, I take the seat next to Poppy, and I instantly feel the anger spilling from her body. Sort of like a fucking fire that someone just threw some gasoline on. In this case, I guess I'm the gasoline. And something about that—something about knowing I have the ability to get under her skin like nobody else can—makes my dick harden the slightest bit.

She shoots me a harsh glare. "There's, like, twenty other open seats, asshole." She waves her hand around. "Pick one."

The bartender, Tasha, slides me a beer and gives me a flirty wink. Which only seems to piss Poppy off more.

Satisfied that she's jealous, I bring the beer to my lips and take a swig. "Nah, think I'll sit right here. It's a bit chilly outside, and I figured Satan herself could put off some warmth."

"Careful. I might melt off some of those fancy clothes you're so fond of these days," she coos, giving me a once-over before she looks at Cade. "Cade,

I'm out. I'll message you in a few days to find a time to meet." Standing, she holds up her middle finger. "And, Walker … fuck off."

Once she's gone, Cade gives me a curious look, and I shrug.

"Think she probably just wants my dick or something. You know how it is."

"Wow," he mutters, shaking his head.

I can't tell him or anyone the truth. I don't want anyone to know where I came from. To them, I'm the rich kid from Charleston. I'm okay with that because they don't actually know who my uncle is, and they don't know that I grew up five minutes from here in a house that was overrun with drugs and rats. Some things are just better left in the past.

Just like Poppy Wilson.

Holding his hand up, Cade orders us a bunch of shots. And even though I really want to warn him to stay the fuck away from Poppy, I don't. Not yet anyway. One way or another, I'll keep them apart. Aside from practice, that is.

Holding the first shot up, he clinks his to mine, and we toss them back. I wish I could get so fucked up tonight that my brain couldn't even begin to think about her. But I know that's hopeless.

That girl is like a tattoo, permanently under my skin. And no matter what I do, I can't rid myself of her. Not completely anyway.

It's always been like a sixth sense I have, knowing when she needs me. Tonight is no different. I just woke up out of a dead sleep, consumed by the feeling in the pit of my stomach, telling me to go to her to make sure she's okay and to rescue her if she isn't.

After throwing on my shirt, I pull my sweatpants over my briefs and slide on my sneakers. Heading through my front door, I move quickly across the dried-out lawn and beeline it to her house.

I don't even make it there before I can hear her somewhere outside. And in the night, I squint my eyes to follow the soft sounds of cries.

"Poppy?" I call into the night.

She sniffles, and when my eyes adjust to the darkness, I barely make out her figure as she sits against the old shed near the edge of the woods. Her knees are pulled to her chest, and her face is buried against her legs.

Running to her, I crouch down, pulling her body against mine. Her head rests against my shoulder, and I kiss her forehead.

"I'm right here," I whisper. "You're safe now. I promise."

For a long time, she doesn't say anything. And I don't push it because I don't want to force anything out of her. Poppy isn't someone who cries very often. In fact, I think this is the third time I've ever seen her cry since we were kids.

Finally, with her voice small, she tells me everything.

"Ron owes the wrong people money." Her voice breaks. "As payment, he offered ..." She cries into her hands. "He offered me."

My heart breaks while the rest of my body fills with anger.

"My own dad was going to let his suppliers rape his child. Just so that he wouldn't be hurt."

I feel like I'm going to puke. "Did ..." I can't even get the words to come out. I don't know if I want to know the answer.

She shakes her head. "I had a bad feeling about those men, so I cracked my door and listened to the exchange. I escaped through my window and hid out here as that deal was made." She wipes her sleeve across her face. "They'll come looking for me. I heard them yelling at Ron once they went into my room and saw I wasn't there."

Crying harder, she looks at me. "And even if they leave, he'll punish me, Walker, because he'll know that I ran to escape them. Leaving him to be hurt and probably lose his supplier."

"Fuck him," I growl. "I'll kill that motherfucker, Poppy. I will."

"I want him to die too," she whispers. "But if you kill him, then the three of us will get put into the system." She pauses. "I'm not scared for me. I'm scared for Jake. He's going to be eighteen in a year and a half. And then he can finally live on his own." She shakes her head. "If he gets taken now, they'll just stick him in a group home for the rest of his life. I can't let that happen. I just can't. He wants so much more than that." Her voice is barely a squeak. "He deserves so much more than that."

"So do you," I say gently. "Poppy, I can't let your scumbag father hurt you anymore." I try to keep my voice soft, but it's hard. "I'm supposed to protect you, and I fail all the fucking time."

At fifteen years old, I know I can't give her the protection she needs. I want to rescue her, but my own life is a mess. I love her more than I've ever loved anything. And sometimes, I think she feels the same way.

"I just wish we could all run away," she whispers. "To someplace better than this. Where our parents aren't high and dads don't abuse their children. Where we get what we need and don't have to be scared every day." Her lip trembles. "I'm so tired, Walker. I'm so tired of this life."

I pull her against me tighter. "I promise you, Poppy, one day, this street will be our past. Van will be running his own restaurant, just like he's dreamed of. Jake will have his own place, be on a football team, and maybe even get to meet Tom Brady," I say in an attempt to lighten things. "You'll be dancing for a huge dance company, and I'll be in the NHL, somewhere near where you're working, I hope." I kiss the top of her head. "One day, Poppy. One day, it'll all be okay."

"I hope you're right," her voice squeaks.

"I'll make sure of it." I kiss the top of her head, wishing it were her lips, but not wanting to push things while she's upset. "I'll always be here."

I drag my hand over my face. The ache from my skull making it almost impossible to sit up. I haven't had a dream or a nightmare in years. I don't dream. Yet, after a ton of liquor and a few encounters with Poppy, here I am.

Sadly, that night wasn't the worst night of our childhoods. There were many, many times when all I wanted to do was be her hero, and I couldn't save her from her own father. Just like she suspected, her dad punished her. She came to school the next day with a black eye and a bruised stomach. And when she was questioned, she said that she was in an accident.

The school let it go. They *always* let it go.

When I saw her, I started toward her house, ready to put that fucker in the grave. But before I could, Poppy got to me. Begging me not to go through with it. She said that it would only make her life worse. In a way, I knew she was wrong. The three of them risking getting separated would have still been safer than the horrors inside that trailer. But because she asked me, I listened.

It fucking killed me. But I listened.

Van had stood up for her, and he had gotten his ass beat too. One thing that worked in Jake's favor was the day program he was in. Ron was smart enough to know that if he laid his hands on Jake, suspicion would rise if he showed up in places with bruises. That gave Poppy a little peace, knowing he was somewhat protected.

My parents died three days later from drugs that had come from her old man.

If I hadn't let her stop me, maybe my parents would still be alive. They could've seen me go pro one day. Maybe they could have gotten clean and stayed clean. Briar wouldn't have been brainwashed by our uncle, and all would be good.

But like always, Poppy took her father's side. Only making everything worse.

6

POPPY

We are days away from the fundraiser, and while I think we're ready, I'm worried about Cade.

Last night, I borrowed Ryann's car and drove by Van's place to check for any signs of life. Because although I'd sent him numerous messages, he hadn't answered. I know he hates me after the things I said to him when I bailed him out of jail. And if it looked like no one else was there, I would go inside and apologize to him and try to get him some help.

Instead of my brother, I saw Cade's truck in the driveway. And right away, it all clicked. Cade Huff is an addict. And while I'm pissed at Cade for deciding to go down that road, I'm more pissed at my brother for doing exactly what our father did—getting people hooked on drugs.

I've been sick about it ever since. I know I need to say something to Cade. Just to let him know I'm here. That he can talk to me. After all, if anyone understands how awful addiction can be … it's me. I've never done drugs myself, but I've seen firsthand the effects they have on others. They can take the kindest person and turn them into a monster. I don't want that to happen to Cade. He's too good of a person for that.

"Hey, Cade?" I say, keeping my voice as soft as I can. "Can I ask you something?"

"You can, but I might not answer." He gives me a playful wink, only making what I need to say harder to come out of my mouth. "This isn't Truth or Dare. So, technically …"

I give him a serious look before walking in front of him. "I know you and I aren't super close. And if it wasn't for this fundraiser, we probably would have gone through our whole lives without speaking. But I just … please don't get mad."

Right away, I know that he's going to be upset. His entire body tenses, just like I expected it to. One thing I've learned about addicts is that they are always on the defense, it seems.

"If you need someone to talk to, I'm here. About Haley. Or … other stuff." I look down, wanting to cower, but I force myself to look him right in the eye and stand taller. "My brother is an addict and—"

"Whoa, girl," he says, stopping me. "I don't know what you're trying to imply, but pump the fucking brakes."

"There're just a lot of signs, you know? That you're … using drugs," I whisper. "You're always late. You're moody. I swear you've lost a little weight since we started dancing together." I pause, swallowing. "But mostly … I saw your truck at Van's last night. He's a bad dude, Cade. I really hope you're not getting tangled up with him."

"How about you just worry about getting this dance the fuck over with and don't worry about me?" He glowers, his face turning red with anger. And maybe embarrassment too. "I'm not your brother, Poppy. Don't ever say shit like that again to me either. If you do, you'll be dancing by yourself at the fundraiser. That's a promise."

Before I can say another word, he turns away and rushes out of the studio. Leaving me feeling even worse about bringing it up.

I'd love to go to my brother and threaten him to stay the hell away from Cade, but what would be the point? The Van I used to know is long gone. There's no reasoning with the person he is now.

And realization hits that I have no one to talk to about any of this. I love Ryann, but I've never told her about where I came from. Not really anyway. In another world, maybe I could run to Walker, and he'd hold me like he used to. And we could sit in silence, and everything would just … melt away. But that other world doesn't exist. There's just this hellhole of one I'm in now.

WALKER

I pull the door open and head inside, instantly spotting the back of Lana's head in the front-row seat. The studio was occupied all day. And since this is the last possible day of rehearsal before the fundraiser event, we're practicing on the theater stage instead.

We missed almost a week of practice because she was sick. When she felt better, I had away games in North Carolina. So, today's practice won't be easy. I know I'm not nearly ready for that fundraiser, but I'm going to try my best.

When she sees me, she cringes slightly. This will be the first time we've seen each other since the night at Club 83, when she was basically trying to dry-hump me on a barstool. I know she was pretty wasted, but she's flirted with me since the beginning of this whole partnership.

"Shall we ... go stretch?" she says shyly, waving toward the stage.

"Sure." I nod, following her.

When we both take a seat on the wooden floor, she blows out a breath. "So ... I'm really sorry for how I acted the other night. I was drunk. And truthfully, the fact that my ex-boyfriend of two years cheated on me has made me act a little ... wild. But even I know I was out of line." She blushes. "If a guy acted that way to a girl, the police would be involved." She chews her lip. "I'm really embarrassed, Walker."

I feel her shame, so I reach over and pat the top of her hand. "I'm sorry about your ex. He sounds like a shitbag of a human. Especially to cheat on a catch like you." I give her a small, reassuring smile. "And I didn't push you away, Lana. And my hand grazed your thigh, you know." I bring my hand away slowly. "I promise, it's all good." I elbow her gently. "And besides, there was a far better man interested in you that night. A much more deserving one."

A smile stretches across her entire face, and her cheeks redden deeper. "Yeah. He's, uh ... he's something all right." She giggles. "Thanks for that."

"Does that mean it worked out?" I ask, pretty fucking pleased with myself for being a matchmaker.

"You could say that. But I'm not looking to jump into another relationship. But, yeah ... he's sweet. And fun." Her cheeks redden, and she covers her face. "Anyway, new subject. I'm going to ask you something, and I want the truth."

I immediately stiffen, scared of what the heck she's about to ask me. "Yeah?"

"If it wasn't for Poppy Wilson ... would I have had a shot?"

When my gaze snaps to hers, she smiles, sighing slightly. "Walker, that night, I saw the way you watched her. And then, when you walked over to her? Well, it was pretty clear there's history." She swallows. "I wanted to ask her about it, but I didn't want her to feel like I was being pushy. One thing with Poppy … she doesn't open up much."

"Yeah." I finally nod. "If it wasn't for her, I promise you … I would have taken you home that night." I laugh. "Hell, probably the first time you rubbed your ass on my dick during practice."

Covering her mouth with her hand, she laughs. "Oh my gosh. I'm awful."

"Hey, guys like Elias? They need a woman who knows what she wants."

She pulls her legs to her chest as her face grows somber. "So, what are you going to do?"

"About what?" I shrug.

"Poppy. Why aren't you fighting for her if you love her?" She looks sad. "You know, for your happily ever after?"

I inhale, looking up at the ceiling for a moment to form an answer. Finally, I look at her. "I'm not sure happily ever after exists for people like her and me." I drop my gaze to the floor. "Especially not now."

"Happily ever after exists for everyone who truly wants it," she says softly. "I've been Poppy's roommate and friend for a while now, and I barely know anything about her. She's so … hard. But I know that she's a good person. And even though she's never opened up to me about her life, I know she's been through a lot." She sighs. "I guess I'm trying to say that Poppy deserves someone to fight for her. So do you, Walker. So, I hope you both figure that out before it's too late."

To an outsider, it must seem too easy. Like a light switch Poppy and I can turn off and back on, resetting everything that's happened. But that's not how life works. I've done things. She's done things. I'm not sure we could ever get past that. Besides, we've both been through so much fucking trauma in our lives that it can't be healthy for two people like us to get together.

So, I don't say anything back to Lana. Because when it comes to Poppy or finding our way back, I wouldn't even know where to fucking start.

WALKER

I try my best, but can't take my eyes off Poppy in her gold sequins dress. She and Cade performed, and I was so fucking glad that it was an upbeat, fun song. And not some romantic, sexy shit. That would have put me over the edge to sit and watch. Not to mention that if it had been slow and seductive, I likely would have had to punch Huff right in the fucking face.

She chugs a bottle of water, laughing with Cade as they celebrate their performance, which annoys the fuck out of me, and I wish I could yank her away from him and lock her in a fucking room forever. That way, no other man would ever hit on her. After all, she was supposed to be mine.

Even though I think our performance went well, I'm just happy as hell it's over with, and I can move on with my life.

And Cade and Poppy can stop fucking hanging out too.

When we were kids, even though I hated dancing, I'd dance with Poppy when she needed help practicing for her performances. It didn't seem that bad as long as I was with her. So, while Lana is great, dancing with anyone who isn't Poppy doesn't feel right. At all.

"You're staring," Nixon mutters, coming next to me. "Don't go pickin' fights with Huff. You know how tight he and Cap are."

It's true. Sterns and Huff are close and all. And I would never jeopardize my spot on the team by picking a fight with Cade. But I'm sure as hell going to keep an eye out to make sure he doesn't cross the line. So far, since that night at Club 83, he and Poppy seem pretty platonic. And it needs to stay that way.

"I am not."

I quickly look away, my eyes finding my dance partner and Elias in the corner of the room. She might have said she wasn't ready for another relationship, but they look pretty cozy to me.

He sits in a chair, her wedged between his legs. I can't help but smile because I like both of them. And I'm happy as hell it worked out for them. Besides, now, she can stop trying to fuck me every five seconds.

"Man, he's giving her the look." Nixon chuckles.

"What look?" I frown.

"The wife look," he says thoughtfully. "He's looking at that girl like he's about to wife her up." He looks her over. "And to be honest, she's looking at him like she's naming their unborn children in her head."

I tilt my head to the side, zeroing in on whatever fucking shit Nixon is talking about. Finally, I shrug. "I don't get it."

"That's because you're like the opposite of Romeo." He laughs, hitting my arm. "I'm not afraid to admit I love me some love. You? You're a loveless grump."

I've never been someone to show how I feel. I guess that's because when Poppy was around, I didn't want Van to catch on to the fact that I loved his sister. Even though he made it clear a few times that he knew all along. And once I left Sunset Drive, I just didn't give a fuck anymore. Not about anyone.

"Whatever," I groan just before Hunter Thompson and his dance partner, Sutton's, dance comes to an end.

Within seconds, Hunter yells for someone to help.

It all happens so quickly. I watch as he attempts to give her a dose of what looks like a rescue inhaler. Like a horror movie, I see her slowly start to lose consciousness as someone yells that the ambulance is almost here. The entire room breaks into chaos, yet everything seems silent as Hunter carries her outside to meet the paramedics.

That's when I see Poppy. Her face is pale, and her shoulders are sagging as she walks into a private room and closes the door behind her.

I've heard some of the guys on the team talking, saying that Poppy was bullying Sutton. I hated to hear it, but I also wasn't really surprised. The saying, *Hurt people hurt people …* well, it applies here. Sutton has everything Poppy could never get, and I'm sure that made her act a certain way.

I hate that nobody knows the real Poppy—the Poppy who took beating after beating and never told on her dad just because she wanted to keep her brother safe. The Poppy who hardly had any lunch money but would give her last few dollars to someone she thought needed it more.

She's so much better than she leads on. She's just afraid to show it because that'll leave her open to getting hurt.

She's not mine to fix, but right now, all I want to do is make sure she's okay. So, rushing through the crowd, I head toward the room she disappeared into moments ago.

I push the door open and find her crouched on the floor. She isn't crying, but she's visibly distressed. She rocks gently, keeping her eyes squeezed shut. It's like she knows it's me in here without even looking.

Closing the door, I sink down the wall next to her. I have no idea why, but something inside of me changes. And I know that at this moment, I just want to be her shoulder to cry on.

Even if she doesn't cry anymore.

POPPY

When Sutton was taken in the ambulance, the girls, Ryann and Lana, looked at me like I was the one who had given her the asthma attack. I could see it written all over their faces. The way I'd treated Sutton weeks prior made them suddenly hate me now that she was sick.

If I could take it all back, I would. I wouldn't act like an entitled brat who deserved the number one spot simply because I had the saddest story. I wouldn't make her want to leave the room when I walked in. I would just separate our differences and not be so nasty.

Looking back, I can see how awful I was. And now, it might be too late to right my wrongs.

I know it's Walker the second the door opens and shuts again. I don't have to look to know he came to me. Just like he used to when he knew I needed him the most.

The same way I ran to him the day his parents died. I held him in my arms for hours in pure silence. He fell asleep with his head on my abdomen, and I would have given anything that day to take his pain away.

Walker sits next to me, not saying a word. Simply ... existing with me. Just like when we were kids and one of us was going through something bad. We could just be together, and that would make it all hurt a little less. The silence didn't bother me then.

Now, it's suffocating.

My body hurts to just give in and crash into his. I miss his friendship and mourn what I always thought we would become one day.

"Do you want to talk about it?" he asks softly into the empty room.

"Not with you," I mutter, staring at my hands.

"Why not?" He cranes his head to face me, but I continue to stare down, only seeing him from my peripheral vision.

"Let's see, Walker. Probably because you aren't someone I would ever talk to about anything anymore," I hiss. "You stopped being that to me long ago."

"And whose decision was that?" His voice grows sharper. "You made that choice."

"Yeah." A bitter laugh bubbles from my mouth. "Like I had any other choice."

"There's always a fucking choice," he growls. Gripping my chin, he forces me to look at him. "You, Poppy, made the choice. And now, my parents are dead, and no one had to pay for it."

"Way to pile onto this already-fucking-awful moment! They overdosed, Walker! Jesus!" I shake my head. "They chose to stick that needle in their arm."

"Those drugs were cut with a deadly amount of fentanyl, and you know it. Your dad knew it back then too." His grip tightens on my chin, and his eyes bounce between mine and my lips. "Just admit that you fucking lied to save your own ass. To keep your family together."

Anger courses through every part of my body. Overtaking my veins and strangling me from the inside out.

How could he think it was that cut and dry?

"I lied to keep Jake from being thrown into a system where he wouldn't get what he needed!" I scream in his face before quickly pulling out of his hold and standing up. "You'll never get that though! To you, all I was back then was the girl who was fucking obsessed with you. The girl who would choose you above anyone else!" I shake my head at him, snarling, "Well, guess what. I'm not that girl anymore, Walker. And sometimes, you have to protect your family! I chose Jake. I chose my family! It had nothing to do with Ron."

He stands, towering over me.

But before he can speak, I poke my finger into his chest. "I will not beg for forgiveness when I did what I had to do to help Jake make his dreams come true," I growl. "Like I said before, stay the fuck away from me."

I don't even make it a whole step before his hands grab my waist and spin me around to face him. He backs me up to the wall, holding my wrists down. His lips are on mine, and his tongue flicks against mine. And I want to be the bad bitch who pushes him away and stands strong. But it's impossible. I've loved him from day one. I've thought about this kiss for most of my life.

He kisses me rough and hard. And stupid me kisses him right back. The room spins, and my head feels dizzy as I feel his erection press into my stomach.

His lips move to my neck, and he kisses my neck before biting down on my flesh and making me cry out. A humiliating loud moan escapes my lips, and before I know it, his mouth catches mine again.

I'm so lost in the moment and lost in this man that I love and hate simultaneously. Suddenly, there's a knock on the door, and I hear Jolene's voice.

Shoving him away from me, I glare up at him. "Be right out," I try to call out, breathless. "Just fixing my dress."

"Oh, okay," Jolene answers, sounding concerned before I hear her footsteps walk away.

I push past him, but his hand catches my wrist.

"Poppy," he rasps, "don't walk away from me."

"I can't do this right now," I plead. "Not with you."

"Well, what was this then?" he asks, signaling his hand between us. "Tell me that."

I stare at him for a second, my heart still beating far too fast while also breaking inside my chest. It hurts so much to love someone so deeply that when you're in moments like the one we just had … nothing else matters.

"This was a mistake. One that won't happen again."

Running my hands down my dress, I smooth it out before exiting the room. And leaving Walker James behind.

Every step is damn near impossible to take with the ache between my legs showing zero signs of subsiding. Damn him.

But mostly, damn me.

I'm supposed to be this bitchy, tough girl who intimidates people. But one touch from him, and I unravel like a pathetic ball of yarn.

WALKER

With the rest of the team, I sit in the waiting room at the hospital. Hunter has barely spoken a word, just sitting with his face in his palms, looking down at the floor. It became pretty clear early on that he had a thing for his dance partner, Sutton. Despite their rough history, they seemed to find their way to each other. And now, she's lying unconscious in a hospital bed, and he doesn't know if she's going to wake up or not.

The entire dance team is here—all except Poppy, who I've seen sitting outside on a bench by herself through the window.

She and Sutton might live together, but they aren't friends. From the sounds of it, they are enemies. I know Poppy enough to know that she wouldn't come in here and try to pretend they were something they weren't. But she must care about Sutton a bit because she's here. And that's something.

I know today isn't about Poppy. But she's hurting, and I'm the last person she wants near her. So, walking over to Lana, who's curled up next to Elias, I take the seat across from them.

"How are you doing?" I ask her, and she looks at me with her makeup-smudged eyes.

She doesn't answer, but shrugs as her lip trembles and her eyes fill with tears.

"She's going to be all right," I whisper. "I know Poppy isn't the easiest person to get along with. And I know she and Sutton weren't best friends or anything—"

"Poppy treated her like shit," she says, cutting me off. "Literal shit."

Sighing, I pinch the bridge of my nose. The last thing I should be doing is blabbing Poppy's business all over campus. She's an extremely private, complex human being. And if she knew I was saying what I was about to, she'd probably cut my nuts off. But I'd rather her be pissed at me than be all alone outside. And the last thing she needs right now is me rushing out there, trying to save her.

I'm starting to learn that maybe she needs to save herself. Because maybe she doesn't trust me enough to be her hero anymore.

"Poppy's tough. Trust me, no one gets that more than I do. She's hard. And she can be really fucking mean." I nod slowly, looking at Lana. "But, shit, Lana, some of the stuff that girl has been through? It's unimaginable to most people." I cringe. "The way I see it, she does good just to get up every single morning and get through the day. Because some people? They would have given up on life a long time ago if they had been dealt the cards she was."

She sniffles. "Why are you telling me this? I thought … I thought there was no happily ever after for you and her?"

I swallow. "There isn't. But right now, she's outside of this hospital, alone. Scared to come in here because she doesn't want to upset anyone by showing her face. I know she cares about Sutton despite how she acted." I reach across the aisle and pat her arm. "I can't be the one to make this better. Right now … she just needs a friend." A lump forms in my throat, and I swallow it down. "She really, really needs a fucking friend. And to know that you all don't hate her."

Looking from me to Elias, she gives a sad, tiny smile. Slowly, she pushes herself to stand and exhales. "I'll go get her."

Standing quickly, I hug her. "Thank you. Thank you so much, Lana."

Releasing her, I watch as she heads outside. Maybe this isn't what Poppy even wants. Perhaps she's fine out there, all alone. But for once, I just want that girl to have someone show up for her. To ride for her. To show her that they care.

Even if that someone can't be me.

POPPY

I wring my hands together nervously before looking around the house to see if everything looks okay. After a week and a half, Sutton is coming home today. And to show her that I'm sorry for how I've acted, I asked Jasmin, a girl I work at the coffee shop with, to cover for me today. I wanted to be here when Sutton first came home.

The girls wanted to keep her homecoming low-key, per Hunter's request, but we put up some decorations and stocked the house with her favorite foods and lots of soups. Because from what I hear, most people like soup when they aren't feeling well. I never really had soup, growing up. We mostly ate things that we could throw in the microwave or plain bread, but it sounds like it would be nice when you're not feeling the best. And since she was intubated for over a week, her throat is healing.

I went and saw Sutton while she was in the hospital once she woke up. I know she was surprised to see me, but it was something I felt like I should do. I'm not sure there's a faster way to make someone realize how awful they have been than seeing the person they've been treating unfairly lying in a hospital bed. It wasn't fair of me to unload years of trauma onto Sutton Savage and make her take the wrath of it all. It has never been about her, but about myself and everything I need to overcome.

I don't think we will be besties and braid each other's hair or paint nails together. But I don't want to hate her anymore. The truth is, we're both dancers. And if I want to be better than her, I just need to work harder instead of playing the pity card.

"She's here!" Lana says, peeking out the window. "Let's not, like … yell or anything." She widens her eyes, looking nervous. "I don't want to send her into another asthma attack. Let's just … calmly say, *Welcome home.*"

"For real? I thought we'd light fireworks and maybe jump out from behind curtains," Ryann deadpans.

Lana's eyes grow wide. "Seriously?" she squeaks.

Smacking her hand to her forehead, she shakes her head. "No, Lana. That was sarcasm." She looks at me, trying to keep it together. "Obviously, we know that after someone has been in a coma for nine days, they probably don't want people screaming and jumping out behind curtains."

"Yeah. And probably no to the fireworks too." I shrug, smiling at Ryann. "Though it would have been a nice touch."

"Oh, thank God."

Lana relaxes and heads to the door. Opening it, she bursts into tears as Sutton and Hunter approach the door.

"I said I wasn't going to cry, yet here I am," she sobs. "Ignore me." Wrapping her arms around Sutton, she hugs her. "I am so happy you're home."

Sutton looks tired. And thinner than she did before her stint in the hospital. But I guess all of that is to be expected. Hunter hovers like a helicopter boyfriend, and I can sense he's scared to even let her out of his sight.

It's funny; Hunter was dating my semi-friend Paige before he and Sutton got together. Paige dumped him and broke his heart. But judging by the way he looks at Sutton, I think everything has worked out exactly as it was supposed to. The dude is head over heels in love with the girl.

Maybe, one day, I'll find someone and stop comparing every person I meet to Walker James. I hope so anyway.

As Sutton gets farther into the house and the others are finished hugging her, I take a few nervous steps toward her. "Glad to have you back." I give her a small smile. "You look good."

Her eyes narrow, but the corners of her lips turn up. "You lying bitch, you know I don't look good."

"Fine." I shrug. "You look like ass. Happy?"

She laughs once before sighing. "Thank you, Poppy."

"Anytime." I nod just as Hunter comes next to her, placing his hand on her shoulder.

"Little Bird, it's been a long morning for you. And you're still recovering." He leans down, kissing her cheek. "Let's get you settled in for a nap. All right?"

Rolling her eyes, she grins up at him. "Yes, boss."

As she turns toward the hallway, she holds her hand up at all of us. "Thank you, girls. For the decorations and for making my homecoming so special."

Hunter takes her hand, leading her to her bedroom.

Ryann comes next to me and throws her arm around me. "Proud of you, biotch."

"For what?" I whisper, knowing exactly what she means.

Resting her head on mine, she sighs. "For being nice. For not being an asshole. And for choosing to believe in the good over the bad. You're growing."

I swallow, inhaling a long breath and letting it out. Maybe I am.

I'm doing my best to just … what's that saying? *Let it be*? I mean, Jake called me yesterday, thrilled because Walker had come and seen his house. And then he took him to lunch. I'm happy for Jake. Really, I am. But I guess I'm envious too. Because between them, things have seemingly just gone back to normal.

But if my brother is happy, I will be happy for him too.

My peaceful moment is quickly ruined when my phone rings. When I look down and see it's the prison, I close my eyes for a few seconds before rejecting the call.

Ron Wilson is not going to ruin this day. He's already done that enough to last a lifetime. But today, I'm choosing to believe in the good. And he … he's the furthest thing from that.

WALKER

I don't know why I'm here. I shouldn't be. There's absolutely no point to it besides to stir up old shit that is only going to fuck my head up more than it already is.

Honestly though, Poppy's already fucked it up to the extreme. What's one more thing going to hurt?

Driving past the trailer Poppy, Van, and Jake grew up in, I frown when I see what looks like Cade Huff's truck pulling out of the driveway.

I've done some digging and found out that Van still lives there. Rumor on the street is, now that his old man is in prison, Van has taken over the drug-dealing business.

God, that makes me so fucking sad and pissed off at the same time. But at least Poppy got out of here. And for that, I'm thankful.

What the fuck? I narrow my eyes to see *HUFF4* on the license plate, instantly knowing it is Cade.

I have no clue why he'd be at Van's. That's no place anyone should be. Well, besides crackheads, I suppose. Clearly, Cade isn't who I thought he was. His demons must run deeper than I ever imagined they did.

Luckily, Huff turns out the other way and doesn't see my truck at the end of the street. Once he's gone, I look out my window at my childhood home. The windows are almost all busted out now. And parts of the roof are falling off. The steps look like someone could fall through if they moved wrong. I need to drive away. I need to get out of here.

So, why the fuck am I pushing my truck door open, walking up to it?

When I peer through the windows, it looks completely trashed. Like homeless people had a party inside once we left it. If I know this street, I'm sure that's exactly what happened.

Flashing before me, I see my dad passed out on the couch after shooting up. I see my mom in bed, unable to get up and make breakfast for my sister and me. I see the times they had to Narcan each other, back when they were given free supplies of it.

I see two kids trying to do their homework with absolutely no one around who could help them. Those same kids scrounged through the cupboards, trying to find something, anything to eat.

I see my sister walking out of her room after losing her first tooth. She held it in her hand, confused as to why the tooth fairy hadn't taken it. It didn't take long for us to grow up and not believe in anything.

But as crazy as it is, I look deeper and also see the good.

I remember those eighteen months when they were both sober. There was a Christmas tree in the living room with a few packages under it—one each for Briar and me. Since my mom knew that Ron never acknowledged Christmas, she got Poppy, Jake, and Van each something too.

I remember when Poppy opened hers. It was a bag with her initials on it to put her dance stuff in. She cried. It was the first time I had ever seen tears fall from her eyes, confirming she was human. For Jake, it was a football of his very own. And for Van, it was a cookbook. Because he loved cooking more than anything. I got my first new pair of skates, and Briar got the Harry Potter books she had been wanting. She loved to read that shit.

I have no idea how they had saved money to buy everything, but each gift was given from my mom's heart. And I'll never forget that. Even when they relapsed shortly after and fell back into their addiction. For a short time, my sister and I'd had our parents.

That's something that Poppy and her brothers will never get the chance to say.

Poppy's mother left a few weeks after giving birth to her and Van. And their father, Ron, has done unthinkable things to his children. From locking them in a closet for days at a time to beating them until they were bruised and battered and even trying to allow men to rape his daughter simply to save his own ass.

The world would be a better place if he were dead.

I don't know why I didn't see it sooner. I don't know why she had to scream it out for me to understand. She couldn't lie for me. She had to protect her brothers. It was never about Ron or even herself. It was about Jake. And making sure that he got the life he deserved when he was eighteen.

I've punished her for years. Abandoned her. Convinced myself I hated her even. And now … I've fucked everything up beyond repair.

Before I left, I always thought that when we got a little older, I'd grow a set of balls and tell her exactly how I felt. I never planned to leave Sunset Drive without her. And then I did.

The damage is done. And I don't know how to repair it. Especially when she doesn't look at me the same. She looks at me with those eyes she looks at everyone else with.

Seeing enough, I turn back toward my truck. And that's where I see him.

Van Wilson. A kid I spent most of my time with back then. He was the brother I never had. But now, he looks like a ghost of his old self. He's scrawny with his hair unkempt, his clothes dirty, and his eyes lost.

I should be scared, but I'm too fucking sad to fear him.

"Well, well, well. Look what the cat dragged in." He lights a cigarette before taking a drag. "Rich boy, what the fuck are you doing back on my street?"

"I was … just riding around and ended up here." I take a few steps toward my truck, keeping the distance between us.

Van always had a heart of gold. But the thing with addiction is that it takes the soul and replaces it with something else. Greed. And selfishness.

"Well, go on. Take your privileged ass off my street." He jerks his chin toward my truck. "Before your truck doesn't look so shiny."

"Touch my truck, and I'll put you in the ground," I growl, my eyes roaming over him. "What the fuck happened to you, Van?" I shrug. "You wanted to get out of this shithole. You wanted to own a restaurant. Now, look. You're just like your old man."

"Well, rich boy, not all of us have loaded uncles who step in and invite us to live in their mansions." He takes another drag from his cigarette, blowing the smoke into the air. "For some of us, this is all we've got. So, we make the best of it." He takes a step toward me, snarling, "You got lucky, James—that's all. If your parents hadn't died, you'd be right where I am. Guaranteed."

I charge toward him, grabbing a fistful of his shirt. "Don't mention my parents again, you fucking loser."

He laughs, his eyes sunken in, and I hardly recognize this person who used to be my friend. "Just like my sister, you think you're too good for me now, huh?" Shrugging from my hold, he shakes his head. "You're not. You're a sellout. A poor kid who left his friends and never looked back." He pauses. "Stay the hell away from my sister. Last thing she needs is for you to fuck with her head. Again."

"Your sister made choices too," I mutter, glaring at him. "I'm not the only one who has done shit that had consequences."

When a car pulls into his driveway, he looks back at it before looking at me. "Stay away from my sister. I've got a lot of people who would love nothing more than to take out the kneecaps of the infamous Walker James."

"What happened to you?" I whisper, looking him over.

His eyes soften the slightest bit. "Stay off of this street, James. Don't come back here again."

As he starts to turn, I call behind him, "Whatever business you've got with Cade Huff, leave him the fuck alone."

A bitter laugh comes from him before he turns. "Protecting your fellow Wolf now?" He looks at me with disgust. "There was a time you would protect the ones who considered you family. Glad to see that's not the case." He turns away from me. "Cade Huff's a customer. Believe it or not, Brooks Wolves can be junkies too."

And then he walks away.

I know I can't say anything to Huff. It won't go well. And I sure as hell can't tell on him because that alone could end his entire hockey career. But, fuck, I wish I had never driven here tonight. And then I wouldn't have this information eating away at me, and I wouldn't have seen how bad things have gotten with Van.

He might have told me to stay away from Poppy, but I'm tired of doing that. And the more time passes, the more I'm figuring out … you can't leave some things in the past.

POPPY

Dozens of students, all decked out in their Wolves gear, stop by the coffee shop on their way to tonight's game. I spot girls wearing jerseys with players' names stretched across their backs. Far too many say James, and I wish I could "accidentally" spill some coffee on them.

No. You're supposed to be choosing good. And being nice.

I wonder if Walker ever gets nervous before a game. He never seemed to back when he was younger, but he'd always listen to music before he hit the ice. That had a way of getting him amped up, I guess. But here at Brooks, the stakes are so much higher. I've heard the buzz; he has the weight of being Cam Hardy's replacement resting on his shoulders.

That must be hard. You have to be great or else you'll let your entire team down—no, the entire campus.

Shaking my head, I wipe off the counter. I don't know why I care if he's nervous or not. I don't. Simple as that. Though I can't even think about kissing him the day of the fundraiser, or my knees basically buckle underneath me.

That was the last time I saw him. Two weeks ago.

Every time I see a black truck drive by the coffee shop or I see a group of guys with duffel bags coming from the gym … I wonder if it's him. But then, before I risk seeing him again, I look down.

Some things just aren't meant to be. I've made choices; he's made choices. All for our own needs. But those choices have been the demise between us.

There was a time when I thought he'd always be in my life. Now, we're on the same campus, yet we're both too stubborn to just let the past stay in the past.

He'll be going pro soon, and then he'll have women throwing themselves at him daily. It's probably best that we don't try to rekindle anything. Then again, I guess we never got the chance to light that fuse to begin with.

"Hey, now that the rush is over, I'm going to restock everything we're down on," I call to Jasmin. "You good out here?"

Looking up from her phone, she nods. "Yep. It'll be a ghost town till the game ends anyway." She walks around the counter. "Which reminds me, you know the boss's rules. We need to put the game on for anyone who might come in."

Throwing my head back dramatically, I groan. "Can we at least mute it for now?" *That way, I don't have to listen to the broadcasters say Walker's name five hundred times.*

Chuckling, she nods. "Good plan."

WALKER

After our halftime pep talk, we all head out of the locker room.

"You're not fucking around tonight." Watson grins, glancing back at me. "Nice work out there tonight, James."

"Thanks, Gent. You too." I nod.

"Must be nice to finally have a game when the name Cam Hardy isn't being shoved down your throat five thousand times, huh?" He chuckles. "Don't feel bad. I felt the same way last year when I was the team's new starting goalie. Soon, the team will be yours."

I know what he means by that. Right now, Link is our captain. But next year, he'll be gone. If I don't get into the NHL next season, the torch will likely be passed to me since I'm the center and one of our best players. I'm not quite sure if I'm ready for it though.

I think this has been my best game yet. For the first time since being here, I feel like the guys are working with me and not like I'm an outsider.

It's about time too. And I'm not going to make them regret it.

As we head back onto the ice, I make my way toward Huff.

Cade is acting out of character tonight. I mean, he's always a little off. But tonight, he's more like a zombie. And he's on edge, and he wants absolutely no criticism. He's on the ice, but he's mentally not here. It's becoming increasingly obvious that he's in deep and he needs help. It's been days since I saw him at Van's. And even though I don't want to get into his business, I'm scared for him. So, later tonight, I'll talk to him. I can't keep it in anymore.

"Huff, get it together," I growl at him. "Everyone out here is doing their job besides you."

"Fuck off, James," he mutters, glowering at me. "I'm fucking here, aren't I?"

"Barely," I mumble, shaking my head.

As I skate away, I see Hunter approach Cade. Huff looks pissed, but I just hope whatever Thompson says works. This is only my first season with the team. But Hunter and Cade have been together for two and also live together. If anyone can reach him, it'd be Hunter or Watson.

I want this win more than anything. Maybe Link gets under my skin so badly because I know I'm a lot like him. Intense. Expecting greatness from everyone. I don't want any half-assed players on my team. And today, that's exactly what Cade is.

POPPY

I'm finishing filling sugar bottles, when my phone rings. My first instinct is to ignore it. It could be Ron calling from a different phone in prison, but because it could also be one of my brothers, I know I need to answer it.

"Hello?" I say, glancing up at the television, seeing none other than Walker James skating across the screen, getting ready for the puck drop.

"Poppy Wilson?" a deep voice says, and right away, I feel uneasy.

"This is she."

"Ms. Wilson, this is Officer Herrick." There's a short pause, and my stomach feels like it's balling up inside. "I have some unfortunate news to share with you. Are you, uh ... are you sitting down?"

"Say it," I whisper, my head feeling like a thousand prickly thorns are poking it as I wait for him to say something that I know is going to change my entire life. It's a feeling in the pit of my being. Something I can't shake.

"I'm so sorry to tell you this, Poppy. But it's about Van, your brother." He sighs. "Sadly, we believe he … well, he overdosed. And now, he's dead."

Every bit of air leaves my lungs, and I collapse into a chair. "I'm sorry. Can you repeat that?"

I must have heard him wrong. He couldn't have just told me that Van was dead. Gone. Forever.

"We got an anonymous tip that someone at your brother's address needed assistance. When we got there … he had passed away. We tried to use Narcan, but unfortunately, it was too late." He exhales into the phone. "I am so sorry, Poppy. But we need you to come down to the station."

"What for?" I blurt out, not even knowing what I'm saying. Or how I'm even forming words.

"Though we know it's Van, because of protocol, we need someone to identify him." There's a short pause. "I know it's an incredibly hard thing to ask you to do. And for that, I apologize."

"You want me … to come look at my brother." I stop, feeling like I might throw up. "My *dead* brother. At the police station. Right now."

"If you can, we really would appreciate it." I can hear how awful he feels in his voice, but that doesn't make it better. "Some people need to see it before they can believe it. Before … their brains will allow them to understand it."

I should cry, but I don't. It hurts, but also feels a lot like nothing. My head just feels dizzy. And I can't organize my thoughts for the life of me.

"I'll be there in fifteen minutes," I mutter. "I need to catch the bus there first."

I end the call, hoping that Jasmin didn't hear any of it. And when I see she's taking someone's order, I pull my apron off.

"I have a family emergency," I mutter. "Can you close tonight?"

Nodding, she gives me a concerned look. "Is everything okay?"

"Not really," I utter and turn away from her.

Maybe it's not him. Maybe … they're mistaken.

"Are you sure you don't need a ride somewhere?" the officer says.

Shaking my head, I cross my arms over my chest, almost hugging myself. "No. Thanks."

I came here tonight, hoping that it was someone else. Knowing that would mean another sister, mother, or friend had lost a loved one. Selfishly, I just didn't want it to be my brother.

But it was. It was Van. The same person who had come into the world at the same time I did. The one who usually knew what I was thinking before even I did. My twin.

When I walked in there to identify his body, I looked at his face. And the craziest part about it was that for the first time in years …

He looked peaceful.

And for a split second, I was happy that he had found that feeling. A feeling of harmony that he and I had never really had the chance to find. And I told myself that maybe, just maybe … he was in a better place. A place that wasn't so hard. And so sad and heartbreaking.

But then I'm hit with the cold, harsh reality that my brother is dead. And I can't help but think of how it all seems like such a waste, that he threw it all away.

Because now, my brother will never get better. He'll never go to college. He'll never get married or have kids. I'll never get to be an aunt to his children and get the chance to spoil them rotten. And if I have kids, they'll only hear stories about their uncle Van. But they'll never know that before he went down the road of darkness, he was a boy who loved to cook. Who loved to make people smile. Someone who was a good friend and an even better brother.

It's such a waste of life. And so sad and vain.

Yet, somehow, when I let the dark parts of my brain take over … I envy him the slightest bit.

He doesn't have to feel this pain that's been coursing through my veins since I was born. The kind of pain that makes it exhausting to just get through the day. He doesn't have to ignore the voice inside my head, constantly telling me I'm not worthy of love and affection, which is why I've never been given it.

He's free of this stabbing sensation in my heart that I've carried for so long, always trying to just … block it out. To dance harder. To be tougher. To not let anything or anyone get under my skin. Never show my weakness. To hurt before I can be hurt. To not give a shit that my mother didn't want me. Or that my father doesn't love me. And that, aside from Jake, I've lost everyone I have ever cared about.

I will never hug Van again. I'll never get to pray that he gets better. Nothing.

And while he's resting peacefully, no longer in pain, I'm here.

I'm here, stuck in a place that has done nothing but take since the day I was born.

After finding out that Van's death was going to be investigated and that agents were sweeping his house, I knew what I needed to do next. It will be a long walk to Brooks and the arena, but I need to catch Cade before he leaves for the night. Before he goes to Van's.

WALKER

I push through the door, my duffel bag slung over my shoulder, just as Coach sticks his head out of his office. "A word, James?"

My heart speeds up, and I panic, immediately thinking it's something to do with Huff and LaConte is going to ask me what I know. But instead, he looks … happy.

I take a seat across from him, my knee bouncing. "Yeah, Coach?"

"Nothing is set in stone, and I didn't want to tell you this before the game tonight because I was afraid it'd mess with your head." He pauses, cupping his chin with his fingers. "The New England Bay Sharks called yesterday, asking a lot of questions about you. Word on the street is, their center is retiring real soon." He sits back, pressing his back against his chair harder. "That's a good team they've got up in Maine, son. I think that'd be a great opportunity for you."

"Are you serious?" I whisper, my head beginning to spin.

He nods curtly. "I am. But like I said, nothing is set in stone, so please don't get your hopes up or send out cards, telling the whole damn campus." The corner of his lip turns up in a crooked grin. "But you're on their radar, James. And that's something to celebrate right there."

"Thank you, Coach." I push myself to stand. "Am I free to go?"

I don't want him to feel like I'm rushing out of here. Especially when he just told me this news—which, even if it's not a done deal, is huge. But I really need to talk to Cade. And something tells me I need to hurry because he's going to rush out of here like he always does.

"Go on." He waves toward the door. "Don't be celebrating our win tonight too hard tonight though, you hear?"

"Yes, sir. Thank you."

I quickly bolt out of his office and head toward the exit, knowing I'm probably too late. Because not only did I talk to LaConte for a few minutes, but Cade also somehow finished interviews before me, so the chances that he's left are already high. But I need to talk to him. I need to confront him on what I know.

That he has ties to Van Wilson.

Walking out of the locker room, I make my way toward the arena's exit. My steps come to a stop when I watch Cade hug Poppy, both of them as pale as ghosts. He holds on to her for a moment, and I can read her body language like a book. Something is wrong. She's upset.

Slowly, he releases her, and she says something else to him before she bolts through the doors and rushes outside. Cade follows but heads straight to his truck.

Rushing outside, I look around to see where she went. I know she wouldn't be walking anywhere this late other than home. So, after throwing my bag in the back of my truck, I take off running.

Within a minute, I see her. She's walking along the dirt path down the dimly lit hill. Her hood is up, hiding her hair, but I know it's her.

"Poppy?" I call out.

Her shoulders tense, but she doesn't turn. Within a few seconds, she starts sprinting, trying her best to get away from me.

"What the fuck?" I groan, chasing her down.

She's quick, but her legs are a helluva lot shorter than mine are. And it's no time when I come up behind her and throw her over my shoulder.

"What the hell are you doing?" I yell. "Why are you running away from me like a fucking crazy person?"

Kicking her legs and flailing her arms, she acts like a damn wild animal.

Then again, that's what Poppy has always reminded me of—a coyote in society. Mean. Dangerous. But also slightly misunderstood.

Coyotes don't redeem themselves after they've eviscerated other animals. Because if you give them long enough, they'll just do it again. Maybe she can't be redeemed either.

"Stop fighting me, my fucking God, Pop," I hiss, tightening my grip on her ass to still her. "Cut the shit. I just want to make sure you're okay."

"Chasing after me in the fucking dark and then throwing me over your shoulder is a weird way of showing it, asshole!" she growls. "Put. Me. Down!"

"If I put you down, will you talk to me?"

She stills, huffing out a breath. "What do you want to talk about, Walker? What could you possibly have to say?"

"What were you and Huff talking about?" I say into the darkness, holding her body over my shoulder.

"None of your business," she snaps. "He's my friend. You are not."

"The look on your face tonight, it was … different," I whisper.

She grows silent. "Yeah, well, not like you'd care, but I guess having to identify your twin brother's body will probably do that." She begins flailing again. "Put. Me. Down."

Immediately, I set her down, but I keep my hands planted on her waist. "Van is dead?" I barely get the words out of my mouth, my throat burning.

"Don't act sad about it," she snarls. "We all know you didn't give a damn about him."

"That's not true." I shake my head quickly. "That isn't true, and you know it."

Her eyes narrow, staring at me like I'm a monster. "I don't know anything when it comes to you. I knew Walker James, the boy down the street who was my best friend. The one who took away my pain and knew the right thing to say to make everything better." She eyes me up and down before exhaling. "The guy in front of me? He's just a stranger."

"It's still me, Poppy," I say through gritted teeth. Out of nowhere, tears blur my vision. "I'm still me. And I'm right here."

She looks up at me, and I watch her face soften as she looks for any sign that I'm full of shit. But the moment is gone as quickly as it came, and suddenly, she's shoving her hands into my chest, pounding on my body as haunting screams come from her lips.

"You aren't the same, and you know it!" Every word she yells at me is filled with anger. "You weren't there for him! He loved you. You were his best friend. And you left!"

She continues beating her fists into my chest. And I let her. Because her brother just died. And because I'm a fucking failure, she had to identify his body alone.

She had to see her brother—her fucking twin brother—lifeless on a table.

Nausea hits me, but I push the thought down of needing to puke. Right now, I need to be whatever she needs. Even if what she needs is a literal punching bag. For her, I'll be it.

She's so close to losing it. I know she's about to fall apart. Years of shit she's tried to push down is going to come to the surface, mixing in with the death of Van.

I'm scared for her. Who can stand pain like that?

"We needed you! And you left!" she screams, almost like she's no longer controlling her actions. "He had no one!" Her movements begin to grow weaker as exhaustion kicks in. "I. Had. No one."

It happens. The tears start, and her voice breaks. Her shoulders slump, and her body sinks. But before she can fall into a pile on the sidewalk, I hold her up.

"I'm so tired of having no one," she cries, letting herself fall against my chest.

Wrapping my arms around her, I cradle her. "Shh," I mutter against her hair.

Her body quivers against mine. I can tell she's tired. Why wouldn't she be? I'm sure this has been the most emotionally draining night of her life.

"Come home with me, Poppy," I say softly. "I don't want you to be alone right now."

"No." She quickly shakes her head, though she doesn't pull away.

"The guys are both gone tonight. You can go back to hating me in the morning." I keep my cheek firmly against her temple. "But tonight, please, just stay with me." I pause. "Let me be your somebody tonight. The way I should have been all along."

The night is so quiet as she lays her body against mine. Finally, she pulls back slightly, wiping her cheeks with the sleeve of her hoodie. "Okay," she whispers. "But only for tonight."

Slowly, I pick her up. Tucking her head to my chest, I carry her in my arms and start back toward the arena.

Sometimes, things just need to fall apart before they can fully come together. I'm ready for us to finally fucking be together now. Because it seems like there's nothing else that could possibly fall apart.

POPPY

Everything hurts. My eyes, from crying. My head, from hyperventilating. And my heart, because my brother is dead. And I did nothing to help him. The last time we talked, I wasn't even that nice.

And then there's the worst part: I have to tell Jake—my sweet, sensitive brother—that his only brother is gone. Because if I don't, who else will?

I decide I'll tell the news to him in the morning after I've processed it and figured out my emotions.

And as much as I hate to, I need to call the prison so that someone can tell Ron too. He's the last person I'm worried about knowing, but Van never gave up on him for whatever reason. In fact, they had weekly phone calls.

Probably to talk about the family drug business. Yes, very important matters.

I stand under the shower for God knows how long. I never thought I'd be here, in Walker's shower, with a pile of his clothes on the bathroom counter for me to sleep in. Yet here I am.

Other than Jake, Walker is the only other familiar person I have.

Which sucks.

Squeezing the excess water out of my hair, I turn the water off and step out. Drying myself off, I comb my hair out the best I can with my fingers and pull on his Wolves sweatpants and T-shirt.

I swipe a circle in the mirror, wiping the fog away with my hand, and look at myself. My eyes are swollen and red, and my cheeks are blotchy. I look as bad as I feel. But I have a feeling I need to get used to it because I'll probably feel this way for a while.

Crying for the first time in years really took its toll on me. I'm ready to go back to not feeling. Or trying to pretend like I don't.

My hand grabs the doorknob and twists it open. If I were in my right mind, I'd probably be anxious right now, walking into a room with one bed and Walker James, likely shirtless. But right now, everything is numb. And the last thing I feel is nervous.

There he sits, on the edge of the bed. His shirt is very much on with a pair of basketball shorts. Even in such a dark time, my heart skips a beat as I take him in. He's that guy who, when he walks past you, you do a double take.

When he sees me coming out of the bathroom, he stands. "You can say no, but I'd really like to sleep in here. With you." He takes a few steps toward me. "But if you aren't comfortable with that, I can sleep on the couch in the living room."

His living room is tiny. Though the dorms for the hockey and football players are still a heck of a lot bigger than average dorms. But I saw the couch. I'm not sure he'd even fit, fully stretched out.

I shouldn't care. But for some reason, I do.

Or maybe it's just because I want him next to me, just like when we were kids.

"It's fine." I walk past him, sitting on the opposite side I saw him on.

I don't know when it happens—I couldn't say the exact second—but suddenly, the air between us is thick. And when his eyes find mine, I suck in a shaky breath, even knowing that it's an inappropriate time to be looking at him the way that I am.

He runs his hand down the back of his neck uneasily. "Do you, uh … need anything from me tonight? Some water? Or a sweatshirt to sleep in?"

Swallowing thickly, I give him a small shake of my head and look down. "No, I don't need water. Or a sweatshirt." Raising my eyes to his again, I bite my bottom lip anxiously. "I need something else. Something … to numb the pain."

He looks uneasy. "What's that?" he rasps.

"You," I whisper, more tears flowing down my cheeks. "Please, Walker. Make it stop hurting."

Slowly, he walks toward me. Each step, it's almost like he knows he shouldn't be taking it. And when he reaches me, he crouches down to my level. "Poppy, I'd give you anything in the world. All you have to do is ask." He stops, looking down and sighing before his eyes reach mine again. "But I want you to be sure. I didn't bring you here tonight for anything other than to just be here for you." This time, a tear falls from his eye, going down his cheek. "The way I should have been all along."

Reaching for the hem of his shirt that I'm wearing, I pull it from my body and toss it on the bed next to me. He drags in a shaky breath before closing his eyes.

"Poppy … what are you—"

"Open your eyes, Walker," my voice croaks, my throat raw from crying. And screaming. "Please. Look at me."

Gradually, his eyes flutter open, but he stares at my face, not so much as looking down at my chest.

"Am I that awful to look at?" I whimper. "Am I so skinny that it repulses you?"

His hand cups my cheek. "You're the most beautiful thing I've seen in my entire life," he whispers. "But right now, you're hurting."

Now, I lean forward, and without permission, I pull his shirt over his head. And when he stands in front of me, I press my palm to his abdomen.

"Please, Walker. Fix me," I whimper. "I can't take it anymore. I can't take this pain."

"I want to, Poppy. So fucking bad that it hurts," he barely whispers. "But I don't know if this is the way. And I don't want you to wake up and regret this in the morning."

"If you ever cared about me at all, you'll do this for me." My lip trembles. "I'll never ask for anything again. I just … need something to make it better." I swallow back more emotion. "It hurts so fucking bad. Everything hurts."

"Tell me what you need," he says, and through his jeans, I watch the bulge grow harder.

"For you to make me forget. For a little while."

He's still for a moment before, finally, he leans forward. Sliding his hands to my waist, he moves me further up the bed. His fingertips go to my waistband, and he slowly tugs the sweatpants from my body, leaving me completely bare.

"I'm going to taste you if that's okay," he says so softly. "I want you to relax. This is for you. But if you feel uncomfortable or need me to stop, just say the word. Okay, baby?"

I'm so scared, yet I want this so bad. But this is my first time being with anyone. And that's embarrassing enough to tell him. And then there's the other part of me that feels so completely messed up for wanting this right now. At a time like this.

"Has anyone ever tasted you, Poppy?" He climbs over me, bringing his lips to mine first.

He kisses me, his mouth tasting like mint as his tongue slowly teases against mine.

"N-no," I say, embarrassment filling my body.

It's almost as if realization hits him, and he stills. "Have you ever been with anyone?"

When I don't answer right away, he kisses my forehead. "Just want to make sure I'm gentle, baby. I don't want to hurt you."

"You're the only person I've ever even kissed," I blurt out before bringing my hands to my face to cover myself up.

Pulling my hands down, he kisses me again. "Do you feel how fucking hard my dick is right now, Poppy? And it just got harder because I'm your first." He stops, his voice growing thicker. "You want me to be your first?"

"Yes," I utter, but then I realize that Cade Huff was actually my first kiss. Even though it was fake and all for show. And looking back, I truthfully can't believe I kissed him at the bar that night, all to make a point. And I completely wasted my first kiss on ... well, him. "Welp, actually ... Cade was my first kiss," I mutter. "But ... he doesn't really count."

His eyes burn into mine, and I can feel how annoyed my words have made him. "You gave your first kiss to Huff?" His voice is low.

"Well, yeah. But ... it was only to prove to him that the girl he likes cares." I pause. "And pissing you off in the process, well, that wasn't so bad either."

"I'm pissed that Huff was your first kiss and not me," he utters.

Moving his kisses to my neck, he sucks gently at first, then harder. He moves down my body to my collarbone, kissing his way across it. And when he gets to my breast, I can't stop the moan that rips from my lips. His tongue feels so good, but I'm terrified for him to go down ... there.

He kisses his way down my stomach before he presses his lips to each of my hip bones. "You're so perfect, Poppy."

I've always been self-conscious about my weight. I'm scrawny. I'm a dancer, but I also have never had the privilege of stuffing my face with three meals a day. Even now, that's not easy to do with work, dance, and school. Not to mention always being low on cash.

But right now, I don't feel like the scrawny girl. I feel ... beautiful and desired.

His tongue moves between my legs, and again ... I moan. He goes slow at first, and my hands can't help but tangle into his hair, pushing him deeper and harder.

This feels like ... heaven. Whatever he's doing with his mouth and the movements with his tongue ... I feel like I'm falling into this mattress, spinning into oblivion. His thumb brushes along what is apparently my most sensitive spot, rubbing small circles. And I'm gone, losing myself to him.

My entire body succumbs to his mouth, and my brain goes dark. I can't tell you how long I stay in this state of euphoria, but when I come to, he's slowly climbing his way back up my body.

"Was that okay?" he asks, his eyes uneasy. "I hope I didn't take it too far."

"It … was … perfect," I whisper before I part my legs further and wrap them around his waist. "Fuck me, Walker. Be my first."

He sucks in a breath, and his cock presses into my thigh. Kissing my forehead, he widens his eyes. "Are you sure, Poppy? It doesn't have to be tonight." He blinks a few times. "I'll wait for you for as long as it takes."

"It has to be tonight," I say quickly. Knowing that there won't be any other time. This can't continue.

But tonight, I just need an escape. And maybe it's not right to use him this way, but he's the only one who can make it better.

Arching my back off the bed, I bring my mouth to his. Not really caring that his mouth was just between my legs. Snaking my hand between us, I palm his dick and slide my hand back and forth, making him moan.

"I need to get a condom," he says against my lips. "Jesus, Poppy. I've wanted this for so long."

"I have an IUD. I got it a long time ago, just in case." I tighten my legs around him. "Please, Walker, I don't want you to wear a condom. I just want … all of you." I sniffle. "Just this once."

WALKER

Maybe I'm a bad guy for going down on her and now taking the virginity of a girl who just lost her brother. But she fucking begged me. And how the hell was I supposed to say no?

I could have come just from eating her tight pussy. The way she squeezed my tongue as her hips thrust against my face. She wanted every ounce of that orgasm she could get. She fucked my face till the bitter end.

Slowly, I push the tip of my dick inside of her heat. Right away, I'm whimpering because she feels so fucking good.

How the hell am I going to last long enough to make this good for her?

"It's going to hurt a little, but because you're dripping wet, that'll help," I tell her, looking down at her pretty face. "But if it's too much, just tell me."

"Okay," she whispers, keeping her death grip on my waist with her legs.

"Promise me, you'll say," I growl this time.

"Yes." She nods. "I promise."

"Good girl," I praise her, and I swear she gets even wetter.

Gradually, I begin to push more and more of myself into her. She hisses, sucking in a breath, but she doesn't indicate that she wants me to stop.

I can't fuck her as hard as I'd like to tonight. That'll take a few more times before I'll even consider that. I want tonight to be about her. And that starts with her being comfortable.

"Christ, Poppy. You feel so good," I grunt, working only about half of my length inside of her, and already, I'm struggling not to blow my load. "You're doing so good, baby."

Her nails dig into my back, and she drives her face into my neck. She's crying now, making me instantly stop moving as I crane my head to look at her.

"Don't stop," she whimpers before angling her face toward mine.

One look in her eyes, and my heart fucking shatters.

"Kiss me," she sobs.

Bringing my lips to hers, I kiss her soft, plump lips as I gently pump in and out of her.

"Harder," her voice squeaks.

"I don't want to hurt you," I murmur against her lips, my forehead on hers. "I've already done that too many times."

I watch tears gather in her eyes and roll down her cheeks.

"I want it to hurt. It takes my mind off my life," she whispers, her voice cracking. "This kind of pain … it's better than the other kind."

There's no universe where I'd fuck Poppy full force on a night like tonight, never mind the fact that she's a virgin. But I'll do my best to give her what she wants. And slowly, I begin feeding more of my cock inside of her, each pump a little faster.

She cries harder but holds my body closer to hers, kissing me rougher.

"I'm sorry," I say, kissing her lips. "I'm so fucking sorry, Poppy."

She digs her fingertips into my back, hugging me tighter.

"I'll do whatever it takes to make it up to you." I kiss her again, feeling her pussy start to tighten around me, sending my balls into a tailspin.

"Walker," she whimpers.

"Let go, baby. Let go of it all and come undone for me."

I move my head down, kissing her neck as my seed spills inside of her, and she moans, coming on my cock. Her nails make my flesh damn near bleed.

Her chest heaves, a mixture of moans and cries leaving her mouth, all at the same time, as she comes back down from her orgasm.

I want to tell her I love her. That I've loved her since we were kids and that I've never stopped loving her. But tonight isn't about what I want. It's about getting her through the toughest day of her life.

And being the man she once thought I was.

POPPY

The dull sting between my legs is nothing compared to the ache in my chest. I woke up, wishing that it were a nightmare, losing my brother. But I'm hit with the harsh reality that it wasn't, and now, I need to break the news to Jake.

I allow myself another gaze at Walker as the sun begins to peek out, waking up the sky and starting the day. The light shines on his face, and for the first time in years, I try my best to memorize every line, freckle, and feature. So badly, I want to lean down and press my lips to his. But one night can't fix everything. And right now, I have bigger fish to fry than figuring out my extremely confusing, all-over-the-place feelings for Walker James.

Slowly, I slide out from under the covers, careful not to let the bed creak. Quickly yet quietly, I pull on yesterday's clothes. Tiptoeing across the floor, I slide my feet into my sandals, looking back at him again. The comforter rests at his waist, and he has one arm above his head and his gorgeous face turned slightly toward the window.

I wish I could stay in the moment when he made love to me last night. If I could, I'd never leave. Because for once in so long, I didn't feel the pain of everything. And just as I'd always wanted, it was us against the world.

Pulling the door open, I walk out. Leaving Walker sound asleep, knowing that when he wakes up, he'll think I'm next to him.

WALKER

Before my eyes even adjust to the light, I know she's gone without physically seeing it. My hand reaches the side of the bed she fell asleep on, and I find it cold.

Shooting straight up, I toss the blankets off and leap out of bed before pulling on my sweatpants. Running out into the main part of the dorm, I look around.

"Poppy!" I yell, knowing it's useless.

She ran.

I wish I were surprised, but I'm not. I stayed awake for as long as I could, just listening to her breathing. And held her closer when she winced in her sleep. None of that will ever be enough though.

Trying to love her will be like bringing a stray animal inside after it's spent its entire life in the wild. Just like that animal, she won't trust me, and she'll always be ready to run.

I'd be stupid to even bother. But I'm going to try anyway.

I still don't have her number, but I know who does.

After dialing Cade and getting no answer five times, I call Lana.

"Walker?" she says after answering on the first ring. "Are you with Poppy by chance?"

"No. I was last night, but she's gone." I drag my hand over the back of my head. "I need her number. Okay?"

"I'll text it to you," she says quickly, and seconds later, I see the text come through. "Done."

"Thanks. I gotta go."

Before I can hang up, she stops me. "Walker, if you see her ... can you call me?" The worry in her voice is clear. "I know you said she was with you, but she didn't come home. And she never does that."

I can't tell Lana about Van. It isn't my place.

So, instead, I nod into my empty room. "I'll let you know. She's, uh ... well, she's going through it right now. And she's going to need her friends." I swallow. "All of you need to be there for her, okay?"

"What happened?" she whispers, her voice breaking.

"I can't tell you. That's up to her. For now, just be her friend. She deserves that."

"I will," she answers softly. "I promise."

Ending the call, I quickly throw my shirt.

She might want to run away from me, but I need to find her.

POPPY

I sit with my brother on the couch as we hold on to each other. The whole bus ride here, my stomach hurt so bad that I felt like I could throw up because I knew that this was going to break him.

Jake cries, and I hug him.

"It sucks." I sniffle. "I miss him already."

Telling him was the hardest thing I'd done in my entire life. Jake understands that Van had demons, like our father had. But he still loved Van and talked about him all the time.

"He didn't get to see my new home," he utters. "I think he would have liked it."

Squeezing my eyes shut, I nod slowly. "He would have loved this place, J," I whisper.

It really is just him and me now. And I will do everything I can to make sure he knows I'll always be here for him. That, unlike our mother, father, and now brother ... he can count on me to never leave.

Thinking of my father reminds me that I still have to call the prison.

Great.

Standing outside of Jake's apartment by myself, I pull out my phone and dial the prison. Once a lady with a thick Southern accent answers, I suck in a breath through my nose and let it out of my mouth.

"Hi, this is Poppy Wilson. My father, Ronald Wilson, is an inmate there."

"Okay? Well, I can't connect you. It's not his day to make phone calls—"

"I don't want to talk to him. I just have a message for someone to pass along." I swallow, trying to ease the burning in my throat. "His son Van died yesterday. I just thought he should probably be told."

"Oh," she says, pausing. "I'm so—"

"Thank you for passing on the message," I mutter and end the call.

My duty as Van's sister is done. Our dad—who is the very definition of the scum of the earth in my eyes, but a hero in Van's—has been notified.

Another thing off my list of awful, emotional shit I have to do today.

Next up … write an obituary for a kid this town has grown to hate.

A loud exhaust startles me, and I look up to find Walker's truck pulling into the parking lot of the apartment building.

"Damn it," I mutter.

I knew there was a chance he'd come find me today. But I didn't think he'd know I was here. Yet here he is, proving me wrong.

Slowly, he gets out of the truck and closes the door. His gray sweatpants immediately make my mouth water, so I look away.

"Thought I might find you here," he drawls softly.

"You didn't take the hint that maybe I didn't want to be found when you woke up and I was gone?" I shake my head. "What are you doing here, Walker?"

"I'm here for you. And for Jake."

He stops in front of me; his Brooks hockey T-shirt hugs his biceps, and I want to crash against him and let him hold me tight.

I can't get used to him always being here to make it all better though. He's proven before that when given the chance, he will leave. So, instead, I take a step back.

"I can't do this today," I whisper. "You need to go."

His hands ball at his sides, and he groans in frustration. "So, that's how it will always be then? You don't trust me, and you never will? Or what? Just tell me what I have to do, and I'll do it."

"I can't do this!" I hiss. "I need to go home and get ready for work. I still have to finish writing my brother's obituary. I need to go to the trailer and go through nearly two decades of shit. All while catching a bus to all of these places." I suck in a breath through my nose, frustrated. "I don't have time to unbox whatever the hell is going on inside your head today."

"You shouldn't work today, Poppy," he says. His eyes stare into mine, making me feel completely naked. "Can I go in and see Jake?"

I fold my arms over my chest, narrowing my eyes. "Are you just going to get his hopes up that you'll be around and then leave again? He has had enough people do that to him. He doesn't need to survive you doing it … twice."

"I'm not going anywhere." He looks sad and almost defeated. "I just want to be there for him through this. For you too."

Glancing back at Jake's apartment door, I sigh. "Go on. But I'm leaving. I have to go get ready for work."

"Poppy, you should—"

"Not all of us have endless money from our uncles, Walker! Goddamn it!" I hiss. "Don't you get it? Even to have Van cremated is going to take every cent of money I've saved up."

Realization flashes on his face, and he swallows before heading toward the apartment. When he gets right next to me, he stops. "I'm here. I will be here from now on."

I close my eyes, and a shooting pain soars through my chest.

"You've said that before," I mutter before I start to walk away.

"Poppy," he calls out.

When I look over my shoulder, he turns to face me again.

"Take my truck. The keys are in it." He jerks his chin toward the Chevy. "I don't have practice until later. I can catch a ride with one of the guys."

I can't drive his truck. Though it would make things easier for the tasks at hand, it would make everything even more confusing in my heart.

"Thank you," I say, dropping my shoulders. "But I'm all set."

"Use the fucking truck, Pop," he growls.

Right now, I can't do this. A month ago, I would have loved for him to act like he cared. But at this moment in time, I'm at my limit of what I can do. And letting Walker into my life isn't one of them.

Between planning this funeral and practices this week for my performance in *The Nutcracker* ... my plate isn't just full. It's freaking overflowing.

I head to the bus stop when he walks into Jake's apartment. Because I'm not about to let Walker James think that I cannot live without his help.

WALKER

What a little shit. I watch out the window as Poppy walks to the bus stop and takes a seat on the bench. Even though I just told her—no, demanded that she take my truck. I want to help her through this week. I want to make it easier on her, though I know that'll be a hard job.

It's hard to help someone who won't accept a damn bit of help though.

"She will come around," Jake says from the couch. "She's just ... tough."

"You're not joking." I breathe out a laugh. "That's one word to describe your sister."

"You love her though," he says, and when I turn around, he's watching the TV screen. "Even though you hurt her feelings. And made her sad when you left." He looks at me, shaking his head. "You knucklehead."

"Yeah, yeah. I know." I look out the window again and watch as the bus stops in front of her and opens its door.

She climbs up the stairs, and I can hardly see her through the darkened windows as she walks through the aisle and finds a seat.

I don't know how to be there for her without being overbearing. And she isn't the easiest person to help through things.

"Van was sad. He's better now." There's no mistaking the pain in Jake's voice as he talks about his brother.

And I'm sure telling him was the hardest thing Poppy has had to do. She loves Jake more than she loves anyone or anything. She'd never want to hurt him.

Walking toward him, I take a seat on the couch. "I think so too." I look down. "Wish I could have been there for him. And for you and Poppy. I'm ... I'm sorry, Jake."

He looks me in the eye for a moment before looking away. "Then ... be there for her now. And don't leave."

He's right. And that's exactly what I'm going to do. I'm not a patient man. Not usually anyway. But I'm beginning to learn that Poppy needs patience from me.

So, I'm about to be the most patient fucker anyone's ever seen.

WALKER

The bus ride home from Florida is long, and I'm thankful we're only fifteen minutes from Brooks now. I've texted Poppy an embarrassing number of times since we left for our away games on Friday morning, and all I've received back are a few one- to two-worded responses.

Between all the shit with Van and then add in that Cade Huff has left Brooks and is in rehab, it's been one shitty week. This whole season, he's been battling drug addiction, and no one knew. Well, besides me, and that's only because I saw him at Van's.

Van overdosed and died. And that fucking sucks for Poppy and Jake. But if he hadn't died, I keep wondering if Cade would have ever gone to rehab. He could have died instead.

Life is so fucking crazy sometimes.

We won our games, but everyone could feel Cade's absence on the ice. The team is a big, slightly dysfunctional family. And without him, our family isn't complete.

I peer over the seat at Coach LaConte, who is staring out the window. I think out of everyone, he's taking it the hardest. He's always had a soft spot for Huff. And I think, in a lot of ways, he feels as though he failed Huff by not seeing the signs.

I know one thing: he's going to be upping how much he piss-tests the team. He's made it clear that this sort of thing isn't going to slip by him again.

It's been five days since Van passed away. I don't know if Poppy is planning a funeral or if she isn't having one. All I know is that whatever she's planning, I want to be there for her and Jake during it.

Even if that pisses her off.

I'm thankful that Jake isn't hanging the past over my head. He's just happy to have me back around. And when I look around at everything he's accomplished, I understand why his sister did what she did.

Three years were wasted with me hating her because I was too fucking stupid to think about everything from her side.

The other night, I got to taste her and bury my cock inside of her, all in the same hour. I'm forever a changed man, and I'm pretty sure any future hookup will be ruined. I knew that was what would happen. I'd thought about doing what we did for years. Then, it happened.

Now, I can't stop thinking about her.

I've spent the past few years sleeping around, hoping it would get her out of my brain. But I don't want to forget her anymore. Who am I kidding? I couldn't even if I wanted to.

"I think the entire ride back from Florida, you've maybe said five words," Hunter says after sliding his headphones onto his neck. "You seem off. Is it because of everything with Cade?"

"I guess," I mutter, knowing there's a lot more going on with me, but not wanting to explain that right now. "Have you heard from him?"

"Huff?" He shakes his head. "Nah. He can't talk to anyone for the first few weeks there."

"Fucking sucks," I utter.

"Yeah, I know." He gives me a small nod. "You know I heard the kid who was dealing him drugs overdosed and died? I keep thinking that could have been Huff." His face pales. "Just goes to show we don't all know each other as well as we'd like to think we do."

I don't tell him that I knew Van for most of my life. Or that despite him being a drug dealer, he had a good heart but had been born into a world that he couldn't escape. That, unlike Hunter and so many others, Van truly did think he didn't have any other option in life but to follow in his father's footsteps. I knew him enough to know that if Van had had more guidance, he wouldn't be dead right now.

"He'll be okay," I tell him, knowing he's worrying about Huff.

"What if he's not though? What if he gets out of rehab and then it gets worse?"

I think back to my friendship with Van—a friendship I abandoned and never looked back. I can't turn back time and be better. But I can vow to be better from here on out.

"Then, we'll all be here for him to remind him of how much he has to lose," I say evenly. "We'll keep a better eye out. We'll be better friends to him."

Giving me an unsure look, he finally nods. "Yeah, we will." He gives me a small grin. "Good job this weekend, James. You're playing like a Wolf now."

"Thanks." I tip my chin down. "I appreciate that."

Just when the team is starting to see me as a true teammate and good player, I'm going to fuck it up by distracting myself with making Poppy Wilson forgive me.

But in a perfect world, it's not just about hockey. Or Poppy. It's both.

And eventually, I will have both.

The bus pulls into a parking lot at Brooks University, and I quickly begin gathering my shit up.

First stop, find Poppy.

POPPY

I furiously hit the keyboard of the laptop the school has been letting me borrow. I'm rarely behind on assignments, but this week has been grueling, and my schoolwork has been put on the back burner.

I have yet to go to the trailer and go through Van's stuff. But I did get his obituary written, as well as worked out a payment plan for his cremation. To add to the craziness, I have been practicing for a huge part in *The Nutcracker*, which I was chosen for at the beginning of the school year. Ryann and I both have big parts in it. And while I'm thrilled to do it with her, it's another thing on my already-full plate.

But it'll be fine. This, too, shall pass.

"Knock, knock," Ryann says, pushing on my door and peeking in at me. "You've got a visitor, babe."

Looking up from the computer, I narrow my eyes. "Who?"

"A tall, delicious Walker James." She winks. "Yummy."

"Don't you have a boyfriend?" I tilt my head to the side. "I've seen you and Watson Gentry lookin' awfully snuggly together. And after all that talk that you weren't interested."

"This isn't about me right now," she says, rolling her eyes. "I told him you'd be right out."

Turning my attention back to the screen, I shake my head. "Nope. Tell him I'm sick. Tell him I have diarrhea or am projectile puking. Anything. Just don't let him in."

"You're going to tell a man who looks like *that*, that you're in here, shitting your pants?" She gives me an *are you serious* look. "For real?"

"No." I smirk. "You are."

"You are too much," she huffs out before leaving the room, closing the door behind her.

I'm just getting back into the swing of typing when my door flies open. Looking up, I shut my computer and shoot Walker a glare.

"For real? Why are you here?"

"You don't look like you're sick, Poppyseed." He takes a few steps forward, stopping at the end of my bed. "In fact, you look pretty fucking healthy."

"So, take the hint that I don't want company." I shrug. "Why do you insist on showing up where I am when I clearly don't want you to?"

"Oh, you do want me to," he says confidently, irking me deep in my soul. "You don't have to lie, babe."

My gaze sweeps over him unwillingly. The Wolves sweatpants instantly make an ache form deep inside of me as flashes of his face between my legs assault my brain. For days, I've refused to think about what happened between us.

Never mind the fact that I lost my virginity the day my brother died. What is wrong with me? That should have been the last thing on my mind that night. I'm truly pathetic.

My phone rings on the bed beside me, and I look at it, knowing it's the cremation company.

"Well, what are you doing? Give me a minute, would you?" I shoot him a glare and shoo him into the hallway.

Once he leaves my room, I slide my thumb across the screen and answer. "Hello?"

"Hi, Ms. Wilson?" a kind female voice says.

"This is she."

"Hi there. It's Martha. I was just calling to say that we have your brother here. He's ready to be picked up." She pauses. "And from what I've read from my coworker's notes, you're going to pay a little today, and then we've set you up on a payment plan for ... one hundred ten dollars a month. Does that sound correct?"

"Yes," I say, feeling my cheeks heat. Even through the phone, I'm embarrassed about how broke I am. "I have two hundred thirty to put toward it. I'm sorry. I, uh, I'm in college. And I just don't have a lot of money saved—" I stutter over my words.

Jake tried to give me some of the money he'd saved from working, but I didn't want to take it. He'll need it to pay for his utilities and groceries now that he's on his own.

"Oh, no. Please do not apologize, darling," she assures me. "Really, it's no problem at all. Do you plan to pick him up today?"

"Um, yes. I don't have a car, but I'm sure I can find a way," I say, tapping my foot as I try to think of how the hell I'm going to get him. I know Ryann will let me use her car. I hate to ask her, but I don't have another option in this case. "I'll be over shortly."

"Thank you. See you soon."

"Bye," I mutter, ending the call.

Walker wastes no time walking back into the room. "Get dressed, Poppyseed." He waves toward my flannel pajama bottoms. "Unless you're going to wear those out."

"Where are we going?" I place my hand on my hip.

"To get your brother," he says matter-of-factly. "I'll be out in the truck."

"Walker ... you don't need to—"

Taking a few steps toward me, he places his hands on my forearms. "I'm not offering. I'm telling." His eyes sweep over my face, stopping on my lips for a moment, making every cell in my body buzz. Finally, he steps back, removing his hands from my arms. "Come out when you're ready."

And then he leaves, and my heart flutters the slightest bit.

Little by little, he's working his way back into my soul.

And that scares the hell out of me.

The lady behind the counter sets the urn before me. "I'm going to go grab a box you can set it in. Be right back."

The urn I chose is the cheapest one they had, but it's sleek and black, and I think Van would have liked it—I hope so anyway.

Walker stands beside me, his hand moving to my lower back. "You all right?"

I don't say anything, but nod my head once. His hand stays on my back, slowly moving back and forth to remind me he's here.

The lady returns, picks up the urn, and puts it inside a box. "You're all set."

I look at her, confused. "Um, I still need to pay. At least the first payment anyway."

Her brows furrow. "Oh, um ... the bill was taken care of."

"No"—I shake my head—"it wasn't."

Walking to the computer, she hits a few keys. "It's paid in full, Ms. Wilson."

"Come on," Walker says, picking up the box.

For a moment, I'm frozen. And then it hits me.

Walker did this.

He did this and didn't even tell me.

WALKER

"Why would you do that?" Poppy asks as I pull out of the parking lot after picking Van's ashes up.

"Do what?" I play dumb, knowing this could go one of two ways.

One, she'll be completely pissed that I paid for Van to be cremated. Or, two, she'll appreciate it. I know she's completely broke, and the thought of her spending every cent she'd made to pay for her brother's death gutted me. I couldn't let it happen, especially when I have an uncle who gave me a credit card for emergencies. And to him, the money it cost for Van's cremation is pocket change.

"You heard me on the phone, didn't you?" She scowls from the passenger side. Before I can answer, she throws her head back against the headrest. "Damn it, Walker. Why do you keep doing nice things?"

I glance over at her. Her jaw is tense, and her breathing is sharp.

"Because I want to."

Her eyes fly back to mine. "Because you want to?" She shakes her head. "And how long will you want to before you take off again? Huh?"

"Would you just stop?" I say, continuing to drive. "It's not a big deal."

"It's a big deal to me!" she yells. "You know what? Pull over!"

"What? No," I say, seeing her hand resting on the door handle.

"Pull. Over," she growls.

"Oh my fucking word! You're such a pain in the ass!" I roar, tearing into an empty parking lot. "Just be a normal fucking person and say, *Thank you, Walker*, and move along!"

When I slam my truck into park, she starts to push the door open, but I reach over, gripping her chin.

"Just let me do something nice for you, for fuck's sake!"

"You did nice shit before, Walker!" Her eyes are wild, and as she sucks in deep breaths, her tits strain against her T-shirt. "You were *always* doing nice shit. And guess what. You still left. No, wait. You made me out to be an awful human being, and *then* you left."

"I was just fucking upset that my parents were dead!" I bark. "I didn't mean to fuck everything up, Poppy. Fuck!"

"You give things. You give me hope," she whispers, her eyebrows pulling together. "And all these nice things you're doing … they will only make it worse when you leave again." She squeezes her eyes shut. "Just be an asshole. An indifferent dick, like you were when you left me on the sidewalk that day." She sucks in a breath, her throat making a squeaking noise as a tear rolls down her cheek. "That'll make it hurt less when you leave again."

I glare over at her before I yank her body on top of mine. Gliding my hand up her cheek and tangling it into her hair, I bring her lips to mine. She kisses me back, grinding her pussy on the hardening bulge through my sweatpants.

When I move my lips to her neck, I watch her nipples pebble through her white shirt, making my cock even harder. Sliding my hands to her hips, I shove her against my dick, feeling how hot she is through the fabric of her leggings.

All at once, it's like I remember that we have her brother's ashes in the backseat of my truck. And if it wasn't bad enough that we did what we did the night he died, this seems worse.

Pulling back, I move my hands to her arms. "We should … we should get your brother to where he's going," I say and watch her cheeks grow red. Embarrassment fills her entire face as she begins to scurry off of me.

"It's not that I don't want you," I groan, tightening my hold on her arms, keeping her on my lap. "You're all I fucking want right now." I cringe. "But not like this. Not right now."

"Okay," she whispers. "I understand."

I take my hands off her body, and she climbs back into the passenger seat and smooths her clothes down.

"Where do you want to take him? Are you going to take him home with you? Or … did you have somewhere in mind?"

She looks shocked before she laughs. "Ummm … I love my brother. But, no, he's not coming home with me." She glances in the backseat at the box of his ashes. "I just want him to be somewhere where he's happy." She sighs. "I'm just not sure where that would be."

I think back to when we were kids. "I have an idea. But we're going to go get Jake too."

She looks unsure, looking from the box to me.

"Just trust me, Poppy. This one time. Okay?"

Slowly, her head bobs up and down. "Okay."

"This is perfect," Poppy whispers before turning toward me. "I can't believe you remembered this place."

I look around before nodding once. "Of course I did. Your brother was so sure that this would make the perfect spot for a restaurant one day." I laugh, pointing at the small pond. "He said he'd have paddleboats in the pond and a big ol' porch where people could sit and eat while enjoying the view." I feel my heart squeeze. "He wanted to name it Van's Tomorrow."

Her eyes fill with tears, and she tucks her hands into her pockets. "He always said, one day, our tomorrow really will only be one day away. And we'll get out of Sunset Drive." She looks around. "Now, he's out of that place. For good."

The land we brought his ashes to is only three miles away from where we grew up, but it is so much different from Sunset Drive because it's on the nicer side of town. And the first time we rode our bikes by it, Van stopped and said it would one day be his restaurant.

Putting her arm around Jake, she rests her head against his. "What do you think, J? Is this a good spot for Van to reside?"

Looking up, he gazes out toward the pond before he drops his hand down and squeezes his sister's hand. "I think … it's perfect."

Her lips turn up in a small, sad smile. And she nods. "Me too, J. Me too."

Eventually, he releases her hand, heads toward where she set the urn on the grass, and picks it up. Her eyes find mine, and I can feel her pain like it's my own. But behind her gaze, I also see something else. Something that I can't place. Hope maybe? Or relief.

Taking a few steps to the huge tree, she kneels down and begins to spread his ashes.

"I hope you're up there, running that restaurant. Just like you always wanted," she whispers. "You are not a loser, Van. You're my family. My brother. And I love you." She sniffles. "So much."

Walking next to her, I kneel beside her and put my hand on the urn while she has it tipped. "I wish that things had been different. I wish you were here, right now, opening a restaurant right here." I wipe my eyes. "I love you, man. Say hi to my parents for me."

Jake's next to sit down on the grass beside us. "I wish you'd gotten to see my apartment. I think you would have liked it," he says softly before his voice dips lower. "I promise I'll make sure that he takes care of P." He pauses before slightly stuttering, "I miss you, Van. I love you."

I glance at Poppy, but she stares down at the urn. Her chest rises and falls faster, and I see the tears gathering in her eyes. Being here today is a gift. And I'm so thankful she allowed me to do this.

POPPY

Walker pulls into my driveway, and I unbuckle my seat belt. After spreading Van's ashes, we took Jake out to dinner, and everything seemed sort of … normal. Well, almost. It just wasn't the same without Briar and Van. And at dinner, I learned that Briar isn't really the same. She's been molded into what her uncle and his wife convinced her to be. That makes me sad because I loved her the way she was.

I chew my lip nervously. "Thank you, Walker." I tuck my hair behind my ear and peek over at him. "For paying for Van's cremation and for finding the perfect place to lay him to rest." I pause. "And for making this day a bit easier. Especially on Jake."

"Poppy, I, uh … I wouldn't have missed it." He nods slowly. "I'm sorry it took me so long to get my head out of my ass and see that I wasn't the victim here. I guess I just needed to be mad at someone, and y'all got stuck with the job." He swallows. "What Jake said—that he'll make sure I take care of you? Well, he's right. Because I will." He looks down. "I should have never stopped."

"It's not your job to take care of me, Walker." I shrug. "It never was your job. It's my job."

"It became my job that first day we met when we were six and I could tell your father was hurting you when I saw your bruises and the cut on your lip," he rasps. "I knew right then that the only job I ever wanted was just to keep you safe." He looks up again, his face strained. "And then I failed. But I won't do that again. I promise. So, whatever you need, tell me. Please, Poppy. I want to make it right. I want to be your best friend again and be there for you when you need me."

When he reaches over, brushing his thumb across my cheek, I suck in a breath. It would be so easy to give in to him right now. It's all I want to do. But I know that I'm still grieving the loss of my brother, and even though I had a great day with Walker, that doesn't mean everything between us is fine because it isn't.

"I just need some time to process everything that's happened. With Van. With … us. All of it," I utter. "I'm not in the best headspace right now."

"I understand," he says, his deep voice stretching across the truck cab, vibrating my chest. "But I'm still going to be around. If you need me, I'll never be far. Okay?"

I flashback to my freshman year of high school. It was the first time we were in different classes now that we were in a new school.

On the walk to school, he glanced at me and said almost the same words. *"If you need me, I won't be far."*

"Okay," I whisper, nodding my head slowly. "I'll, uh, see you later." Reaching for the door handle, I smile. "Thanks again, Walker. Night."

His eyes grow sad, and he holds his hand up. "Good night, Poppy. If you need me ... you know where to find me."

Pushing the door open, I climb down from his truck and head inside.

My mind can't help but wonder ...

Does he mean what he just said?

And if he does, where does that leave us?

POPPY

I peer out into the crowd, seeing hundreds of smiling faces. Christmas is coming, and so many mothers have brought their children tonight to get in the holiday spirit. I guess *The Nutcracker* will do that.

Brooks has been putting on *The Nutcracker* since I was a kid. And this particular show at this venue has always been special to me. Because I remember the first time I watched it live onstage. I was in the sixth grade, and our class took a field trip. Most of the kids' parents had sent them with money to buy snacks. I didn't have any money, but Walker had been helping an older lady who lived the next street over from ours. She'd pay him to mow the lawn and keep her yard picked up. He used most of the money for hockey necessities. But saved a little here and there too.

The field trip was optional. And while Walker came with me, Van said hell no and skipped.

I remember when Walker told me he'd be right back, only to return with popcorn, drinks, and candy. I swear he spent all the money he had brought just for me. And I knew if I hadn't gone to that show, he wouldn't have either.

The Nutcracker isn't even supposed to be emotional. But I watched those dancers onstage, and I felt every emotion possible. I was in complete awe of their talent and how they captured the audience.

I knew right then that I wanted to be onstage one day even if it was just a performance for the local community to come out and watch or if it was on Broadway. I wanted to be good enough for other little girls to watch and think to themselves … *One day, that's what I want to do.*

That was exactly what I felt when I first saw *The Nutcracker.* And he was right next to me, holding my hand, when he saw the emotion on my face.

After that, he'd save money just to take me every year. The last time was during my freshman year, before he left.

"I've got a surprise for you, babe." Ryann's voice pulls me from my thoughts, and when I turn, I find her holding out a huge bouquet of the most beautiful flowers.

Slowly, I take them and frown. "Did you get these for me? Or …"

"Watson just brought them in." She shrugs. "Says you have a secret admirer. He didn't tell me who it was." She winks. "Spill the tea, baby girl. I'm mighty thirsty."

I give her my best confused look. "I have no idea who these are from."

"You lie like a rug," she whispers, shaking her head. "I will find out. I allllways do."

I keep my face unfazed before, finally, she struts away. And then I move the flowers around until I find a card.

> *I remember the first time I watched The Nutcracker. Somehow, I think I'll like it more this time. Watching you dance has always been my favorite thing.*
>
> *—W*
>
> *P.S. Good luck, Poppyseed.*

My heart squeezes before it beats faster—and faster—almost like I'm running on a treadmill or doing some insane cardio workout.

Walker is here. Like … here. To watch me perform.

Sure, he was at the fundraiser, but that was different. He was performing too. And I was doing a silly number with Cade. This performance tonight challenges me. It pushes me. And also, it's a lot of choreography.

But most of all, we used to come to this together, he and I. He knows how much this means to me.

I could screw up. And he'll be out there, in the crowd, watching me.

Peering up into the crowd again, I wonder where he's sitting. I know he can't see me because I'm hidden in the dark wing of the stage. And though I wasn't all that nervous before … I sure as hell am now.

There are hundreds of people here. But really … he's the only one who matters.

WALKER

I'm not sure how I'm still alive right now. I swear I've spent this entire performance hardly breathing. My eyes were fixed on Poppy and how her body and soul moved around the stage so gracefully.

When she dances, the pain that usually lives on her face disappears, and the hardness in her eyes melts away. Left behind is an angel—one who was born to be on a stage.

"You're staring at my sister," Jake says, elbowing me gently.

"I can't help it," I admit just as she leaps into the air, stretching her legs out before landing on her feet again.

"I know," he whispers, patting my arm with his hand.

Jake is dressed to the nines tonight. He was so excited to come to this when I picked him up. I found him in a tuxedo, smiling like a fool.

His sister might be his biggest cheerleader, but he's hers right back.

"She doesn't look sad when she dances," he says slowly and thoughtfully. "She used to have that same look when you were around."

I know he didn't mean to, but his words cut me deep. Just knowing that for a long time, she trusted me. Probably more than she trusted anybody else in the world. She'd smile at me. Like … really smile. Not the forced one I see her give people sometimes.

Now, she'll barely look me in the eye. And I can't help but think about all the bad things that could have happened to her when I was gone. I wouldn't know because I wasn't there. I have no clue what she had to endure, and the thought alone makes me sick.

The show ends, and as they call her name and she takes a bow, I stand, cheering loudly as I clap my hands together. Jake brings his fingers to his mouth and whistles loudly.

"I still haven't figured out how to do that!" I tell him, laughing. "I've tried so hard to learn."

"What can I say? I'm the man," he tosses back, clapping his hands.

Once everyone starts to exit the stage, Watson Gentry heads toward me.

"Ryann delivered the flowers to your girl, man." He holds his fist up, bumping it to mine. "How long has this thing between you two been going on anyway?"

"Since they were kids," Jake says, answering for me. "He's very in love with my sister."

Watson laughs before holding his hand out to Jake. "I've heard a lot about you from my wife, man. It's nice to finally meet you."

"Wife?" I say, my mouth hanging open. "You and Ryann are fucking married?"

"You know it," he says with a grin.

Jake steps forward, narrowing his eyes. "If you hurt her, I'll have to hurt you," he says, giving Watson a harsh glare. "Ryann's the best."

"She is." Watson nods. "I'll never hurt her. You have my word."

"But if you do—" Jake starts, and Watson pats his shoulder.

"If I do, I give you permission to beat me senseless."

Seeming satisfied with that answer, Jake finally shakes Watson's hand. "Congratulations on marrying the prettiest girl on the planet."

"Thanks, man." Watson smiles. "I appreciate that." He turns his attention back to me. "So, you and Poppy Wilson." He laughs. "And here I thought, I had it tough with Ry. Poppy is … man, she scares me a little. I can't lie."

"Yeah." I laugh. "She's … she's tough." I glance at Jake. "Didn't you say you wanted to tell her good job? Let's go get her before she finds another ride home."

Jake gives me a pointed look, tipping his head down. "You are the one who wants to tell her good job."

I shrug. "Yeah. Okay. That's fair." Holding my hand up to Watson, I tip my chin up. "See you at practice, big dawg."

"See ya. Good luck." He chuckles. "With women like Ryann and Poppy, you'll need it."

That's putting it lightly.

POPPY

I feel how I imagine a teenage girl feels when going on her first date. When the guy picks her up and she's dressed up and feeling all bashful. That's what it feels like, seeing Walker all dressed up, knowing he gave me flowers and just watched my performance.

"Good job, Poppy," Jake says, throwing his arms around me. "I didn't even fall asleep."

I burst out laughing, shaking my head once he releases me. "Ummm … thanks, I guess?"

"What?" He shrugs. "It's a long show."

My gaze finds Walker, and he looks down at me, smiling. A smile that reaches his eyes, which isn't something that I've seen too many times on him.

"You did great," his deep voice says softly before he drags his hand down the back of his neck, shifting anxiously. "And you look … gorgeous."

I've known Walker my entire life. He's not a man who gets nervous. Even as a boy, he was confident, cool, and collected. But right now, he's nervous.

Are his cheeks red?

"Bonnie … my girlfriend, and her mom are here to pick me up," Jake says, stepping in and giving me another hug. "Love you, Poppy."

"Love you too, J." I squeeze him with one arm, my other holding the flowers, before he steps back and walks away.

And now, it's just Walker and me. And this pulling force between us that makes me do crazy things. Things like losing my virginity an hour after identifying my dead brother. Or dry-humping him in his truck with ashes chilling in the backseat.

I have no control over what happens once our lips touch.

For some reason, the silence becomes too much, and I can't stop myself from laughing at the debatable things I have done with this man lately.

"Sorry." I put my hand to my mouth to silence an awkward giggle. "Thanks for coming. And for the flowers." I pause, holding up the bouquet slightly. "They are beautiful."

"You're welcome. I wouldn't have missed it," Walker rasps, his expression growing serious. "I missed watching you dance."

"I missed watching you play hockey," I say softly, feeling the tension growing between us. I pull a breath in but still feel like I'm suffocating.

We stand there with people moving around us, all having their own conversations. Yet it seems like it's just us and a bunch of background noise.

Brushing a strand of hair from my cheek, he slowly pulls his hand back. "Can I give you a ride home?"

Butterflies take flight in my stomach, thousands of them, all running rampant. If I leave with him right now, I'll have this dress torn off before we even leave this parking lot.

Giving him a sympathetic smile, I wrinkle my nose. "Sorry. But I actually have plans with some of the other dancers after this." I take a breath. "Thanks for coming. And for bringing Jake." I narrow my eyes. "But how did you know I was dancing tonight in this?"

He gives me a sly smile and shrugs. "I can't reveal my sources, Poppyseed." He leans in, wrapping his arms around me and giving me a squeeze. "Have fun tonight. Be safe." Kissing the top of my head, he murmurs against my hair, "I'm so proud of you. You did so fucking good."

When he releases me, my body immediately misses him. And I stand here, rooted to this spot, forcing myself not to dive back into his arms.

He looks so good tonight in his dress shirt and pants. And he smells even better.

He smells like … home. And that's coming from someone who's never even had a real home.

"Thank you." I wave. "Have a good night."

"You too, P."

As he turns and heads toward the exit, it takes every ounce of my control not to chase after him and climb into his truck.

WALKER

"Look at you, all dressed up and shit," Nixon says with a grin when I walk into the dorm. "Hot date or what?"

"Something like that," I mutter, looking around. "Where's Elias?"

"No idea. Probably out with that Lainey. Or Lorna. Whatever her name is."

"Lana," I say.

He points. "Yep, that's the one. Dude's in fucking love with her already." He holds up the remote to the Xbox. "Whatcha say, James? Up for a game?"

"You know it." I head toward my room. "I just gotta change real quick."

After the show ended, I drove around for a while in an attempt to clear my brain. It was useless, of course. So, now, I'm just hoping I can eventually fall asleep and stop thinking about Poppy.

Walking to my dresser, I pull out my gray Wolves sweatpants and my white T-shirt and change out of the stuffy-as-hell clothes I wore to Poppy's performance. I'm not going to lie. I wish I were hanging out with her right now. I was pretty tempted to find out who she was hanging out with and where and show up there. The thought that she's out partying right now—maybe around other dudes—well, it pisses me off. But this is also one of the first times she's gone out and had fun since her brother died, and the last thing I want is to take that away from her. So, I guess it's video games with Nixon instead.

Just as I finish changing, my phone goes off, and I see Gentry's name on my screen.

Gent: Where you at, man? I see your better half, but you're nowhere to be seen.

Me: We aren't really a thing, I guess. She told me she had plans with the other dancers. I must have missed you dancing up on the stage in tights.

Gent: Trust me, if I were in tights … there'd be no missing it.

I chuckle at the eggplant emoji, shaking my head.

Gent: I'm here with my wife. We're at Club 83, and I'm telling ya, there are a lot of dudes fixin' to piss on your property and mark her as theirs.

That has my blood boiling.

Me: What the fuck do you mean? Who is it?

Gent: Question is, who isn't it? There are a lot of football players, baseball players, and even a few basketball players here tonight. Lot of attention on your little dancer, my friend.

Gent: Oh, and she's also hammered. So, there's that.

Me: Be there in ten.

Gent: Yeah. That's what I thought.

Pulling my Wolves hockey hoodie on, I rush out of my room.

"Sorry, B. I gotta run to Club 83 to check on a friend."

I yank the door open, and he leaps from the couch and charges behind me.

"Well, guess what. I'm going too." He stuffs his cell phone into his pocket. "And don't worry; I'll find a ride home so you can thoroughly check on this … friend."

Heading outside, I tread toward my truck. Because the idea of my girl getting drunk with a bunch of horny college dudes around doesn't sit well with me.

Not one bit.

Watson wasn't lying. She's pretty fucking drunk.

And that's just my observation from across the room, watching her sway to the music with her eyes closed. She's not with dudes though, but surrounded by other chicks. But the way she moves, the swinging of her body, it's blatantly obvious she's intoxicated.

She's still so beautiful, even if she isn't in her right mind. There's always a slight frown on her lips, but right now … it's gone. And the corners of her lips are turned up. She's either happy or she's just feeling the liquor a little too much. Either way, her cheeks are red, and her hair is no longer in a neat bun, but flowing over her shoulders, flying in every direction as she sways.

I nurse my beer, continuing to monitor her. This is her night. *The Nutcracker* has meant everything to her since the first time we watched it. And now, she was in the show, performing for all the people in the Brooks area. And she's having fun. So, until some sorry motherfucker walks up to her, I'll sit my ass here and just observe her beauty.

"Figured you'd show up about the time I mentioned your old lady was getting hit on," Gentry drawls, taking the stool beside mine. "Also, I give her about fifteen minutes, and she'll be puking her guts out."

"How much did she drink?" I scowl at him. "And why'd you let her?"

"Uh, well, let's see … she's not my responsibility. And, oh yeah, I suggested she take it easy, and she told me to piss off and fuck a couch. So … I sort of just walked off."

"She's pretty spicy," I mutter, glancing at him. "I figure I'll let her have her fun for a little while longer. She's had a rough few weeks."

Bringing his beer to his lips, he takes a sip. "Yeah. I heard that Huff's dealer, who died, was her brother. That really sucks, man."

Turning my attention back to Poppy, I sigh. "It does. But right now, she looks happy." I swallow. "I don't want to cut the night short. Because, to be honest, Gentry … she doesn't get to be happy very often. I fucking love it when she smiles."

He's silent for a moment before tapping his bottle to mine. "Ryann does this thing where she smiles at people to be polite, but it's not a true happy smile. When I get to see her, like, really smile, fuck, man, it makes everything else in the world not matter one bit." He clasps his hand on my shoulder. "Make her smile more, man. Be the reason why she smiles."

"Trust me, I'm trying," I mumble just before one of Brooks' top basketball players, Victor Jacobs, approaches her.

As soon as he dips his lips close to her ear and speaks, her eyes fly open, and she stares him down. Getting up from my stool, I vaguely hear Watson laugh before he mutters something. I don't stop to ask him what he said because my girl is drunk. And as far as I'm concerned, that asshole can back the fuck up.

"No thanks," I hear her voice yell over the music. "I'm here with friends."

"Come on, beautiful. One drink." He gives her his best grin, leaning a bit closer. "And if you don't want to hang out with me after that … I'll leave you alone."

"Um …" She looks nervous but takes a few long blinks, clearly feeling the effects of whatever she drank.

"She's had enough for tonight, thanks," I grumble, stepping between them and tucking my arm around her waist. "Let's get you home, babe."

She snorts before slapping the palm of her hand against my chest. "Walker *motherfucking* James. In the flesh." She laughs harder, tears gathering in the corners of her eyes. "Always here to saaaave the day!"

Victor's eyes widen as he looks her up and down. "Yeah. She's, uh … all yours."

Once he walks—no, scurries—away, she belts out another laugh. "Look, you scared my friend away!" She pokes her lip out. "Big, scary Walker James." She drives her finger into my abdomen, talking in almost a baby voice. "No one wants to piss you off, big fella."

"Good," I utter. "I'm fucking glad." Putting my arm around her, I angle her face up at me. "I'm taking you home. You're drunk, and you need to sleep this off."

"Soooo bossssy," she whispers, now touching her finger to my lips. "So cute though. My little grouchy cutie pie."

She stands on her tippy-toes, moving her face closer to mine. "Are you going to take me … *home*? You know, *home*. Wink, wink." She attempts to wink but instead squints one eye before blinking both.

Suddenly, she frowns. "I don't feel that good." She gazes around. "Whoooa, the room is spinning."

Scooping her up in my arms, I push through the crowd. Tonight has been a good night for her. The last thing she needs is people videoing her puking all over Club 83 and posting it on social media or some shit.

When I pass Watson at the bar, who now has Ryann between his legs, he holds his hand up and waves at the same time Ryann's eyes find Poppy, and she cringes.

"She'll be fine," I assure her before she can say anything. "Y'all have a good night."

Pushing through the door, I head to my truck and gently set her inside on the passenger side. Once she's in the seat, I stretch the seat belt over her chest and click it into place. Her head hangs forward, making all of her beautiful, thick dirty-blonde hair fall over her face.

Gently, I push her hair away from her face and dip my head closer. "Let's get you home, Poppyseed."

Before I can back away, her hand grabs my forearm. "I got drunk because I kept wanting to call you." She hiccups. "I thought ... *I just need to drink enough to not think about Walker freaking James for one night of my life.*" Her eyebrows pull together, and she's somewhere between laughing and crying in her drunken stupor. "All I do is think about you. And I'm tired. I'm tired of it. So, if you could please just get out of my brain so that I can go back to my life, that'd be great," she slurs, swaying her head back and forth.

"Poppy, I'm here right now because I couldn't stand the thought of you drinking and getting taken advantage of." I cup her face. "Also, for years, I've woken up every morning worried that today would be the day you met the man who'd be yours forever. And it's still no different." I swallow before breathing in her sweet cinnamon scent. "I'm not ready to let you go." I breathe out a laugh. "What the fuck am I saying? I'll *never* be ready."

Her bloodshot eyes look up at me. "I'm sorry I didn't tell the police officers the truth." Her lip trembles. "I haven't been a good friend."

I think those words are something I've waited to hear for so long. But now, they don't really matter because I realized weeks ago that I never had a right to be mad to begin with. Not really anyway.

Pressing my lips to her forehead, I kiss her warm skin. "You have nothing to be sorry for. I'm sorry that I abandoned you. *All* of you."

She's silent before she pulls back, pushing her head into the headrest. "Walker ... I don't feel so good."

All at once, she unbuckles and slides out of the seat and pukes in the parking lot. Pulling her hair back, I find an elastic on her wrist and tie it up before rubbing her back.

"It'll pass," I mutter as she throws up again.

"I've never drunk this much before," she croaks out, still keeled over. "I never want to again either."

Once she stops getting sick, I wipe the tears from her eyes, causing her makeup to run under them, making black streaks. Normally, she doesn't even wear makeup, but given her performance tonight, she has it on.

"I'm so embarrassed that you just saw me do that," she groans. "Literally want to die right now."

"I've seen you throw up a lot more times before tonight." I chuckle. "You forget those times you had the flu as a kid."

"You always stayed home from school to be with me," she whispers. "And miraculously, you'd never get sick."

"Tough immune system, babe." I wink before taking her hand and directing her back into the truck. "Let me give you a ride home so you can sleep this off."

She doesn't protest, but instead climbs into the truck and closes her eyes again.

POPPY

I wake up, and right away, I'm greeted by a pounding so deep in my skull that I can hardly lift my head. And the nausea? Oh … the freaking nausea.

I'm never drinking again.

The last thing I remember is leaving Club 83 with Walker. I don't really know how he got there, but I know he was there.

Memories of me puking my guts out and him tying my hair up and rubbing my back float back into my mind. He was so sweet. But I'm still so embarrassed. It's one thing that he saw me throw up as a kid. It's another to know we've hooked up, and he saw me splattering all the contents inside my stomach into the parking lot.

Kill me now.

Turning slightly, I see the note on my nightstand with two pills and a glass of what looks to be Coca-Cola beside them.

> *I had early practice, and from the sounds of you sawing wood, you were sleeping pretty well, so I didn't want to wake you. Take the Tylenol and drink the flat-ass Coke. It'll help, I swear.*
>
> —*W*
>
> *P.S. You still drool when you sleep.*

I quickly wipe my mouth, but my head is pounding too hard for me to be embarrassed right now. I'd probably care more if he was someone new in my life. But the thing is, he and I have been through everything together. He's seen it all. Embarrassingly enough.

Throwing the pills into my mouth, I swallow them down with what has to be the flattest glass of Coca-Cola in the world. And slowly, I slide out of bed and head to the shower.

I have no idea where last night left Walker and me. But I know one thing: when I think about seeing him again … my heart races a little, and my chest warms.

I know that I'm not in a place to give him all of me. And to be honest, there's not much of me to give. But staying away from him is impossible. Because just like when we were kids … we always found our way to each other. I'm not sure if that will ever change.

POPPY

"**A**re you sure it's okay if I pop out?" Mandy, my coworker says, chewing her bottom lip. "I just started here a few weeks ago, and I don't want it to seem like I'm flaky."

Yet here you are, asking to duck out of your shift an hour early.

But what do I care? It's dead in here. Besides, I like being alone. Mandy is nice, but she likes to talk—a lot.

"Nah. It's fine." I look past her at the empty café. "I think I'll manage. Go on."

She sighs in relief before nodding eagerly. "Thank you, Poppy. I'll cover you next time you need to slip out early." Gathering her things, she quickly darts out the front door like she's scared I'll change my mind.

Once she's gone, I take a deep breath and slowly let it back out. Closing my eyes for just a second, I take in the silence and allow myself a moment of just … nothing.

I like working in the café alone. It's quiet. And calm. And I don't have to try to make small talk with someone that I barely know. I mean, unless it's extremely busy. Then, yeah … working alone would suck. But tonight isn't going to be like that.

Looking around the café, I shake my head at myself. "Enough rest for one day."

I've always had this idea in my head—well, more of a belief—that if I sit still for too long, all the demons I've been running from will catch up to me all at once. In my mind, I see them tackling me to the ground in dark, thick waves of pure horror. Draining the life from me, holding me hostage to my own experiences. Almost as if they are cutting my air supply off and suffocating me to death.

Until the night Van died, I had spent years running from my pain. Hiding it behind my bitchy face and snarky comments. Always hurting others before they ever got the chance to hurt me.

I guess I sort of became a bully in other people's stories.

I don't want to be like that anymore. I just want to be … peaceful.

In the past, I'd mute the hockey game just to avoid having to hear the mention of Walker James's name. But tonight, I hit the volume button, turning it up enough to hear. I watch him move across the ice, knowing it's him right away, before seeing his name stretched across his back with the number ninety-one below it.

My chest squeezes as he assists Link Sterns, who slaps it in. They celebrate before getting right back to attack mode. He's found his place. And I'm so happy for him that he has.

Sighing, I tear my eyes from the TV and start wiping down all the tables for the second time tonight, trying my best to make the last leg of my shift pass by a little quicker, which is absolutely useless because the next hour passes at a snail's pace. I check the clock every now and then. And finally, like watching paint dry on a wall … it's time to close this bitch down. And I get to go home.

Turning the sign on the door, I grab my hoodie from behind the counter and pull it on. As soon as I walk outside into the night air, my nose is freezing. Winters in Georgia can get cold despite what people think because it's in the South.

Locking the door, I give it one good pull to make sure it's latched before I start my trek home. Ryann would have undoubtedly picked me up on her way back from Watson's hockey game, but I didn't want to be a bother. At some point, I'm going to need to get my own car. When I finally have the money.

I guess that'll be sooner than I thought, thanks to Walker since he took care of the bill for Van to be cremated.

Pulling my hood up, I hear a vehicle coming up behind me. I don't panic because this is Brooks. And though the hockey game ended a while ago, a lot of spectators are probably just now heading home.

The car gets closer and closer, but it doesn't pass by me. And even though I try to push it down, that feeling of dread fills my gut, chilling me to the bone. As the car comes to a stop and I see the headlights in my peripheral vision, the hair on the back of my neck stands.

I'm overreacting. It's probably just one of the girls on the dance team messing with me.

As much as I want to believe my own reassuring thoughts, that ends quickly when two doors open and I move my focus to the car to see two men, wearing black ski masks, running toward me.

For a second, I freeze. I don't think I take a breath as paralyzing fear spreads through my body, taking up every ounce of my being.

But when I snap back to the present, I realize that no matter how useless it is, I need to at least try to run away. And so I do. Unfortunately for me, they are much faster than I am. And within seconds, I'm being dragged between two buildings. One of the men throws me down on the hard ground, and the other pulls my head upward by my hair.

"Be quiet. Or I'll fucking kill you. Listen here, you fucking bitch," the deep voice growls, tightening the grip on my hair. "Your brother owes us money. And since he's fucking dead, guess that leaves you to pay up."

The one standing above me takes his foot and drives it into my stomach. "Hand it over, you stupid bitch. Pay up. Pay for your brother's fuckups."

Reaching in my pocket, I take out every dollar I earned tonight. It's not much, but maybe it'll be enough for them to let me go.

He snatches it from my hand, and I wince when the one behind me pulls upward even more. My scalp screams in agony.

Taking his flashlight, he holds it over the money before his foot comes down again. This time, with a lot more force. "This is, like, forty fucking dollars!" he roars, kicking my side now.

I bite my lip so hard that I taste blood. I'm afraid if I cry out in pain, it'll only make this all worse. I blink a few times, willing myself to wake up. Maybe this is a nightmare. Perhaps in a moment, I'll wake up in my bedroom.

Yes. That must be it.

There's no way that there's a reality where someone could lose their brother and get attacked by his dealers in the same week. No. I mean, life sucks. But it's not *this* tragic.

Any hope I had that this wasn't real is taken away when I'm pulled to my feet, and the guy releases my hair, only to land a blow in the face—first in the nose. Next the lip. The cheek. The stomach again.

I lose track. I let my mind go to a place far, far away. A place where things like this don't happen. Somewhere there are more good times than bad.

A mouth hovering right by my ear pulls me back to my shitty reality as a hand grips my cheeks, sending pain over my entire face as I feel wetness that I know isn't tears on my flesh. It's blood.

"Six fucking grand, bitch. That's how much your useless brother owes us." Squeezing my face harder, he shoves me backward, knocking me onto the ground yet again. "If you don't have our money the next time we come back, you'll be in a grave right next to him. Oh, and if you even think about going to the cops, we'll kill every bitch in that house you live in."

I don't bother to tell them that my brother isn't in a grave. Or that he's free now. Not confined. Or in pain. Instead, I silently wince as his boot kicks my stomach once, then twice. And then, through blurry, tear-soaked eyes, I watch them get farther and farther away from me before they get in their car and squeal away.

Through the pain, I force myself to stand. Each step I take feels like a thousand knives are stabbing my body. But finally, I walk … and then run toward my house. Knowing I don't want anyone to see me this way and that I'll have to spend the next few days hiding from the entire world.

Until I can come up with their money.

WALKER

I let the music play, resting my hand on the wheel as I head away from the arena and toward Poppy's place. I know I can't go in. It's late, and I can't just show up whenever I want to.

But, fuck, I wish she had been at my game tonight. I hated that she wasn't.

I had her. Three years ago, I fucking had her. She looked at me like I'd hung the moon and all the stars. Now, she'll never see me that way. Even if we have moments, they always end.

You can't change the past. That's for damn sure.

Heading past the library, I drive down the hill and past the coffee shop. But when I turn the corner, I see a figure walking and limping. As soon as my headlights cast over them, they disappear between a few buildings.

Driving to where I saw them last, I peer into the shadows.

I should just go home.

Whoever I saw clearly doesn't want to be seen. But I keep thinking about the fact that it looked like a woman.

What if she needs help?

"Fuck it," I huff out before throwing my truck into park and climbing out. "Let's hope this isn't a serial killer," I mutter, heading between the two buildings.

At first, I see nothing. But then the light of a phone catches my eye, and I squint.

"Hey, uh, are you all right?"

For a second, it's silent before I see movement.

"Walker?" Poppy's voice sobs so quietly that I almost don't hear her. "Walker, is that you?"

On instinct, I run toward her, reaching her within seconds.

"Poppy, what the f—"

The moon peeks out from behind the cloudy night sky, illuminating her face. My heart drops, and I feel fucking sick as my eyes take in the bruises, cuts, and scrapes all over her beautiful face. Droplets of blood drip from the cut and down her chin.

"Who—" I stop, sucking in a breath. "Who fucking did this, Poppy? Who did this to you?! I will fucking kill someone right now."

When I reach for her, she stumbles backward. "Please—" She puts her hands in front of her abdomen like a shield. "Please don't touch me," she cries. "It hurts."

Dipping my face closer to hers, I cup a spot on her face with no marks. "What hurts, baby? Tell me what hurts."

Her lip trembles as she falls against me, sobbing uncontrollably. "*Everything*," she whimpers loudly. "Everything fucking hurts."

Carefully, I slide my hands down her body and lift her up. With her head against my chest, I kiss her hair. "I'm taking you to the hospital."

"No!" she screeches. "If you take me to the hospital, the police will get involved." She shakes her head softly. "I can't do that, Walker."

Heading out of the alleyway, I walk to the passenger seat of my truck and gently slide her in. "I know where to take you." I dip my nose close to hers. "Do you trust me?"

Her mouth quivers before she gives me the slightest nod. "Yes," she cries. "I trust you."

Pressing a kiss gently to her forehead, I carefully close the door and head to the driver's side. I don't want to press her for answers right now, but I know one thing to be true.

I'm going to fucking murder whoever did this to my girl.

WALKER

Reaching for my energy drink, I tip it back, draining every last drop. My body is tired. I guess playing a college hockey game and then finding the woman you love beaten to a pulp will do that. But my mind couldn't be more awake. Racing a thousand miles an hour. Yet I can't focus on anything besides the fact that I wasn't there. I failed her.

Again.

It's all I do. I fucking fail. I couldn't save my parents. Now, my sister has been brainwashed by my uncle and is acting like a lunatic, and Poppy was attacked. Whoever I get close to goes down in flames.

Bringing my uncle Beckett into this is the last thing I want to do. But I have no choice. Beckett has a lot of money and resources at his fingertips. I'm going to need her protected until we find the attackers. But I know my uncle enough to know that, despite how the public might see him, he runs in some pretty bad circles.

I glance over at her as the sun begins to peek along the horizon, ready to start the day. A day that I'll make sure is better for her than yesterday was.

If I knew who did this to her, I would have already found them and probably killed them with my own bare hands. I would have beaten them senseless. Because I know that once I started, I wouldn't be able to stop. Not until they were a bloody mess on the pavement at my feet.

In her sleep, her lips form a frown. Like even asleep, she has no peace. There's no escaping her reality. And seeing the cut on her lip brings me back to the very first time she crashed into my life. Or I guess I should say, I crashed into hers.

We moved to Sunset Drive when I was six. But I still remember the very first time I saw her. She had a bruise on her arm and a swollen lip with a cut on it. She wore jean shorts overalls, and her hair was tangly. When Briar and I were walking on the sidewalk with our parents, Poppy and Van were playing outside. He ran right over, black eye and all. But Poppy, she barely spared us a glance.

My mom might have had her demons and her struggles, but she had a heart of gold. And when she saw Poppy and Van both living in hell, she wanted to help—even if she wasn't really able to.

When Van caught me watching Poppy curiously, he tapped my shoulder and said, "She just doesn't trust new people." He glanced back at his sister before giving me a small smile. "She really loves sour stuff. Warheads are her favorite. If you bring her those, she won't hate you as much."

"She hates me?" I blurted out. "She doesn't even know me."

He let out a long sigh. "Look, we're not really used to people stayin' in our lives. Y'all seem nice. You and your family. But … my sister will take more convincing."

On that day, I decided I'd buy a pack of Warheads with all the change I had hidden in my sock drawer and give her one once a day. For the first four days, she ignored me or ran away.

But by day five, she whispered, "Thank you."

And on day seven, she asked if I wanted to go for a walk.

Her hair was still tangly, and her clothes were worn, just like mine. And for the first time in my entire life, I felt like I had someone who had been made just for me.

But looking at her now, I'm realizing I was wrong all along. Maybe it was me who was made for her.

My phone vibrates, and I'm thankful when it doesn't wake her up. We still have forty-five minutes until we get to my uncle's, and I want her to get all the rest she can. Because when she wakes up, she's going to be in pain. And I really fucking hate the thought of that.

Quickly pulling over, I quietly open the truck door and gently close it behind me, making sure she stays asleep on the passenger side.

"Hello?" I say, leaning against the truck.

"How far out are you?" Beckett's voice clips, making me grit my teeth.

"About forty-five minutes."

"Hurry along. I don't have all day," he says. "Do you want me to break down the conditions of our agreement in front of this little piece of ass of yours? Or should we go over the details right now?"

I drop my head, balling my free hand up into a fist so tight that it actually hurts. "Go on. Let's fucking hear it."

"Well, first off, when you go pro, I'm going to need you to invite me to some events. For, you know, marketing reasons. But more importantly, you remember the Romano family, right?"

"Yep," I utter, trying to push away the thought that I slept with Marco Romano's daughter a while back when I was drunk. Because it meant nothing. Just like every other hookup.

Besides Poppy.

"Well, from what I hear, you're quite familiar with Gia. Which is good because you're going to marry her," he says callously. "I need more pull in Italy with some of our … suppliers. And what better way to gain that than becoming family?" He's more pepped up now, excited to break the news to me that my life is fucking over.

"You can't be fucking serious, Beckett. That's insane," I growl, praying he'll bark out one of his annoying laughs and tell me he's kidding, but I know deep down that's not how this is going to go. Far from it.

"Oh, I'm very serious. And before you even consider backing out, I'll have you know I've already called Romano. And men like him? Well, you know as well as I do that people don't change their minds on things." Greed drips from his voice. He's so impressed with himself for sealing this deal. "See you soon," he says smugly.

I instantly feel sick.

What the fuck have I done?

I look over at Poppy, knowing that this is going to break her. She's a girl who asks for nothing. She doesn't expect anything, and she never wants to inconvenience anyone. She's too stubborn for that.

What's done is done. And even though I was scared and really fucking pissed when I called Beckett in the first place, I can't turn back the clock and take the phone call back.

Even if I really, really wish that I could.

Poppy

The movement of being in a vehicle hits me before the pain of my entire body does. But when it does, holy shit, I'm freaking hurting.

When I finally open my eyes, I see Walker behind the wheel, and it all comes back to me—the attack. Walker finding me. Him going into Walgreens and getting me Tylenol and Motrin, plus every sort of hot and cold pack he could find.

And some sort of sleeping pills. Because I'd begged for something to knock me out. To take me out of this nightmare.

I'm regretting them now because I can hardly keep my eyes open.

I yawn, and the pain that sears through my stomach brings an uncontrollable wince from my mouth. Resting my hand over my abdomen, I suck in a few shaky breaths.

"Shit," I whisper. "Shit. Shit."

"We're almost there," Walker says, reaching over and resting his hand on mine.

"Where?" I utter, attempting to scooch up in my seat.

He never told me where he was going to take me. He asked me if I trusted him, and I told him yes. The truth is, as scared as I am that he's going to leave again, aside from Jake, Walker is the only person I trust.

"To my uncle's," he says almost hesitantly. "He's a doctor. And ... he'll be able to look you over."

"Look me over?" I ask. "I ... I don't—"

"Poppy, it's okay," he answers softly, pulling up to a gate and putting his window down.

Reaching out, he types in a code on the keypad, and seconds later, the large gate slowly opens.

I stare straight ahead at the paved driveway with the manicured lawn on both sides of it. And up in the distance, I see one of the biggest houses I've ever seen in my entire life.

Walker must sense my intimidation because he gives me a small, reassuring smile. "Trust me, it's not as great inside of that house as it might look from the outside."

I gulp, looking upward at the house as he pulls his truck in front of the ginormous garage. "If you say so," I mutter.

Quickly opening his door, he turns toward me. "Don't move. I'm helping you get down."

Jumping out, he shuts his door, races to my side, and pulls mine open.

"Walker, I think I can get out of the truck by myself. I'm not completely useless, you know." I roll my eyes as he slides his hands under my armpits. Even that small action alone sends pain shooting through my abdomen, and I grimace.

Carefully, he sets my feet on the ground, keeping his face angled toward mine. "Oh, really? You don't look so good right now, Poppyseed."

Remembering my face, I quickly look in his truck mirror. "Oh my God! How am I supposed to go in there, looking like this?" I wave my hand toward my face. "I look like I just walked off *The Walking Dead* set and I'm here to eat other people's faces." I throw my head back, pouting. "On a scale of one to ten, what do you rate how bad my face looks right now?"

"A fifteen," he says low.

Snapping my gaze to his, I shoot him a glare. "You were supposed to say that it's not that bad. Don't you know anything about what women want?!"

"You tell me." He cocks his head to the side. "When my head was buried between your thighs, did it seem like I knew what I was doing?"

Every ounce of blood rushes to my cheeks, which somehow seems to only make the bruises on my face hurt more.

When he dips his mouth to my ear, I can hear the smirk in his voice as he says, "When you came in my mouth, your pussy clenched my tongue so fucking hard that I thought you might cut it right off. So, yeah, I think I know what women want."

My mouth hangs open in disbelief, but before my brain can come up with something to say, he nods toward the front door.

"Come on, Poppyseed. Let's get you looked over."

After checking me over, Beckett, Walker's uncle, leaves the room, and I sit straight up, glaring at Walker.

"Are you fucking kidding me?" I hiss. "Your uncle is *Dr. Boobs*?" I shake my head in pure disbelief. "Why didn't you say you've been living with a *freaking reality star*?" I growl the last words.

When Beckett Benson walked into the room, I couldn't believe my eyes. This dude has been a reality TV star for years—all for doing plastic surgery for celebrities and fixing botched procedures for them too. One nickname he earned is Dr. Boobs simply because he had done breast implants for so many famous people. And they certainly weren't crappy boob jobs. No, the dude knows what he's doing.

"I didn't feel the need," he mutters. "And you'd better not tell anyone. There's a reason why no one knows."

"I feel like I'm either dead or I'm in a hospital, pumped full of happy gas, because there's no way I'm in Dr. Beckett Benson's kitchen." I gaze around the room at the most insane kitchen I've ever seen. "Walker, he's like … a boobie goddess. But with a penis."

"Why, thank you." Beckett chuckles, walking back into the kitchen with a first aid bag. "Boobie goddess with a penis. I'll take it."

Walker shoots me a harsh glare, and I shrug, widening my eyes.

What? I mouth.

He simply shakes his head and continues to grumble something I can't make out.

Apparently, Dr. Boobs is a sore subject for him. Who would have thought?

Cleaning a cut on my cheek, he takes a small package out of his bag. "Just so this doesn't leave a scar on this pretty face, I'm going to put a few butterfly stitches here." He looks me up and down. "Ever think about implants?"

I open my mouth to say something back, but nothing comes out because I'm in shock that this grown-ass man just looked at my breasts through my shirt and asked me about implants.

"Fuck no," Walker growls from across the room. "Don't even look at her fucking chest, Beckett."

"Easy, easy." Clearly amused, Beckett laughs. "Just saying, with a face like this, she could do more with the chest area."

"Shut the fuck up." Suddenly, Walker is right next to him, towering a few inches over Beckett. "Say one more thing about her body, and I'll fucking make sure you never perform another surgery again. Your fingers will be too mangled."

Unfazed, Beckett leans forward, gently applying the butterfly stitches. "If I didn't know any better, Walker, I'd say you're not over this old flame of yours." He glances back. "Careful, boy. You know the deal. And it certainly doesn't involve you getting more tangled with this one." He looks me over, clearly unimpressed. "You seem like a sweet girl and all, but we all know that wherever Ron Wilson goes, there's trouble. And you, sweetheart, have his blood pumping through those veins." He shrugs. "No Wilson can be trusted. Including you."

"I am *nothing* like Ron Wilson," I snarl, snapping my gaze to Walker. "I want to leave now."

Walker's face looks pained. "But when we first got here, he said that you should have an ultrasound of your stomach. Just to make sure you don't have internal bleeding." He swallows. "If you don't get it with him, you're going to have to go to a hospital."

Squeezing my eyes shut, I lean back in the chair and throw my head up. When I finally open them up again, Dr. Boobs himself is smirking.

"So, doll, what will it be? I'll even use my fanciest machine on you. After all, for the price Walker's paying, the sky is the limit."

When my eyes find Walker's, he looks down. And I know that whatever deal he made to get me looked at today … he's going to pay a price.

I just wish I knew what the hell that price was.

15

WALKER

Poppy has been quiet on the drive back to Georgia. Too quiet. But I know she's over there, in the passenger side, just stewing. Wondering what my uncle could have possibly been talking about when he said I was paying a price.

After her ultrasound showed no internal damage, we headed home. But little does she know that part of the deal I made with my uncle on the phone last night wasn't just for him to check her over. But also for him to help me keep her safe. She told me that Van owed some bad people money and they were coming to her to pay them. But that's really all she's told me so far, and because it just happened last night, I don't want to push her to open up right now. But tonight, I'm going to need to find out exactly how much he owed them before he died and everything else about her attackers. My uncle has friends in the police force who agreed to help find them. So, that's what we need to do.

Unfortunately, when I asked him for his help, I basically signed my life over to him. But what choice did I have? Poppy is in danger. I've failed her so many times, and I'm not going to do that again. Especially because if I don't protect her, who will?

Even if it means that, just like Briar, I'll be stuck marrying someone of my uncle's choice once Poppy is better. Marrying into a family strictly for my uncle's benefit is sick and fucking insane. But then again, that's who Dr. Beckett Benson is. The TV just doesn't show that side of him to the people watching him on the screen.

Briar has spent the past few months with Beckett's wife, Natasha, in Italy. This is all because Beckett brainwashed my sister into an engagement with the son of a powerful couple.

My uncle's circle is much like that of a cult. And if you stick around too long, you're going to drink the Kool-Aid. One thing my uncle couldn't stand about me while I was living with him was, I refused to drink that shit. I'd never get that thirsty. But now, I don't have a choice. Poppy needs the type of protection that I can't afford without Beckett's help.

"Are you going to talk at all or just sit over there and be bitchy?" I finally mutter.

I basically feel her anger radiating now.

"That depends. If I talk, will you lie? Because it sure seems like you're hiding something for a dude who was just begging me to trust him last night," she sasses, her eyes fixed on the window.

Keeping one hand on the wheel, I run the other over the top of my head and groan. "There's nothing you need to know right now. It's not going to make this entire situation any fucking better—I can promise you that."

"You're so predictable." She laughs bitterly. "You are good though—I'll give you that. Just when you convince me that it's all good, that I can trust you, and that you are the boy I grew up with … you remind me that isn't the case."

"Fucking A, Poppy!" I roar. "That is not true! Everything I do is for you!" I slam my fist against the console. Instantly regretting it when she flinches. "S-sorry." I grimace. "I didn't mean to scare you. But, Christ, Poppy. Everything I'm doing, I'm doing with you in mind."

"Then, tell me the truth," she bellows. "What is the deal you made with your uncle?"

I grind my back teeth together, staring straight ahead at the highway. I could tell her right now, but it would only make her entire fucking situation worse. She won't want to hear that I'm about to be engaged to someone who isn't her. And she certainly won't want her safety to be the reason why. Nothing good will come out of me revealing the truth right now. Other than I wouldn't be lying to her.

"I'll tell you soon enough, I promise." Glancing over at her, I cringe. "I can't say the words out loud myself. Just give me a little time, okay? To see if … to see if I can change Beckett's mind."

She looks at me for a split second before snapping her gaze back to the window. "Fine," she mutters. "Whatever."

The only girl I've ever wanted is sitting beside me. Battered and bruised. But last night, I had to choose between her safety and knowing that I'll never get the chance to be with her again.

I have to keep her safe. I'm the only one who can.

POPPY

"Why are we here?" I look at the swanky hotel we're parked in front of. "Like … why?"

Killing the engine to the truck, he stuffs his keys into his pocket. "You said yourself that you don't want anyone to see you beat up," he says, shrugging. "You're going to stay here until you're healed." He pauses. "Oh, and until your attackers are found and … dealt with."

My eyes must grow to the size of saucers, and my mouth hangs open. "Walker Samuel James, I know that you are not bringing me to this hotel and holding me hostage." I poke my finger into his arm. "No freaking way have you lost your mind enough to do that."

"Actually, that's exactly what I'm doing," he says, unfazed. "Deal with it, Poppyseed."

"You've got to be joking," I snarl. "You're going to, what, force me to stay here? Like Cinderella trapped in her tower?"

The corner of his lips turns up. Clearly, I said something to entertain him.

"Christ, Poppy. Even I know it was Rapunzel in the tower, not Cinderella." He shakes his head, laughing lightly. "You are literally the least romantic human being on the planet."

"I'll be romantic one day," I sass, "when the right man comes along."

I watch as his grip on the steering wheel tightens and his eyes narrow.

"Oh, yeah? Maybe I'll keep you in there forever then."

"Right. You're going to tie me to the bed and force me to be your prisoner." I huff, rolling my eyes. "You don't scare me, big guy."

He sucks in a breath, and I watch as he shifts in his seat. And when my eyes float downward, I bite my bottom lip when I notice the growing bulge in his pants.

"Sounds like wishful thinking on your end, babe. Be careful. I'm going shopping for some clothes for you later. I can easily pick up some rope or handcuffs," he drawls slowly. "It's obvious that's where your mind is right now."

It takes me a few seconds to unclog my brain enough not to act like a pathetic idiot. So what if I'm now having thoughts of him tying me to the bed and devouring my body? Who cares? That doesn't make me a weak bitch.

Not at all.

"Come on," he says, sighing when he looks me over. "Everyone in here is about to think I'm a fucking woman beater."

He has a point. I'm rough-looking, to put it lightly.

"I'll just wait in the truck until you get the key."

"Fuck no. We're too close to Brooks. Those two lowlife thugs could be anywhere. For all I know, they are tracking you." His eyes widen. "Which reminds me, I'm going to have Hudson look at your phone later to make sure they didn't put anything in it to track you."

"They never had my—" I pause before scowling. "Who the hell is Hudson?"

Pushing his door open, he jumps out, and I can sense the hesitation all over his face. "He's going to be your security guard while I'm not here."

He closes his door and comes over to my side.

I shove him backward when he tries to help me down. "A guard? Now, you're not only keeping me here hostage, but I also have to have a babysitter." I shake my head. "No. This is absolutely absurd."

"Yeah, see … it's not a request." He shrugs. "Besides, don't get your fucking panties in a bunch. You can order room service all day long. You can use the pool and hot tub once you're healed enough. Oh, and they have a spa. I know you're not really into that shit, but you could test out being a chick for once and do girlie stuff. And, oh, I don't know … enjoy yourself."

"Fuck you," I hiss, folding my arms over my chest.

"Such a dirty girl." He tsks me. "So eager for me to fuck you again." Sliding his hands onto my waist, he dips his forehead to mine. "Just think, if you have a fit right now and cause a scene, someone could call the cops. And I'm pretty sure we just drove all the way to South Carolina because you didn't want to get cops involved, right?"

I huff out a deep breath and groan. "Fine. But move and let me get out of this truck alone. I don't need your help."

Stepping back, he holds his hands up. "Suit yourself."

As I step down from the tall truck, my stomach screams in agony, but I force myself to keep it together. I refuse to show him how hurt I am right now.

I don't need someone to save me. I've been saving myself my entire life.

WALKER

Such a sassy girl.

Here she is, limping along in front of me on our way to the elevator, acting like a tough guy, not wanting any help. When I got our key cards from the front desk, I saw the receptionist giving Poppy a look of horror. I'm sure she thinks I did that to her, and that makes me sick to my stomach. I'd never hurt her. Hell, I'd fucking jump in front of a bullet just so that it couldn't get to her first.

Under her eyes, she is black and blue with a purple hue in some spots. Her cheek is the same, but it also has a pretty deep laceration that Beckett put butterfly stitches on.

Stopping in front of the elevator, I can tell she's uneasy, being in a place this fancy. Especially looking the way that she does in the Wolves hoodie and sweatpants I grabbed for her from my dorm before we headed to South Carolina last night.

The doors to the elevator open, and out walk two middle-aged women, all dressed up with their hair perfectly curled. They openly gawk at her face, not so much with empathy because of her bruises, but more with disgust. Especially when their eyes rake over her attire.

"You should see the other guy," Poppy mutters with a small smirk before brushing past them and onto the elevator.

Following behind her, I can't help but chuckle and shake my head.

"Real funny, Poppyseed. Real funny." I press the button for the twelfth floor, and the doors quickly close.

"What?" She shrugs. "They were staring. Staring is rude." She sighs. "They look like their names would be, like … Margaret and Eloise or something. Stuck up and offended by everything." She pats her legs. "They don't know what they are missing. Sweatpants are life."

She has a point there. They did look like they'd be like that. Then again, I bet ninety percent of the people in here look like that too.

Her eyes widen when we step out of the elevator after the doors open.

"There are only two doors up here? Which means …" Her voice stops.

"A penthouse suite. And before you get even more annoyed, I only did it because it seemed the safest. Plus, this way, Hudson will have the room next door." I shrug. "No matter if we stayed at the sketchy Super 8 downtown or the most expensive place in the area, my uncle was going to keep the deal the same. I figured … fuck it. Might as well make it nice. Right?"

"So, this Hudson dude isn't going to stay in the same room as me then, right?" She raises an eyebrow. "That's what you're saying."

Rearing my head back, I scowl. "Fuck no, he's not staying in a room with you."

I trust Hudson. I really do. But the dude is attractive. And covered in tats. And pure muscle. So, no, he isn't staying in a room with my girl while I'm gone.

"Walker, this all seems too—"

Putting my hand on the small of her back, I lead her to the door and flash the key card in front of the black pad. When it blinks green, I open the door and usher her in.

"Holy shit," she whispers, walking through the kitchen and into the living room. Looking out the windows for a few seconds, she quickly heads toward the bedroom. "Wow. This is the nicest bathtub I've ever seen," I hear her call out. "There are those fuzzy robes. The ones I've seen in movies."

Moments later, she emerges. Only now, with her eyes narrowed and a hand on her hip.

"You said that Hudson will be here when you can't be. So, let me get this straight. Since Hudson gets the room next door, that means you're staying there when he's gone. Correct? Because there's only one bed. And … yeah. Not happening."

"What's not happening?" I ask, amused.

"You. And me. In a bed. We're not sleeping together. Like, not *sleeping* together. As in real sleep. And we're not … you know, hooking up." She stops, clearly flustered. "So, anyway, you're staying in the other room. Right?"

"First off, we already did sleep together. And I enjoyed it, in case you were wondering. And second, no," I say as I walk over to the window and look out at the parking lot. "I'm staying here. With you. Will that be a problem, Poppyseed?"

"Umm … yes. Yes, it will." She stomps her foot down. "We can't … you know … do what we did," she whispers.

"Why are you whispering?" I grin. "Who exactly are you afraid is going to hear you?"

Even with the bruises, I can see her face turn red.

"Shut up."

Pulling her phone from her pocket, she presses the side button to turn it on. And within seconds, it's vibrating like crazy as messages come through.

She looks anxious, chewing on her bottom lip. We've spent enough time together that I'm confident she doesn't have a boyfriend. But some of those messages coming through could be from guys. And I don't fucking like that.

"I'm going to go into the bedroom and make some phone calls," she says softly. "I need to figure out everything with the school and with Jolene too."

"I emailed the school from your phone last night," I say casually. "They said they'd pass the message on to Jolene."

She's pissed now. Stomping toward me like a kid who wants a lollipop or some shit.

I'll give her something to suck on any day of the week.

"What exactly did you say?" she hisses through gritted teeth. "That is such an invasion of privacy."

"I said you had some family things going on and that you would be out of town for the next week or so. And that if they could email you your assignments, that'd be fucking awesome." I stop, winking. "I didn't say fucking awesome, so don't panic." I nod toward her phone. "It's all in your email. You can see exactly what I said, Poppyseed."

"You had no right," she growls, tipping her chin up at me. "That's like … stalker, creepy, Lifetime movie ex-boyfriend type of shit!"

My eyes involuntarily roam down her neck, and my cock twitches. I always love when she gets feisty. I find it incredibly fucking hot, to be honest.

"What I think you mean to say is … *Thank you, Walker. That was nice of you to take care of that in all your spare time,*" I say smoothly. "So, you're welcome."

Her nostrils flare as she continues to glower up at me, but eventually, she trudges off into the bedroom, slamming the door behind her.

In a perfect world, she and I could use this next week or so of her healing to build back everything we lost. But what would be the point when she can't be mine in the end anyway?

I'm already ruined for anyone else. But one more taste of her, and I'll never want anything besides her. Another time inside of her, and I'll be in too deep to get out.

Who am I kidding? I've been in too deep since we were kids. Everything in my life begins and ends with Poppy Wilson. And now, because of it, I'm about to pay the ultimate price.

I sit impatiently on the couch, staring mindlessly at the TV. Poppy went into the bedroom and locked the door over two hours ago and has yet to come out. Eventually, she needs to eat something and take her meds.

Fuck, her meds.

I look at my phone to see the last dose she had. Because, yes, like a fucking weirdo, I wrote it down. Given her family's history of drug addiction, she refused anything from my uncle for pain, but has been steadily taking Motrin and Tylenol, and it's seemed to help.

She has fifteen minutes until her next dose. If she isn't out by then, I'm going to break the door down if I have to.

There's a knock at the door, and even though I know it's Hudson, I still check through the peephole. Sure enough, I find his handsome, gigantic self-standing there.

Hudson's sister owns the strip club near Brooks, the one a lot of chicks who attend Brooks work at. Hudson's worked there as a security guard every now and then for the past few years. But he's also traveled with a lot of celebrities and rich people—my uncle included.

When Beckett and Natasha took Briar to Italy weeks ago, Hudson went with them as Briar's personal bodyguard. But a few days ago, he flew back to the States. And perfect timing because he's one of the few I'd trust with Poppy. He might be terrifying to some, but I know Poppy will be safe with him when I can't be around.

Though I'll admit, I worry she might be checking him out. I've only been around him at a few events, but women would turn into blubbering idiots when he so much as looked at them. Which makes me wonder how it went with him being Briar's guard. Though my sister isn't one to throw herself at any man. She's tough. But for whatever reason, my uncle has turned her into a meek girl who does shit like agreeing to marry a man she doesn't know.

Opening the door, I hold my hand out, and he clasps his hand with it and leans in, bumping his chest to mine.

"Well, if it isn't Uncle Boobies' biggest problem child," he says with a grin. "You know, my sister is pissed at you. I was supposed to be working at Peaches these next few days."

"Hey, I'm not his child at all," I point out. "He's just lucky that I haven't gotten a chance to talk to Briar alone. When I do, I'll make her an even bigger problem child."

His face grows somber for a moment, and there's no mistaking his sense of sadness. "Yeah, I, uh … how's she doing?"

His fumbling over words surprises me because he's not a man who does that. "Guess she's getting married sometime soon," I mutter, dragging my hand down the back of my neck. "Fuck if I know with that screwed up bunch."

"Yeah," he mumbles, looking off in the distance. "It's … it's pretty fucked up. Isn't it?"

"You ain't kiddin'," I drawl, opening the door wider. "Come on in, man. My … guest is in the bedroom right now. So, we can go over details."

"Guest, huh?" He chuckles. "I'm going to start callin' your ass Mr. Lewis."

I scowl. "Who in the fuck is Mr. Lewis?"

"You know, Edward," he deadpans. "The dude from *Pretty Woman*."

I stare blankly at him. "Yeah, sorry, but I don't watch chick flicks in my spare time." I shake my head. "Isn't that movie about a fucking hooker? Poppy sure as hell isn't a hooker."

He looks amused, and his lip twitches. "You ought to watch it in your spare time, young gun. Anyway, moving on since your ass clearly doesn't appreciate a good movie, tell me … what's the job? I got the gist of it on the phone earlier, but I want more details."

As he takes a seat on the barstool, I lean on the counter to face him. "So, last night, when she was leaving the coffee shop where she works, she was attacked by two guys wearing masks." I try to keep my voice even as I talk, but it's really fucking hard. "Her brother Van recently overdosed. But apparently, he owed people money." I speak low, not wanting her to hear me in the bedroom. "Bad people."

"Shit," Hudson mumbles. "So, what's your plan? You can't keep her locked up forever, you know."

"Poppy's the most private person I know. I knew she wouldn't want anyone to see her beat up the way she is. So, while she heals, we can keep her safe." I pause, looking down for a moment. "And while she's here, safe, Beckett's hired a few officers to find out who the scumbags are. And to take care of them somehow."

He pulls in a deep breath, leaning back on the stool. "Fuck, man. Officers?" He waves around the room. "Two penthouse suites?" He shakes his head, pointing toward himself. "My protection?" Grimacing, he swipes his hand over his face. "With a dude like your uncle, that must be one fucking deal you made. Did you sign your life over or what?"

My stomach churns. Hudson knows how my uncle works. He's traveled to enough events with him to understand how selfish and calculated he is. I think that's why he isn't working with him anymore.

"Yeah. Pretty much," I mutter, tipping my chin up toward the closed bedroom door. "But just like her old man, her brother ran with bad people. So, if selling my soul to the devil means I get to keep her from ever getting hurt again or dragged into that shit, so be it. Beckett can do his worst. I don't care." I shrug. "I've seen it all. There's nothing he can do that scares me. As long as that girl in there gets out of this and can go on to live her life and I can keep playing hockey, fuck the rest."

"You know, that sure sounds like love, brother." Hudson grins. "And don't you worry. We'll keep her safe. You and me."

"Fucking right we will." I nod. "I appreciate you being here, man."

"First things first," he says, taking his phone out. "Every call that comes through her phone will be coming to mine too."

I relax a little because I know that she's in the best hands with Hudson being involved in keeping her safe. The dude knows his shit. And if her attackers are dumb enough to actually contact her, it'll be game over for them. Because he's smart.

My eyes find the door again, and I know I'm going to have to force her to open that door soon because she needs her medicine.
And I'd also really, really like to sleep in that bed beside her.

POPPY

I wake up, stretching my arms over my head. Right away, a pain shoots through my stomach, and I wince. I'm hoping the bruises will begin to be less sore by tomorrow and I'll start feeling better.

After calling Ryann, Lana, and Jake last night, I passed out. And besides Walker breaking into the room at some point to basically force Tylenol and Motrin down my throat, I was dead to the world.

I guess the events of the past few days finally caught up to me. And I slept.

A lot.

The left side of the bed is perfectly made, and I can't help but wonder where Walker slept last night. But it obviously wasn't next to me. This is nice because, according to Ryann, who shares the room next to mine, I cry in my sleep sometimes. And I really don't want to risk Walker seeing that.

Slowly, I scooch my ass to the side of the bed and stand up. Day two of looking like a battered wife, and I think I feel worse today than yesterday. But maybe that means I'm healing.

Heading into the bathroom, I see a purple toothbrush still in the package, and I know Walker put it here for me. After brushing my teeth and washing my face, I head out to the main area. Only he isn't out here. In fact, the only sign he's been here at all is the folded-up blanket and pillow on the couch. But when I walk into the kitchen, I see a note on the counter with Walker's scribbly handwriting.

P,

I had to leave early for practice and class, but I'll be back soon. Order room service for breakfast—the menu is right under this note. Don't even think about not eating. You skipped dinner last night. They have your favorite, Belgian waffles.

Oh, and, yes, you still snore. Even from the couch, I could hear you. Thinking about investing in some earmuffs.

—W

P.S. Please look at the picture below. That's Hudson, the security guard we talked about. Please make sure that if someone knocks on the door, it's him. Don't open it for anyone else.

P.P.S. I'm fucking serious, Pop.

I can't stop smiling when I read his note. I feel guilty as hell about ordering room service though. Especially because everything on the menu is probably expensive as hell. But I know Walker, and if I don't eat, he'll be pissed. So, I decide I am going to order some waffles and a coffee, but I'm going to jot down the total cost on paper so that I can pay him back once I get my next paycheck.

Speaking of paychecks, I never called the café.

My next shift isn't for a few days, but I know even by then, my face will still look like this. Plus, the thought of working there and walking home after the attack … makes me feel sick.

I'll call my boss later tonight to explain that I need the rest of the week off. I know he'll understand if I say I have family matters to attend to.

Picking up the room phone, I hit the button for the restaurant and order myself some Belgian waffles and a coffee. As if my stomach can hear my voice, it rumbles embarrassingly loud, likely reminding me it's time to eat. I consider ordering two plates of waffles but decide that'd be a bit much and stick to one.

Twenty minutes later, I hear a knock at the door, and when I rush over to open it, I see a large, tattooed man grabbing the cart from another man dressed in a chef's coat.

"I'll be taking this to Miss Wilson," the tattooed man says.

I should say, the hot, tall, tattooed man.

The server looks incredibly confused, and I'm internally telling myself I failed my first test because I didn't do the one thing Walker wanted me to do. Check the damn peephole to make sure it's Hudson before opening. All I was thinking about was waffles and coffee, and I threw that bitch open without so much as wondering about who was on the other side of it.

Oh well. If he asks, I'll lie and say I checked first. He'll never know.

Giving the server a nod, I smile. "It's okay. You can go."

He holds my gaze awkwardly for a moment, and suddenly, Hudson reaches into his pocket, grabs some cash, and hands it to him. Graciously, he takes it.

"Thank you, sir," he says and quickly leaves.

My entire neck and face burn with shame. *Of course you're supposed to tip them when they drop food off, you dumbass.*

I want to crawl into a hole and hide. But how the hell am I supposed to know this type of shit? The fanciest place I've ever been is the Olive Garden. And that was because Ryann insisted we take Lana there for her birthday.

Holding the door open, I look Hudson up and down. And then it hits me. I've seen him before when I had to use Ryann's car and pick her up from work. He works at the strip club. Ryann's always saying that all the girls who work there have the biggest crush on him. And even though he does nothing for me because of my stupid, Walker-obsessed brain ... this guy is hot.

He pushes the cart into my room, and I follow him, shifting uncomfortably on my feet.

"Does Ryann know where you are?" his deep voice asks, pulling the cover from my waffles and carrying it to the table, along with my coffee.

He recognizes me. I didn't know if he would because our interaction was so short.

Grabbing a few napkins, I head to the table. "No. And I'd like to keep it that way."

"Hey, not my business to tell." He steps back before heading toward the door. Every step he takes screams swagger. "Oh, and, Poppy?"

"Yeah?" I mutter, taking a seat as my mouth waters when the sweet scent of waffles, strawberries, and whipped cream hits my nostrils.

"Next time, check the damn peephole before yanking the door open." He looks back at me. "Yeah?"

Rolling my eyes, I blow out a sigh. "Yeah ... okay."

"Thanks," he says, making a clicking noise with his tongue. "If you need anything, Walker added my number to your phone. Don't come in the hallway. Just call."

"Okay, okay," I whisper. "So dramatic he is."

"Well, I mean ... his girl got the shit beaten out of her by two thugs less than forty-eight hours ago. Dude's got a reason to be dramatic," he deadpans.

And then he's gone.

Leaving me to ponder two words he said.

His girl.

He thinks I'm Walker's girl.

And I could have corrected him, but I didn't. Because maybe … I liked being called that.

WALKER

I walk into the hotel with the two big bags in my hand. I could have gone to Poppy's house and picked some of her own shit out, but—let's be honest—the girl could probably use some new clothes. Besides, she doesn't want anyone to know what's really going on, and I'm pretty sure my rolling in there, rifling through her drawers like a perv, might come off as a red flag.

I wanted to get her comfy stuff because, for the next few days, her bruises will be healing, and I want to make everything easier for her right now.

I also picked up a formfitting black dress. Because apparently, this place has a fancy restaurant, and I'm going to have Hudson stand guard outside one night while I take her down for a nice dinner. Once she's feeling well enough, of course.

I know that I can't be with Poppy forever, so this next week … I'm going to make sure that whatever she wants, she gets.

I hit the button to open the elevator doors, and I step inside.

Hudson's kept me updated the entire day, but aside from her breakfast order this morning, he says she hasn't contacted him or room service.

It's after two in the afternoon, and she should have ordered lunch by now.

Getting off on floor twelve, I text Hudson, letting him know I'm back in case he wants to step out for a while, and I head into the room. Unsure of what version of Poppy I'll find today.

Sweet Poppy, who looks at me like I'm her hero. Sexy Poppy, who demands me to fuck her. Or sassy Poppy, who mouths off and rolls her eyes every five minutes.

Or maybe, if I'm lucky, I'll get a mix of all three.

Sweeping my eyes over the kitchen and living room, I set the bags on the table and rush toward the bedroom.

"Poppy?" I call out.

No fucking answer.

The bedroom door is open, so I walk in. And again, no Poppy. The bathroom door is closed, but I don't hear the sound of the shower running.

Putting my fist to it, I knock a few times. "Poppy?"

Still, no answer.

I don't want to invade her privacy, but she could be there … hurt. Or worse, what if she hurt herself? Her life has been complete fucking trash lately. Who the hell knows what's going on inside that beautiful yet fucked up mind of hers?

"If you don't open the door on the count of three, I'm breaking it."

As I start to count, I take a card from my pocket. This place is swanky as fuck; I'm not going to break their door down if I can just jimmy the damn thing.

"One … two … three," I say slowly.

And when the door remains closed, I jam the card in again, wiggling it around until it unlocks.

Stepping inside, I suck in a breath at the sight of her. Earbuds in, bubbles covering all but her face, and eyes closed. She doesn't sing, but hums low, gently bobbing her head.

I should leave her alone. She looks so relaxed. But, Christ, I can't pull my eyes away from her. I can't even see her gorgeous body, and I'm still fixated on her.

Strands of loose hair frizz around her face from the humidity from the steam. She doesn't have an ounce of makeup covering her bruises, and her split lip is starting to heal.

She's so beautiful. But so fucking broken. And all I want to do is be the one to put her back together.

Only I can't.

When her eyes flutter open, they widen for a second before she screams. Ripping the earbuds out, she takes her hand and splashes a blob of water and bubbles at me.

"Get out! You creep!" she screeches. "Get out! Get out!"

"I can't even see your fucking body, Poppy," I holler back. "And even if I could, I've fucking seen it before!"

When she sinks further into the water, shooting me a glare, I smirk.

"Do you not remember when my face was buried between your thighs and I was eating your pussy like a fucking ice cream sundae?"

"You're annoying!" she hisses. "No girl, especially one who's been attacked two freaking days ago, wants to be in the tub, thinking they are allllll alone, and then realize that someone is looking at them." She gives me an annoyed look. "Even if we did … you know … the other day. Still, it's weird."

I instantly feel really fucking bad. "Sorry," I mutter. "I … I just didn't know where you were. And then when I yelled, you didn't answer." I shrug, dragging my hand up the back of my neck to the top of my head. "I got worried. I wasn't trying to creep you out." Turning, I take a step toward the door. "I got you some clothes. I'll put them on the bed for when you get out."

"Walker," she says softly.

I don't turn around. Instead, I just stop. "Yeah?"

"I don't think you're creepy. I'm just … overly sensitive, I guess. And, well, bitchy." She sighs. "But you already knew that last part."

I swallow, inhaling sharply. *Of course she's overly sensitive right now. And how fucking dumb am I to be so inconsiderate of that?*

"No worries. I'll, uh, try to be better."

Walking out of the bathroom, I close the door behind me.

POPPY

Looking in the mirror, I run the brush that magically appeared in the bedroom through my hair and glance at the new loungewear Walker picked up.

Six sets of new pajamas and loungewear outfits. A bunch of black leggings. A Wolves crewneck sweatshirt—my size. And lying on the bed is a gorgeous black dress and a pair of simple black heels. Oh, and every pair of panties I could think of, as well as a few new bras.

How he got the sizes right on everything, I have no freaking clue.

I go with the gray-and-white striped lounge pants, which are as soft as a feather, and a matching tank top. After looking like a slob for a few days, I'm still in pajamas, but at least my clothes and I are clean.

He got all of this for me, and I called the guy a creep.

I feel awful for what I said. It just … came out.

When I opened my eyes, at first, my vision was a little blurry, and I just made out a figure. I panicked, and even once I realized it was Walker, I was a complete bitch.

Walking out of the bedroom, I find him on the couch, flipping through the channels mindlessly. And when I take a seat at the other end of the couch, he doesn't look my way.

"How are you feeling?" he asks, his gaze fixed on the screen.

"I feel okay. The bath felt nice." His mouth opens to speak, so I stop him. "And before you ask, no, I didn't let the cut on my face get too wet."

"Good." He nods, stopping the TV on a cooking show. "Every time I see a show like this, it reminds me of Van." There's a sadness in his voice that can't be mistaken, and even his eyes seem to glass over a bit. "I hope he's somewhere in heaven, running his own restaurant."

A lump lodges in my throat, burning and making my eyes water. Though I'm pretty sure the real reason my eyes are watering is because I'm trying to fight off crying again. I cried so hard the night Van died. It was the first time in years, and I felt everything.

I'm not ready to feel things that deep again. It was horrific. And exhausting.

And it made me feel weak.

But right now, I'm having a hard time fighting it. Because I'm seeing Walker. Really seeing him. And what I see is a man who's in pain.

Just like me.

"Yeah, me too," my voice squeaks. "I wish he could have done it in real life though."

He looks down, his head hanging. "Yeah, me too." He sniffs. "I should have never left him. I shouldn't have been so selfish." His chest heaves. "I'm so fucking sorry, Poppy. I … I didn't know what else to do."

Walker didn't fall apart the night that Van died. I did, and he glued me together, ragged edges and all. And he didn't fall apart when we sprinkled his ashes.

But right now, he's going to fall apart.

"I saw him," he whispers. "Just days before he died. I saw him." Pinching the bridge of his nose, he squeezes his eyes shut. "He wasn't the Van I'd known my entire life. But still, I could have hugged him. I could have fucking dragged him away from the trailer and forced him to get help."

I watch a tear and then another run down his cheeks.

"Instead, I didn't do a fucking thing. And now, he's dead. He's fucking dead." He glances at me for a split second, grimacing. "He's dead, and you were attacked." He stops, and I can feel his sadness. "All I do is fail you, Poppy."

It's like seeing my best friend again. Like he never left me. Or us. And suddenly, I'm in his lap. My body might hurt, but I don't care because my bruises aren't nearly as deep or painful as the history between us.

Cupping his face, I force him to look up at me. "It's okay, Walker. I know I've said things, but the truth is, it wasn't your job to keep him safe." I swallow. "It wasn't mine either." I dip my forehead closer to his. "I understand the guilt. Trust me, I do. The last time I saw my brother … I …" I pause, my voice cutting out. "I called him a loser. I told him he was just like our dad." My lip trembles. "I'd give anything to take that back. To not let that be the last words I spoke."

Bringing my lips closer to his, I look him in the eyes. "He forgives you. I know he does."

"But do you, Poppy?" he croaks. "Do you forgive me?"

I feel my heart stop, but gently, I nod. "Yes," I whisper against his lips. "Do you forgive me?"

"You've done nothing that needs to be forgiven," he utters. "I'm just sorry it took me so long to understand that." He swallows. "I needed someone to blame. And I guess … you were that person."

Something has been weighing heavy on my mind since I first heard about whatever deal he made with his uncle.

"I want to move on from the past, but you're keeping secrets," I whisper. "I need to know what deal you made to keep me safe." Gently, I press my lips to his. "Please, Walker, talk to me."

"It doesn't matter," he whispers. "You'll be better off without me anyway, Poppy." He brushes my uninjured cheek. "You can do anything you set your mind to. I hope you know that."

"Talk to me," I plead, my eyes blurring with tears.

He squeezes his eyes shut for a moment, and I pull back enough to look down at him, still straddling his lap.

"There's this family in Italy. Two brothers, both very powerful and very rich." He stops, blowing out every ounce of air from his lungs, it seems. "One has a son. The other, a daughter." He swallows, making his Adam's apple bob.

The silence in the room is suffocating, and I hold my breath, waiting for his next words.

"Briar is engaged to the son. And I … well, soon, I'm going to be engaged to the brother's daughter." He looks down. "It was the only way I knew you'd be safe. My uncle has resources. And a lot of money. And a shit ton of connections. But everything, Poppy—every single thing when it comes to that man—has a price."

As quickly as my body will allow me to, I scurry from his lap. Backing up to the wall, I rake my hands down my hair. The swelling from having my hair yanked hurts, but nothing like this news does.

"Walker," I croak, "how could you make a deal like that? You're here with me. Buying me clothes, making sure I take my meds. And what? You're going to marry someone else?" I sob, holding my chest. "All to … what? Keep me safe?"

When he stands, slowly walking toward me, I suck in a shaky breath.

"I'd rather be in danger than ever see the day you marry someone else." I say the words I've felt my entire life. "I have loved you forever, Walker. How could you do this?"

I can't breathe. My chest is burning, and I feel like someone is squeezing my lungs, clenching their hold tighter and tighter.

"Because I've fucking loved you forever too, Poppy. And not as a friend," he growls, and my heart pumps harder before squeezing. "I couldn't take the chance of something else bad happening." He throws his arms around my waist. "Not to you."

When I look up at him, it's like a thousand memories flash through my mind. All of him and me. Back when, even though life sucked … it didn't seem impossible, not like it does right now. I'm losing him again. But this time, it's for good. It's forever.

He's going to marry someone. Someone who isn't me.

"I can't be here." I crash my hands into his chest before slipping out of his hold. "Just go. Call it off. Let me leave."

As I march into the kitchen, he rushes in front of me, blocking the door. "You're not fucking leaving, Poppyseed. We're in this now. It's a done deal."

"So, what?" I cry like a pathetic idiot. "We just spend the next week pretending like everything isn't about to change? Like … any of it is going to matter once we leave this hotel?"

"If the most I get with you in this life is this week, Poppy, then I'll take it," he utters. "Will it make it harder to leave? Yeah. Will it hurt you more than help? Probably." He reaches for me, gently touching my chin. "But I'm being a selfish prick right now because all I want is you."

All at once, I lurch toward him, my lips on his. The second my cut stings is the same time he pulls back.

"You're too hurt for that, Poppy."

I grimace. "It's because of how I look, isn't it? I wouldn't want to do anything with me either."

I start to back away, but he stops me.

"You're fucking beautiful. And just looking at you, bruises or not, makes my cock hard. Every. Single. Time. And I mean that with everything that I am." He looks pained. "But you're still hurt. And I don't want to do anything that'll cause you pain."

The way he's looking at me right now, I see it. He really does think I'm beautiful. And his eyes eat me up in a way I've never felt. Despite how scary I look, he wants me still. And that means so much.

Sliding my palm under his shirt, I rest it just under the band of his briefs. "Let me decide what I'm too hurt for, okay? I can take a lot of pain."

"Poppy," he rasps, "this will be twice now that you've been in pain and I've fucked you to make it better." He gives his head a slight shake. "It can't fix anything. You know that."

Moving my hand lower, I feel the bulge through his jeans, and I gently massage it before dropping to my knees. Reaching up, I unbutton his jeans and pull them down enough for his hard cock to spring free. My lip might be busted up, but I don't care. Right now, all I want to do is make him realize that there will never be another Walker and Poppy. I want to make him realize how much he'll miss me when he's gone. How much he'll miss us.

"You don't have to do that, baby," he groans low. "Your lips ... they're—"

"My lips are eager to suck your dick," I hiss, loving the pure shock I see in his eyes as his pupils dilate. "Now, be a good boy and let me do that."

I've never done anything like this before. And to be honest, I'm terrified that I'm not going to be good at it. And his soon-to-be wife ... she will be.

God, I can't think about that right now.

Reaching for his thighs, I give him a shove until his back is up against the door. I open my lips and spring up on my knees enough to welcome him inside. The second my tongue touches his flesh, his hips buck toward my face, and he hisses.

I take him deeper, opening my throat as much as I can and letting him slide across my tongue. Closing my lips around him, I bob back and forth, angling my head upward to look him in the eyes just before moaning around his length.

"Jesus Christ," he growls. "Feels so fucking good."

Cupping my tongue, I work my way down his dick before flicking my tip around his head.

His hips buck again at the same time I try to take him deep, and he hits the back of my throat. I gag but keep him inside of my mouth.

"Fuck, baby ... I'm going to—" he hisses.

I quickly move my lips up and down his wet cock, craving to bring him to his finish. He hisses a slew of curses as his hips jerk up and back. The taste of salt hits my throat, and I force myself to not flinch.

"Look at me while you're swallowing my cum," he snaps, barely choking the words out.

Staring up at him, I focus on my breathing as panic builds in my chest. I don't want to disappoint him by not finishing him off the way I want to. So, I refuse to do that, and I relax my throat.

"Swallow," he utters, his eyes rolling back as the last bit spills from his head.

Gazing at me again, he stares at my throat as I work to swallow down the rest of him, never taking his cock from my mouth.

I run my tongue around him once more, and his mouth hangs open as he moans.

"Fucking A, baby. You even licked me clean." He reaches down, brushing his thumb under my chin. "Such a good fucking girl for me."

Slowly, I release him and push myself to stand. Looking down bashfully, I chew my bottom lip. "Was that ... okay? I can learn to be better ... you know."

"The fact that it was your first fucking time sucking dick, and it was the best head I've ever had ... Jesus Christ, Poppy." He gently swipes his thumb over the side of my lip that's not cut. "This mouth was made to take my cock." As he slides his hand to my neck, his eyes darken. "And this throat ... to swallow my cum."

My legs are shaky, and I didn't even orgasm. But the pain that I've been accustomed to since the attack has somehow disappeared, and all that is left behind is a throbbing between my legs and a sting on my bottom lip.

"I bet you're fucking dripping, baby," he utters, sliding his hands to my waist. "I bet sucking my dick has that pussy of yours soaked."

"Y-yes," I breathe out.

"I don't want to hurt you. You're still healing. So, if anything is too much, you're going to have to tell me, okay?" he says, sliding one hand to my ass and giving it a squeeze.

He gazes at my chest, and already, his length hardens, standing out straight.

"Hmmm ... do I want to bury my face between these thighs? Or do I want to drive my cock so deep inside of you that you scream?"

Gently, he spins me around so that his erection is pressing into my ass, and he marches me to the couch. As he pushes me forward, I feel my bottoms being pulled down, and he palms my asscheek.

"No panties, huh?" he mutters into my ear. "It's like you were just waiting to take my dick, weren't you?"

"Yes," I whisper.

"Tell me, Poppy, did you think of me in that bathtub?"

I should blush, but I'm far too turned on to even care. The truth is, I did think of him. I turned my music on, and I imagined all the things we could do in this penthouse. But afraid that he'd barge in, I didn't dare to take it further than that.

"No," I lie, craning my neck to look at him.

"Don't lie. You fucking slid your hand between your legs, and you imagined it was my fingers slipping into this tight pussy." He drags his hand up my inner thigh, brushing my heat, but not pushing his fingers inside of me.

"How many times, Poppyseed?" he grumbles. "How many times over the last three-plus years have you fucked yourself with your hand, just picturing me?"

With my ass still to his front, he leans forward and kisses my neck. "How fucking many?" he growls.

"So many," my voice croaks as he pulls my shirt over my head, leaving me completely naked. "Did you ..." I swallow, looking down.

"Did I think of you?" he mutters into my ear. "Baby, I've covered my hand in cum, imagining it was your pussy, more times than I can count. I've also pictured you sucking my cock the way you just did. Or riding my dick with that sweet ass slapping against my balls while these perky tits bounced for me."

My mouth hangs open, and I moan just as he drops to his knees behind me and spreads my legs further apart before his tongue is inside of me. Unable to keep myself completely upright, I press my body into the couch, and I whimper as he buries his face deeper. My hips instinctively rock back against his face, and his hand reaches around the front of me, brushing his thumb against what I've realized is my most sensitive spot while his tongue continues to work me over.

It feels so damn good. Too good. Everything in my brain melts away, and all I can focus on is the amount of pleasure my body is feeling in this moment. I'm at his mercy, so close to coming undone. All for him and what he does to me. But before I cross that finish line, he's pushing to his feet, and he moves me to the window.

Even though I know it's blacked out from the outside world, I can't stop my heart from racing when I imagine the people who could be below.

I feel his growing cock press against my ass.

"I know you're sore, baby. You're healing. So, the last thing I want to do is make it worse," he mutters into my ear.

"Take me," I whisper, craning my head to glance at him. "The first time, you were so scared to hurt me because it was my first time. And I … I wasn't in my right mind." I push back slightly, enough so that his length presses into me harder. "Take me, Walker. And don't hold back. I want all of you."

"Fuck … me," he growls before pressing his body to mine, forcing me against the window.

The sting from the bumps and bruises on my body is quickly diminished when he parts my legs and works the head of his dick inside of me.

"Jesus, your pussy is so fucking tight. It practically sucks my cock in and holds it prisoner," he groans, pushing more of himself inside of me, inch by inch, until I feel so full that I could combust. "And, baby, I'd like to fucking stay here forever. Just like this. Buried inside of you, feeling you squeezing around me."

It hurts, but it's not the bad kind of pain that I'm used to. This pain is welcome. This pain feels like … living.

Before I know it, he takes a few steps back, bringing me with him before he pushes my head forward. Instinctively, I bend over, grabbing the windowsill and arching my back and bringing my ass up to meet his thrust.

Every time he pumps in and out, it hurts a little less. And not long after, we're working in a rhythm.

"Goddamn, you're fucking soaked," he growls. "You're just about dripping down my thighs, baby. Coating my dick and making me want to come inside of you right now."

"Walker—" My voice breaks when, all at once, my orgasm hits me, and the edges of my vision start to fade to black, making it hard for me to keep hold of the window. "Oh fuck," I cry out, almost screaming as my body starts to fall forward, but he keeps me still, coming inside of me abruptly.

"Fucking A, I love how your greedy pussy feels while I fucking spill my cum inside of it," he bellows. "Taking every ounce like a good girl and my little whore."

My legs are shaky as his body jerks forward a few more times. And when he kisses my shoulder before slowly pulling out of me, I suck in a few shaky breaths and hide the wince coming from my abdomen, proving that I really, really overdid it.

Turning me to face him, he cups my cheek and kisses me. "You're fucking killing me, Poppyseed. Ruining me for anyone else."

I freeze, looking at his disheveled hair and his rising chest as he tries to catch his breath. "Walker … I don't want you to marry someone else," I croak. "You can't."

"I know," he whispers, not giving me anything else besides those two insignificant words. "Let's go to bed. I want to hold you."

Why is he avoiding talking about this? Is it because he knows he'll never get out of this deal and the time in this hotel is really the end for us?

God, I hope not.

WALKER

"You can't avoid talking about it forever, you know," Poppy says softly against my side. "Eventually, the day is going to come for you to go marry this girl."

Right after we fucked, she brought it up. And being the coward that I am, I couldn't bear to talk about it, so I tried to shut it down. But she's right. It's not going away. She deserves to know everything about this other girl and the deal. It's the least I can give her.

"I know," I whisper into the semi-dark room. "I guess I just keep thinking if I don't talk about it, it'll go away. Which is stupid for me to even think because my uncle isn't the type to not collect debts."

"Why does your uncle care if you marry this girl or not? If Briar is marrying into the family already, isn't that enough?" She shrugs her slender shoulders. "Why drag you into it?"

"Because in Beckett's eyes, it gives him more control. He's always been able to control my sister. But me? Not so much."

"Until now," she mutters. "All because of me."

I tighten my grip around her. "I will gladly take the wrath of my uncle and all his stipulations if it means that I get to make it right with you, Poppyseed." I run my fingertips on the bare skin of her back. "Since I left you, thoughts of you on that sidewalk have haunted me every single day. But that wasn't nearly as bad as thinking that you were in danger all those years." I sigh. "At least this way, we're leaving on a good note, and I'll know that you're safe because these lowlifes will be taken care of."

"Yeah, probably just in time for Ron to suddenly get out of jail," she says with a laugh, but it's laced with sadness.

She doesn't know that I've been keeping tabs on her father since I left. He still has a year to serve in prison. But once he gets out, I wouldn't be surprised if he tried to reconnect with Poppy.

Just thinking about it, I ball my hands up, and my nails dig into my palms. Whatever I can do to make sure that doesn't happen, I will. I might have to be married to someone else, but I'll always protect Poppy first.

When I don't say anything, she carries on. "I understand why you left, Walker. Back then, I was being selfish, and the only thing I could focus on was the pain of losing you. But now, I get it." She kisses my flesh. "I'm going to be okay. But it's not fair that your life is being dictated by someone else. You deserve so much more than that."

"Yeah," I utter under my breath before glancing down at her just as she angles her head upward. "What about you? What happened to Juilliard? I thought that was your dream."

It's almost as though her body stiffens at the mention of her dream school. And I feel her sighing before her lips part, and she answers, "I didn't end up applying there."

"Why the hell not?" I can't stop how annoyed I sound, which isn't a good thing because, with Poppy, I need to remember to tread lightly.

"I mean, when it came time to apply, Jake was still living in the trailer with all of us, waiting to hear back about the housing program he had applied for. I couldn't just leave him, you know?" She stops for a few seconds, looking away from me. "Van had gotten himself into drugs, and I couldn't leave Jake with Ron. So, I applied here. And I got in."

Brushing some loose strands of hair from her face, I exhale slowly. "You deserve to follow your dreams, Poppy. You are allowed that."

She's colder now, her body more rigid. "I probably wouldn't have gotten in anyway, so what's it matter now? This is a good program, and I can go visit Jake—in his very own place—anytime I want." She looks up at me again, clearly begging for a change of topic. "Well, I can once this crazy hockey player guy stops holding me hostage."

I force myself to chuckle, but only to appease her. Deep down, I keep thinking about how much this girl has given up. And how I'd give anything … anything at all, to watch her dreams come true.

Even if I can't be next to her while it happens.

145

POPPY

I watch the screen before dunking the crab rangoon on my fork into the duck sauce, slathering it with an ungodly amount, and shoving it into my mouth. I love Chinese food, but it's not something I get to have very often. Eating out at restaurants or getting takeout isn't something I can afford. But Walker must have given Hudson instructions on what I would want to eat while he was away because, judging from the vegetable lo mein, crab rangoons, and a crap ton of duck sauce, someone gave him some pointers. Someone named Walker.

Walker left for his game in Ohio early yesterday morning. He wasn't planning on waking me up, but I set my own alarm so that I wouldn't miss wishing him luck. My good luck ended up in a morning quickie, which made it even harder for me to say good-bye to him. The good news is that I have a ton of classwork since I've been out, so his being gone has given me more than enough time to complete that.

The Wolves won last night's game, and even though they are currently down by one, I know this game is far from over.

The night that Walker told me about the deal he made with his uncle to keep me safe, I sort of decided right then and there that I wanted to throw all caution to the wind and just live life for the next week or so. After all, once I get out of here, he'll be someone's fiancé and then husband.

Even thinking about him and the word *husband* when it doesn't involve me makes me sick.

Though I've never been one to picture a white picket fence or a grassy backyard with a swing set and things like that, I always thought we'd somehow be connected. And I hoped we'd end up together.

He gets me. He isn't exhausting to be around because he understands pain and grief himself. I don't have to plaster on a fake happy face and pretend to be something I'm not because Walker knows more than anyone that … life is sad.

I watch the screen as Walker flies down the ice. One of his teammates, whose name I don't recognize, slaps him the puck, and before anyone can even think about stopping him, he scores a goal. His team all huddles around him, cheering with excitement. Even on the screen and through his helmet, I can see his smile.

He's so happy when he's on the ice.

Every time we kiss or have sex, I know that I'm making this thing between us grow even bigger than it already is. I'm creating a monster because neither of us will want to pull away when time runs up and we have to say good-bye.

I'm playing with fire—I know that. But I'm so used to being burned that right now…I'm the one sparking it up and dumping the gasoline. There's nothing that could make me stop.

My phone vibrates on the table, and since I'm watching Walker on the screen, I know it's not him. But since it could be Jake or maybe even Ryann, I jump up from the couch and go to it.

I don't recognize the number, but because it might have to do with Jake, I decide I'd better answer it. I've been worried about him getting pulled into this mess Van left behind, but luckily, not many people that Van was associated with knew he had an older brother because Jake had already moved out. Me? I was living in the crack house for months before I got out of there, which is why I've been chosen to pay Van's debt.

"Hello?" I say, nervous about what's going to come from the other line. Between the random phone calls from Ron since he went to prison and the worst call of my life when I was told my brother was dead, I'm scared for what else could come from my phone ringing.

"Look at you, little fucking bitch. Jumping campus and hiding?"

I instantly recognize the voice, feeling sick.

"Guess what. Joke's on you because we know where you live and where you work." The voice laughs bitterly. "Guess it's time for your coworkers to pay up. Or maybe those other dancers who live in that big ol' house with you. The legs on that blonde one? She could pay in other ways than just the cash."

"No," I cry out. "I have your money. I'll … I can meet you with it," I lie. I have no money. None. But I can't let them go after my friends or the girls I work with. "Can you give me forty-eight hours? I promise, I … I'll have it."

"Hmm … tell you what, you dumb bitch. You can meet us at the same alleyway where we … visited you three nights ago. Tomorrow, nine p.m." His deep, cold voice pauses. "Don't even think about bringing someone with you or calling the cops. If you do … it won't be good. Not for you and not for your roommates."

Suddenly, my door slowly pushes open, and Hudson holds his finger up to his mouth, instructing me to be quiet.

"Okay," I whisper, a tear running down my cheek. "I'll … I'll be there. Just please don't hurt anyone else. I'll have your money."

I went from not crying for three years to having no control over the tears spilling from my eyes. It's like the second Walker stepped back into my life, everything went to hell, but I also got my ability to feel again.

"You'd better. Or we'll finish what we started, and you'll be dead. Just like your brother."

The line goes dead, and when my hand drops to my side, Hudson rushes toward me to take my phone.

"You good?" he asks, looking down at the screen.

"Not really," I squeak. "I've been here, eating room service, sleeping in the comfiest bed, and taking bubble baths." I shake my head. "Freaking bubble baths! All while they could be hurting the girls I live with. Or my coworkers—and anyone else associated with me." My eyes widen. "Jake! What if—"

"We've been keeping an eye on Jake's. Nothing has seemed out of the ordinary there." He reaches forward, patting my shoulder. "Just … breathe. Okay?"

He looks at the screen again before his lips turn up the slightest bit.

"The good news is … oftentimes, druggies and drug dealers aren't all that complex. They sure as shit didn't think a girl like you from Sunset Drive would have people backing you to stop them in their tracks."

He holds my phone up. "I've gotta send this number to my buddies. The ones who Beckett hired to find these scumbags." He grins. "I don't think they'll be looking much longer. These idiots didn't even block their number." He shrugs. "Rookie mistake."

"So … they won't hurt my friends?" I sniffle. "Or go to the coffee shop?"

"Doesn't look like it." He takes his own phone out of his pocket, and when he turns around, swiping his finger across the phone, I see the silhouette of a girl on his screen.

She's got her back to the camera, but I recognize her instantly.

It's Briar.

He walks into the kitchen, muttering some things into the phone before returning moments later. "I should call Walker." He nods toward the TV. "Once the game's done. He'll want to know about that phone call."

I sigh, looking up at the screen. There's only a few more minutes left in this game, and now, Brooks is up by one goal. This team is one of their toughest competitors. If they win this, it'll be huge for them. And they're doing it all while Cade is away at rehab.

"Can we just wait and tell him when he gets back tomorrow morning?" I give him my most pitiful look. "Please?"

"Ma'am ... James is a wild card when it comes to you. Keeping something like this from him?" He breathes in through his teeth, making a slight hissing noise. "He'll fucking kill me."

I look back at the TV, and my heart hurts as I watch the clock run down. "That boy right there has put everyone ahead of himself for his entire life. He never asks for anything in return, never expects it." My gaze finds Hudson's, and I tilt my head. "To keep me safe, he signed his life over to his uncle. Something I'll never forgive myself for allowing to happen. Please, Hudson, if he finds out that I got that phone call, he'll try to find a way to rush home tonight. And that won't fly with his coach. So, I'm begging you, don't tell him tonight. Let him enjoy this win with his teammates." I swallow. "For kids like us? It's a miracle to even make it to the point he's at. We didn't have support or love. Or anyone to cheer us on. Besides each other. Give him this night."

He stares at me for a long time. Finally, he drags his hand over his head. "Fine, but if he's pissed at me, I'm throwing you under the bus."

"I'm more than okay with that. Thank you." I smile before chewing my lip nervously. I know what I want to ask, but I don't want to make him feel uncomfortable. "The girl on your screen? Is that Briar?"

His shoulders tense, and he looks down at his phone before tucking it into his pocket. "Uh ... no."

I chuckle. "It is. And I promise, your secret is safe with me." I exhale slowly, sadness spreading through my chest. "Aside from her brother, she was my best friend, growing up. I sure miss her."

His face pales, and there's no mistaking the sadness that covers not only his face, but also his entire body as he slumps slowly, seeming pained. "Yeah. Me too. She's, uh, about to be married to someone else, apparently." His nostrils flare with anger. "Her sleazeball uncle has an odd way of controlling every person close to him. Even her."

My heart hurts for not only him, but also myself. And for Walker.

"Yeah, I'm beginning to see that," I whisper. "Maybe we can stop it, you know?" I try to smile, but it's hard. "Not just for Briar, but Walker too." I swallow. "Because he's in the same boat."

Hudson cringes, leaning against the couch. "Fuck. I knew James had made some sort of deal with Beckett, but I didn't know it was that."

"Yep," I say, emphasizing the P. "I guess when it comes to Dr. Boobs, nothing is free."

He bursts out laughing, shaking his head. "No. No, it sure isn't." He hands me my phone, jerking his thumb toward the door. "I'll be just outside in the hallway if you need anything. If your phone rings again, get me." He stops. "But remember, check the—"

"Peephole first," I say quickly. "Yes, yes. I will." I frown. "You aren't going back to your room?"

"Not tonight. Not after—" He stops himself like he doesn't want to say anything that might upset me.

"Not after the phone call?" I guess, raising my eyebrows.

Slowly, he nods. "If James were here, he wouldn't close his eyes tonight because he'd want to make sure you're safe. Least I can do is sit outside the door until he gets back tomorrow." He chuckles, cringing a little. "After all, I'm keeping this secret from him."

"Annnnd your wallpaper is his sister," I point out. "There's also that."

"Yeah, there's also that." He laughs before nodding toward the TV screen. "Looks like the Wolves are taking home the W. Night, Poppy. If you need me, I'll be right out here."

"Night," I mutter as he goes into the hallway.

When I look at the television, the camera zooms in on the Wolves as they all leap together, hitting the top of each other's helmet with excitement.

For once, I wish I could have been there in the stands, cheering him on.

Maybe someday. Even if it's from afar.

18

WALKER

I sit in the chair, glaring forward, staring at absolutely nothing. I keep my mouth shut because anything that comes out of my mouth won't be nice. That's for fucking sure.

I got back an hour ago, only to learn from Hudson that Poppy received a threatening phone call last night and that even though the attackers think she's meeting them later, they'll be caught before then.

All of this shit happened minutes before my game ended. And neither Hudson nor Poppy filled me the fuck in. In fact, I talked to her on the phone not long after it happened. She sounded fine. She mentioned nothing about that phone call.

"Are you going to continue sulking, or can we go about our day?" she calls from the kitchen.

When I don't answer, she walks into the living room, and I keep my eyes hard as I glare at her. Her bruises are now a yellowish hue, slowly fading from her skin. And from the way she moves, I can tell that her body is much less sore than it was when I left for Ohio a few days ago.

"You should have told me," I snarl, avoiding her and keeping my hands on the armrest and looking away from her. "I know damn well Hudson would have. But I guarantee you didn't let him."

"You're right," she says calmly. "I did ask him not to tell you. Because, for once, I wanted you to enjoy something."

Out of the corner of my eye, I see her across the living room. "You can be mad all you want, big guy. I'm not sorry for caring enough to want you to enjoy your win with the team."

I snap my eyes to her, narrowing them. "I'm so fucking pissed right now, Poppy."

Taking a few steps forward, she shrugs her shoulders. "What do I have to do to make it up to you?" she coos in a breathy tone. "Tell me, and I'll do it."

I stare at her in her baby-blue tank top and matching cotton shorts. Through her shirt, I can see her tits perfectly, and my cock twitches.

"Get on your hands and knees and fucking crawl to me," I growl slowly. "Crawl across the rug, to my feet and beg for me to forgive you enough to give you my cock."

Poppy has never been one to do what she's told. I expect her to argue or sass me. Instead, she sinks to the floor, gets on all fours, and crawls to me. Her eyes never break contact with mine, and she tilts her chin up when she's at my feet. "Please, forgive me. I didn't want to ruin your night. You deserved to celebrate with your teammates," she whispers as her tank top hangs forward, giving me a direct view of her tits.

I swallow a groan before it escapes my lips.

"You're going to suck my cock. You're going to make me come, but don't you even think for a second that I'm going to let that greedy pussy of yours do the same," I hiss before I push forward to stand and pull my sweatpants down enough to let my cock spring free.

She looks at my dick, still on all fours, as her eyes grow hooded. But when she starts to lift her hands, I shake my head.

"Nope. You stay on your hands and knees, my little whore," I grumble. "Now, open up that deceitful mouth and suck on my dick."

Keeping her back arched, she leans forward, bringing me into her mouth slowly. Now that her lip is healed, I jerk my hips forward, plunging deep into her throat and making her gag. Normally, I wouldn't consider being this rough with her, but she lied, and I need her to know I'm angry about that.

But the thing is, she fucking loves it. She gags slightly before moaning.

"Maybe I read it wrong, huh, Poppyseed. Maybe sucking my dick is too much of a reward for you. You don't deserve a reward right now."

She moves her lips up and down my cock, soaking my length and making it impossible for me to force her to stop.

I watch her hand lift from the floor and move it between her legs. Pulling my cock out of her mouth, I reach down and grip her chin.

"Don't even think about touching yourself, P. Hands on the floor. Don't make me ask again."

Whimpering, she does as she was told.

"Look how fucking turned on you are. Just like I said, sucking my dick is too rewarding for you. We can't have that, can we?"

Standing up straighter, I tease her by brushing the tip of my dick over her lips and along her cheek. But instead of sliding back between her plump, now-reddened lips, I palm myself. Sliding my hand back and forth, just half an inch from her face.

"Walker," she whimpers, moving her mouth closer to my cock. "Please—"

I continue to jerk my dick, glaring down at her. "Please what, Poppyseed?" I bark.

"Please … let me. Let me …"

Her lips part, and she stares up at me. I'm so fucking turned on that I can hardly keep myself from blowing my load all over her face right now to teach her a lesson. Then again, she'd probably like that too.

"Say the words, angel." I tilt my chin up. "Say it like a good fucking girl who wants a mouthful of my cum."

"Please, let me suck your dick," she says, somewhere between a whine and a growl, and I love it when I see a pinkish hue fill her cheeks.

Shaking my head, I make a tsk noise at her. "No, you've been too deceitful for that. Instead, I'm going to fuck your mouth. Hard, too, so be ready to gag and breathe through your nose. You won't have an ounce of control, and here's your warning to hold still and take it. Because the second you try to take the reins, I'm going to pull my cock from your lips, and I'll fuck my hand and come all over your face. Because right now, this isn't for you." I glide my cock into her mouth slowly. "Do you understand?"

Her big eyes stare up at me, and she nods once.

"Good girl," I growl, pushing myself further down her throat, loving the feel of it closing around me.

She's begging for air before I pull back. Her body moves back and forth slightly with every thrust of my hips, but she tries her best to stay rooted to the floor.

"Look at you," I murmur, barely choking the words out because it feels so good and looks even fucking better. "Swallowing my cock, taking every inch like a good girl." I fist her hair gently, not wanting to hurt her. "Are you a little whore for my cock?"

She moans on my length, her eyebrows pulling together as I pull my dick from her mouth.

"Answer me, Poppy."

"Y-yes," she moans.

"But only for me, right, baby?"

"Only for you," she whimpers. "Always for you."

"That's right," I snap, thrusting myself back into her mouth and making her gag. "No other man has ever fucked this mouth."

I stop myself before saying anything else. What I want to say is no other man will ever fuck this mouth. But that'd be a lie. What's she supposed to do, wait for me forever?

I fucking wish she would.

I don't warn her when I lose it and come into her mouth, trembling as her eyes stare up at me, and I watch her throat swallow me down. She keeps her tongue cupped on me as my hips jerk slower and slower until I'm fucking spent. And once she pulls back, I wait a solid few seconds, making her believe that I'm really going to punish her by leaving her hanging while I know she's fucking soaking wet.

Pulling her to stand, I tear her clothes from her body until she's completely bare. Reaching between her legs, I slide my fingers into her heat, and my breath hitches.

"That fucking wet from tasting my dick?" I swallow down a moan before I take a few steps to the couch and slide my back down so that I'm only half on it. "Come here and sit on my face," I demand. "Grab the back of the couch and fucking ride my face until you come all over my tongue."

Her thighs squeeze together before she takes a few shaky steps and straddles me. Moving her body up, I can tell she's nervous, so I reach around and grip her ass, pulling her upward until she's sitting directly on my face.

"I fucked your mouth; it's your turn to fuck mine," I grunt before my tongue pokes out to taste her. She's so fucking wet that she soaks my face right away. "Come on. Ride my fucking face, baby. Fuck my tongue. I'm starving."

Slowly, her hips start to move, my tongue working right with them. And after a moment or two, the shyness wears off, and she grips the back of the couch and rides my face like she's a bull rider.

Her ass bounces up and down on my chin, and she cries out as I eat her pussy like a fucking meal. I drag my hands down her body, gripping the backs of her legs, and hold on tight as she thrusts forward and back. Finally, I feel her tighten around me, and against my tongue, I feel her pulsating.

"Walker," she moans slowly. "Walker, oh … my … God."

Her movements get faster as she bucks against my face while she continues to cry out my name like I'm God and she fucking worships me just before she slows, her entire body trembling.

Moving down my body, she buries her face into my neck. "Thank you," she breathes. "That was … yeah."

I hold on to her, feeling her heart racing against mine. I never was all that mad, I guess.

Maybe I just wanted to punish her a little.

"So … when are we leaving?" she asks nervously.

"To go where?"

"You know … to meet the attackers to pay them."

I pull back, looking at her. "Poppyseed, I'd never let you ever meet those scumbags."

"But what about—"

"Shh," I say, stopping her. "Trust me, in the next few hours, they won't be thinking about that money. And you won't have to worry about them anymore either."

She relaxes against me, and I listen to her breathing softly.

"What's going to happen to them?" she whispers.

Rubbing my fingertips up and down her back, I rest my head against hers. "Let's just see how it all plays out, okay? But no matter what, they'll never hurt you again."

No one will ever hurt my girl again.

POPPY

After showering and putting on a pair of sweatpants and Walker's hoodie that basically hangs to my knees, I walk out of the bedroom and find him on the couch.

I silently giggle because, to be honest, I'm not sure I'll ever look at a couch the same—especially *that* couch. At first, it felt a little awkward to literally … take a seat on his face. But once I let myself enjoy it … holy shitballs, I can feel my heart fluttering, just thinking about it.

He grins at me as if reading my thoughts, and I bite my lip.

Holding the remote in one hand and Sour Punch Straws in the other, he shrugs slyly. "So, here's the thing. Hudson called me the dude from *Pretty Woman*, and I don't have a clue what the fuck that means. Well, aside from there's a hooker in it. So, we're watching it."

"First off, you got me one of my favorite candies?" I grin before walking toward him. "Second, you and I? We're going to watch what could debatably be the biggest chick flick in the history of movies."

"I mean, I guess we don't have to. I could always go hit the gym and—"

"No!" I yell, practically leaping onto the couch and curling up beside him. "No. A movie sounds great."

Throwing his arm around me, he plays with my hair softly before kissing the top of my head. "Let's see if I'm Edward. The rich, hooker-loving fella."

I shoot him a glare before twisting his nipple. "Shut up."

This feels good. This feels … just like it did before.
Before he left me the first time.

POPPY

I give Jake one last hug good-bye, squeezing him probably a little too aggressively. Until an hour ago, I hadn't seen him in ten days. That's the longest we've ever gone without seeing each other. Walker stopped in to visit Jake several times before or after practice. I didn't want him to see me until the remains of my bruises could be covered with concealer.

"Good to see you, stinker." I release him. "I hope you didn't enjoy that little hiatus from me too much. Because it'll never happen again!"

His grin only spreads more, and he moves to Walker and hugs him.

"Thank you," Jake says. "For making Poppy smile again."

Walker tenses but pats him on the back. "Talk to you later, buddy." He steps back, glancing at me. "Ready?"

Blowing out a breath, I bob my head up and down. "Ready."

Hudson was able to trace the call I received from my attackers and locate the scumbags. And because of the connections Beckett has, those men are now in prison—probably the same one as my dad, where they can all conspire against me. Nonetheless, I'm free to go about my everyday life again.

And yet I'm kind of sad about that.

It's like doomsday is coming, and I know Walker and I both feel it. His uncle has demanded he come to South Carolina this weekend, and we both know that the girl he is going to soon be married to will be there.

As we head outside to his truck, I'm lost in my thoughts. *What if she's prettier than me? What if he falls for her and forgets I even existed?*

And the thing that's killing me the most is thinking that I might never get to see him again. Like, really see him. Sure, I'll see him in passing. But we'll never be the way we are right now. Not when he becomes someone else's other half.

He turns out of the parking lot and reaches over, putting his hand on mine. "Hey, you all right?"

Glancing at him, I give him a weak, half-assed smile. "Yeah. I'm … I'm good."

"If you don't feel up to going to Sunset Drive today, we can pick another day," he says, looking at me with pure understanding in his eyes.

What other day? I want to scream out. This is one of the last days we'll be together. And this is something he and I need to do. Without him, I don't think I could get through it.

For weeks, I've known that I need to go to the trailer and get Van's belongings out of there, in case, for some stupid reason, Ron gets let out of prison early. Because the second he returns to Sunset Drive, I'll never step foot on that street again for as long as I live.

It's now or never.

"Today is fine," my voice barely squeaks as I make a pathetic attempt to sound okay. "Let's just go get it over with."

He eyes me over suspiciously, and I know that he can read my every thought. He knows that I'm dreading going back to that place. But he also knows that if I don't, I'll never forgive myself.

And eventually, he nods. "All right."

WALKER

I sit on the worn, definitely-not-safe steps, happy as fuck I'm up to date on my tetanus shots, looking out at the street as I wait for Poppy. I didn't want her to go inside alone, but how can a street hold so many good memories and so many bad ones at the same time? Sunset Drive is where I made my first friend. Learned to ride a bike. Threw a football for hours on end with

Jake. Lit off firecrackers with Van while Poppy stood on the steps, shaking her head at us with that annoyed yet amused look on her beautiful face.

It's also where I knew, with every single cell in my body, that I loved Poppy Wilson more than I would ever love another human being because we both had this darkness inside of us. Something that could only come from growing up the way that we did. We just got each other. We still do.

I know that the more time we spend together before we say our good-byes, the harder it'll be to leave. But I don't have a choice. Not as far as I can see anyway. My uncle is a ruthless man. Once he sets his sights on something, there's no going back. And right now, his sights are set on me getting married to Gia Romano. A girl I've literally met twice at parties that Beckett hosted during my senior year of high school.

And, yeah, I got way too drunk, and we hooked up. But it's not like I can tell Poppy that. The girl fucking waited for me, never so much as kissing another man. Well, besides Cade. But I'm sure as hell not going to think about that fucking shit right now. Pisses me off too much.

But aside from Huff, she waited. All while I did the opposite. I tried to drown my sorrows in meaningless sex, pretending each girl was her.

It's one thing for Poppy to know I've been with other women. It's another for her to find out I'm marrying a girl I've been with in that way. But it didn't mean anything. In fact, after it was over, I couldn't get away from her fast enough.

She's the opposite of Poppy. And that's why I can't stand her.

The door creaks open, and I turn my head to see Poppy before she takes a seat next to me and sets the cardboard box of random things on the ground.

Her head rests against my shoulder as we sit in silence. The light breeze rushes through the trees, making the leaves dance on their limbs.

I gaze up, not seeing this shithole the way I used to. When everything looked dirty and abandoned, I resented everything about it—even the pavement. We'd all talk about how, one day, we'd get out. I guess we all did in some way or another.

Now, I just want to go back. Back to a time when Poppy looked at me like I'd hung the entire fucking galaxy. Or when Van hadn't taken his first hit of heroin and he had dreams of getting out of here. Jake had both siblings alive and healthy. And most of all, to a time when, in my heart, I thought I'd end up with Poppy. The NHL isn't far away now. LaConte has gotten multiple calls from teams interested in me. I have all the money I could dream of, and I no longer live on a street where no one is safe.

Yet I feel like I've lost everything. And she's not even gone yet.

Loving and letting her go is like a Band-Aid that's sitting on a wound. You know it's better to just rip it off and get it the hell over with, but it's the hardest fucking thing I'll ever have to do. And that says a lot because we both went through a lot of shit during our childhood on Sunset Drive. A place where we learned about life, loss, and pain. And even heartbreak. It sucked, and it didn't make for the easiest life. But it made us who we are today, in this moment.

She's strong. She's so fucking strong. And to be honest, I know she'll be fine without me. But I can't say the same for me. Because those years without her, I was so fucking lost. And since that night that her brother died and she let me back in, I am finally starting to feel like everything makes sense. Even as fucked up as that sounds because Van died. I'd give anything to change that, but the fact is, that terrible, fucking awful moment in time brought us back together. And now, we're about to get ripped apart again.

And I can't stomach it. But I also don't know what to do. My uncle is not above getting those two thugs out of jail and having them go after her again if I don't play my part in his game.

The way I see it, either way, I can't win. But if one of the options keeps her safe and the other doesn't? Come hell or high water, I'll always throw myself in front of a bullet for her.

Finally, she sighs, keeping her head against my shoulder. "I can't say I'll miss this street, but I wouldn't change a thing about it as far as me and you. You know?"

Of course, I know what she means. I wouldn't change anything either. Because as shitty as the circumstances were, it brought us together.

I don't think I could love anyone who had never known the pain she and I have felt. Because of that pain … I know how tough and resilient she is. And that's what makes me love her as fiercely as I do.

"There will always be you, and there will be me. But without this street, there would be no you *and* me. So, as much as I'd like to … I can't hate this place," I mutter softly. "I can't hate anything that led me to you."

She nuzzles her cheek against my hoodie. "At least this time around, we're not leaving angry." She pauses. "That's got to count for something, right?"

"Right," I mutter lifelessly.

It doesn't matter if we leave each other happy, angry, or fucking hating one another. Any universe where she's leaving or I'm leaving her behind makes zero sense.

I nod toward the box, seeing one of the hats Van always wore and a piece of pottery he made in, like, fifth grade. But when I see the MVP baseball trophy Van got in seventh grade, I almost lose it. He stopped playing the next year, which was a damn shame because he was quite the player.

"I hated baseball. Literally couldn't fucking stand it one bit. But I always wonder, if I had just played a few more years, if I could have stuck it out for him … maybe he would have kept playing and ended up with a scholarship." My eyes glance around. "A scholarship to get him the fuck out of here."

"You had to chase down your dreams, Walker," she whispers against my hoodie. "If you hadn't, you could have ended up in the same boat as he did." She stretches an arm around the front of me. "Watching you on the ice again just solidifies what I've known all along." She cranes her neck so that her face is tilted up toward mine. "You were born to play hockey. And I love watching you do something that sets your soul on fire."

My chest warms while my heart hurts, all at the same time. "Hockey just doesn't seem like that big of a deal anymore." I shake my head. "I'm losing you. We lost Van." I stop, feeling the dread spreading through my body. "I've felt guilty since the night I saw Van when I came back here. Right when I looked at him, I knew in my heart that I had abandoned him and that if I hadn't, he might have never gotten into drugs or dealing them to begin with. Just because I moved away didn't mean I had to stop being there for you all. But that's exactly what I did. That's something I have to live with. And to be honest, P, it fucking kills me." I take a long breath, slowly letting it out, though it comes out shaky. "My sister has lost her mind. Van is dead. Jake will likely hate me when he thinks I'm leaving you again." I look at her, my eyes growing blurry as I squeeze her hand. "I just want you to be happy, Poppyseed. That's all I've ever wanted."

Slowly, she reaches up, brushing my hair over. "I refuse to think that after everything we've been through," she says, stopping as her eyes fill with tears, and she smiles before pouting sadly. "Our families addiction, abuse, betrayals, hunger, feeling filthy ..." Her lip trembles. "After all of that, Walker James, I refuse to think that someone they call Dr. Boobs is going to be our demise." She attempts to lighten the mood but only cries harder. "I was never with another man because I had never given up on the idea of us." She squeezes my hand tighter. "I'm not about to throw in the towel now."

My lips attack hers, and I kiss her, tasting the salt from her tears on my lips as her body shakes against mine. Pulling back, I cup her cheeks. "I love you. I have loved you since we were kids, and I will love you until the day I die." I kiss her again—happy as fuck that her lip is healed because I'm almost certain I just bruised it without meaning to.

"I think I've loved you for my entire life." She sniffles. "And even though I've never thought of myself as wife material, I can't let you marry someone who isn't me."

I don't make a promise that I can't keep. And I don't tell her it'll all be okay and that my uncle will drop the deal and let us ride off into the sunset and leave me the fuck alone. I might have hurt her in the past, but I don't want to lie to her and give her false hope. So, instead, I kiss her again and touch my nose to hers.

"Please, let me get you out of here," I whisper, sliding my hand to her thigh. "Let me take you home. I need to feel you, my perfect fucking girl."

"Okay," she utters, nodding her head up and down.

But before we stand, my phone rings in my pocket. Pulling it out, I see an out-of-state number with an area code I don't recognize.

"Better see who it is," she whispers, nodding toward my phone.

Slowly, I drag my thumb across the screen and bring it to my ear.

"Hello?" I say, expecting a telemarketer or maybe even my uncle to respond.

"Hey there. Is this Walker James?" a deep voice replies quickly.

"Uh, yes." I glance at Poppy, who watches me closely. "This is Walker James."

"Walker, this is Jack Dow, GM of the New England Bay Sharks here in Portland, Maine." There's a short pause, and I swear to God my heart fucking stops beating as I wait for his next words. "You've probably heard that our starting center, Kenneth Smitten, is retiring after this season. Leaving us in need of some fresh blood on the team. We've watched you this season. And we're impressed. You came onto a brand-new team as a freshman, stepping into the shoes of Cam Hardy. Which we recognize was no easy feat. Anyway, we'd love to offer you a position on our team next season."

"For real?" I barely register myself saying. My brain feels like it's spinning.

"Hell yeah, son." He laughs. "We'll send over a contract for your agent to look over. Talk about it with your family and get back to me in the next few weeks. Okay?"

I'm still so shocked by the phone call that it takes me a second to even respond. "Yeah ... yeah, that sounds great. Uh, thank you." I run my hand over the top of my head. "Thank you so much."

"Look forward to hearing from you, James. Enjoy your day."

He ends the call, and I look at Poppy, whose big eyes stare at me, wondering what the hell is going on. And I'm scared to tell her because if the odds weren't already stacked against us for being together ... they really are now.

Playing in the NHL is all I've wanted to do since I was a kid. But if I had to choose between the pros and her, I'd hang my skates up right now.

All I know is ... I'm not letting Beckett find out that his nephew just made it into the NHL. Fuck. No.

POPPY

Judging by the look on his face, it's obvious that he just got big news. Huge news even. And as the call comes to an end, I patiently wait for him to share with me what's going on.

Slowly, he stands. "That was the general manager of the New England Bay Sharks." He swallows, looking straight ahead. "They want me to come play for them next season." His eyes find mine, and he cringes the slightest bit. "In Maine."

As hard as the sting in my chest hits me, knowing he'll be gone and I'll be here, I'm so happy for him. Because this has been his dream for his entire life. Everything he's done has been for this moment. And what better place to find this out than here, where it all began? To remind him that where he came from isn't where he's going to end up.

Pushing to my feet, I stand, looking up at him. "You're going pro?" I barely whisper, tears gathering in my eyes because I'm the one who's right next to this boy when all his dreams are coming true. Not his arranged wife. Me.

"I mean … yeah," he croaks. "I guess I am."

I leap into his arms as the tears flow down my cheeks in a steady stream. "You're in the NHL," I cry. "You did it!"

His arms squeeze me, pulling my feet from the ground as he buries his face into the crevice of my neck. "Maine is a long ways away from Georgia," he murmurs, an unmistakable anxiousness in his tone.

When he sets me down, I keep my hands on his waist and angle my chin up to look at him. "I'm losing you anyway, Walker." My voice croaks. "I'm finally starting to understand that whether you're one mile away or a thousand … you'll always be with me." I sniffle harder when his thumbs brush the tears gathering under my eyes. "No matter where you go, I'll be with you. Always."

"It's not the same," he growls. "It'll never be the same."

It's like watching a clock run out of time when you still have so much more you need to do or want to say. There will never be enough time with Walker. I could be promised eternity, and I'd still watch the clock, scared it would eventually come to an end.

"I always knew you'd be the one to chase down your dreams and make them become reality," I whisper, smiling through my tear-soaked lashes. Releasing one hand from him, I wave toward the street that once was our home. "You came from here and look where you're going next."

I stand on my tiptoes, pressing my lips to his. "I love you, and I am so proud of you, Walker James. And I know your parents are looking down, so proud of you too." I kiss him again. "So, you're going to go to Maine because you deserve it. And you're not going to feel bad."

His eyebrows pull together, and his eyes grow misty before he lifts me up, forcing my legs around his waist. "I fucking love you, Poppy. And I promise you, when it comes to this arranged marriage, I'm not going down without a fight. I'm going to try like hell to come back to you."

I nod, my nose rubbing against his. "I believe you." I say the three words, trying to sound so calm. But the truth is, I'm terrified.

Because deep down, I know I'm going to lose him. Again. Only this time, I don't think he'll come back.

WALKER

Life's a fucking weird thing. One minute, you're balls deep inside of the woman you love, staring into her eyes as you both come together, all while the rest of the world melts away. And for a while there, it really does seem like it's just the two of you. But then, the next thing you know, you're at your uncle's, and he springs on you that he's brought the chick he's demanding you to marry here early.

Gia sits across from me on the patio. Her brown eyes cut into mine, but I can't look at her directly. Her dark hair is perfectly curled, just like it always is when I see her. Her outfit consists of designer clothes pressed to perfection.

She's a ten by anyone's standards. She comes from old, old money. For her entire life, she'll want for nothing, as will I once we tie the knot.

"You can stop ignoring me. I don't want to be here either, you know," she whispers, taking a sip from her sweet tea. "Believe it or not, living in the United States, married to a toothless hockey player, isn't exactly my childhood dream."

I open my mouth, pointing inside. "I have all my teeth, *wife*," I answer sarcastically with a scoff.

"Yeah, for now." She rolls her eyes. "Look, we had sex. It was fun. I enjoyed myself. But this?" She waves her hand between us. "I don't want to be your fiancée or wife, Walker."

"Gee, thanks." I feign being hurt.

She gives me a pointed look. "What girl would want to marry a dude who is clearly spoken for?" She shakes her head at me. "You couldn't be more emotionally unavailable if you were a rock."

I sit up straighter. I just assumed before today that she was on board with this entire thing. I guess I should have asked sooner.

"So, you're saying you don't want this either?" I glance toward the door to make sure Uncle Fucking Titty Man isn't listening. "Like, you don't want to get married and all that happy horseshit?"

"Hell. No," she says quickly before inching closer to me. "What deal did you make? You know … to end up in this situation."

"I'll tell you mine if you tell me yours," I utter, widening my eyes. "Go on, girl. What do you get out of this fucking mess that they've created for us?"

She looks down, picking at her nails. "My father will pay for the boy I love to attend college. Something that certainly would not have happened if I hadn't agreed to this." She shrugs. "When do you think enough will be enough? Both of them are already powerful and rich. Why on earth do they need to join forces?"

"Because they are greedy," I say matter-of-factly because it's the fucking truth. "And with people like that, nothing will ever be enough."

"So, go on then." She raises a perfectly shaped dark brow. "I told you my secret. Tell me yours."

I huff out a breath, sitting back in my seat further. "This girl, Poppy, she got in a bit of a mess. I needed to make sure she was protected. And that the people who hurt her were taken care of." I pull my sunglasses down. "And now, well, here we are."

She gives me a small smile. "You love this girl, correct?"

"Yeah," I say instantly. "What's it matter though?" I jerk my chin toward the house. "He'll make sure that if she's tied to me in any way, she'll never dance for any major company."

"Did he say that?"

"He didn't have to," I deadpan. "I know how my uncle's mind works. And if I go against this deal—a deal I agreed to—Poppy can forget chasing her dreams. So can I. He'd never let it happen."

She opens her mouth to speak, but before she can, Natasha and Beckett walk out onto the patio with Gia's parents close behind her.

"Look at y'all coupled up," Beckett drawls, taking a sip from his whiskey. "Guess it's a good thing that your daddy and I talked, Miss Gia." He smirks from her to me. "Y'all are getting married early."

"What?" Gia blurts out, standing abruptly and throwing her hands up into the air.

I just sit there, tossing my head back, not really surprised at all.

"Papa, is this true?"

"My dear, Walker's hockey schedule is very grueling," Beckett chimes, coming beside me and putting his hand on my shoulder. "Isn't that right, nephew? But he has tonight and tomorrow off. So, that means … it's the perfect time for a wedding."

"I don't want to marry Gia, Beckett," I growl, finally standing, and I tower over him by a few inches. "And she sure as hell doesn't want to marry me."

"Well, unlucky for you, both of you knew this was part of our agreement." He shrugs, sipping down the rest of his drink.

As always, Natasha says absolutely nothing. She just stands there with her long, silky blonde hair brushed over her shoulders. A stoic look on her face, though she smiles when he looks her way, as if on cue.

"Papa," Gia cries, going in front of her father, "I am your only daughter. How can you do this to me?" Her head swings toward her mom. "Mama, you can't possibly be all right with any of this, can you?"

There's no denying the look of sadness that crosses her mother, Serena's, face. But when her husband squeezes her hand, it quickly vanishes.

"Your mother agrees that this will be a good thing for you, princess." He looks from his wife to his daughter. "Right, Serena?"

"Yes," she barely chirps. "Walker will make a good husband," she says, her eyebrows barely pulling together with emotion. "Everyone is not this lucky, you know."

"You call this lucky?" Gia hisses, looking around at the people who are supposed to be our role models. "You all make me sick. Papa, when will enough be enough? Now what? You need to attach me to Walker James because you think there's a good chance he's going pro, and you're going to try to use him to build your sports connections here in the States?" Her nostrils flare. "I am so disappointed in you. I really am."

She takes off, running into the house, and I glare at Beckett.

"She's right. This is fucking insanity." I step closer to him, tossing my arms out at my sides. "You can do whatever you want to do to me. I'm not playing your games anymore."

His dark eyes stare into mine. "Oh, what? You think you have a choice?" He chuckles, looking around at everyone else. "If you love your sister or … what's the name of that nice piece of ass? Right, Poppy. Daughter of a drug dealer. If you love either of them or care just a smidgen"—he holds his fingers up—"you'll cooperate, Walker. Because I promise you, things can get really ugly, really quick."

The old Walker would have beaten the fuck out of him until he could hardly move. But that was before Beckett knew Poppy. And had complete control over Briar. The stakes are too high for me to act stupid right now.

"You're a fucking prick," I growl.

Backing away, I head into the house, slamming the door before putting my fist through the drywall.

Maybe we will have to go through with this wedding, but in the end, they never mentioned we weren't allowed to get a divorce.

POPPY

I walk back from the coffee shop, feeling completely defeated and annoyed. Walker left this morning to go to his uncle's, and I have yet to hear from him since. I've texted him, but the messages aren't going through. And I have this bad feeling deep inside my gut that something isn't right.

A car stops next to me, instantly putting me on edge, but I'm thankful that it's daytime and the streets are full of other students walking to and from places.

The tinted window, so dark that I can't see into it, rolls down, and Hudson's stoic face stares back at me, stopping me in my tracks.

Jerking his head toward the passenger side, he rests his hand on the steering wheel. "Get in."

Maybe it's because I know he's no threat or I'm desperate to find out where Walker is. Whatever it is, I bolt to the truck and climb inside.

"What's going on?" I ask, buckling my seat belt. "Why are you here?"

"I'm here because, in a little bit, Walker will be at the arena for practice—but he won't be alone." He side-glances at me. "Beckett and Walker's soon-to-be father-in-law have set up their wedding for tomorrow." He looks ahead again. "Walker's a good kid. And if he marries that girl, he'll be miserable. I can't let it happen." He blows out a long breath. "I have dirt on his uncle. Enough dirt to bury him so deep that he'll never resurface." He pulls into the arena parking lot, parking between two cars. "Let's stop this shit, yeah?"

Stunned, I relax my head back on the headrest before nodding. "Yeah," I mutter with wide eyes. "Yeah, okay. Just tell me what to do, and I'll do it."

"First things first. You need to get Walker alone. If I know that hothead, he's on the verge of losing his shit. He needs to pretend like he's going with the flow." When he sees the irritation on my face, he shrugs. "It's the only way my plan will work. We can't set off any red flags."

"Fine," I whisper and notice Hudson's eyes focus on something behind me.

I turn slowly and watch Walker and a girl I've never seen getting out of his truck before heading toward the arena. Neither smiles, but it doesn't matter. Physically seeing him with her hurts my heart.

She's beautiful with her long, dark hair and the perfect amount of curves. And there's no missing her ultra-trim stomach that pokes out from her crop top that's matched perfectly with her leggings and cardigan, falling from one shoulder. I look down at my Hanes crewneck and my leggings and cringe. My hair is pulled into a messy ponytail because I've been working all day. Something I'm sure she doesn't have to do. But I can't hate her for that. This isn't her fault.

"Now, I can see why he's ignored my messages all day," I huff out, watching as they disappear inside the arena doors, sulking like a baby.

"Nah, I'm sure Dr. Boobman blocked your number," he answers nonchalantly. "Walker called me earlier. He said the same thing about you. That you weren't answering his messages either. Didn't take long for me to assume his uncle is severing all connections."

My hands ball up, my fingernails digging into my palms, and I groan. "That man is a major controlling douchebag."

Hudson leans forward on the steering wheel. "He's worse than that, babe. He's a monster. I've watched him do shit for years, and I've always just stayed out of it. Not anymore."

Unbuckling my safety belt, I turn my body toward him. "And Briar? Does this have anything to do with her?" I say as gently as possible, not wanting to make him uncomfortable.

He stiffens before his shoulders slump the slightest bit. Something I've never seen in Hudson because he's always been so strong and sturdy. Someone who seems untouchable.

"She's too far gone, I'd say," he mutters. "Walker's fighting his uncle. I know he is. Briar gave up. She threw in the towel long ago." He turns the key to his truck, killing the engine. "Come on, girl. Walker's always telling stories about how feisty you are. I haven't seen it yet. So, show me that fierceness. He saved you, and now, it's time for you to save him back."

His words hit me like a ton of bricks. Maybe I'm not as tough as I used to be. Maybe I have relied on Walker James to make everything okay. But not anymore. Right now, it's my turn to be the hero for once in my life.

Hudson strolls in behind me, heading into the stadium, and when a few coeds walk by, I don't miss the smirks they throw his way or the drool that runs down their chins as they look him up and down. Hudson's got that broody bad-boy look to him. And I honestly can't imagine him with good-girl Briar at all. But he's attractive and incredibly smart, and she's beautiful and quirky, so, hey, I guess it works. Or did until she went and got engaged to someone else.

"Heads-up," Hudson mutters from behind me.

Off to the side, where the apparel shop is, I can barely see Gia approaching us.

I slowly breathe, begging for her not to notice me. But then again, why should I worry? I doubt she even knows who I am.

"Poppy," she calls, quickly walking toward us. "Is that you?"

Swinging my gaze toward her, I'm so freaking mad at myself for not being better dressed today. Or curling my hair and maybe applying a little freaking mascara.

Would it have hurt you to just try not to look like you live in a trash can?

Smoothing my clothes out, I stand a little taller and look toward her. "Yes?"

Hudson doesn't speak, but he stays close, observing intently.

"I thought that was you," she says with a smile. "Walker has shown me pictures before." She rolls her eyes playfully but giggles. "My fiancé sure likes to talk about another woman to me a lot."

Right now, I don't know if she's a threat or an ally. I don't know her. I have no clue what her intentions are. So, I'm not about to let my guard down.

"Umm … okay?" I shrug. "I'm actually headed to him now, so …" I take a step, and she stops me.

"Look, I don't blame you for giving me the cold shoulder. When we slept together, we were both drunk and hurting, and it just happened."

My eyes must widen to the size of dinner plates, and I feel sick.

"When the fuck did you sleep with Walker?" I hiss, all but frothing at the mouth.

Her face turns beet red, and her eyes fly to Hudson's before mine again. "A very long time ago. I thought … I assumed that's why you didn't want to talk to me. I'm so sorry. I thought … I thought you knew."

"Nope," I say quickly. "Sure didn't."

I walk around her, but her hand catches mine, and I spin around.

"Look, I don't know what the hell your deal is. Coming in here with your fancy clothes, hair extensions, and fake lashes, but back. The. Fuck. Up."

I swear I hear Hudson chuckle, but I don't take my eyes off Gia long enough to find out.

"I'm sorry," she whispers. "If it's any consolation, he had his eyes shut the entire time. And when it was over …" She pauses when she sees me squeeze my eyes shut, not wanting to imagine Walker and her together that way. In any way actually. "He couldn't get away from me fast enough. And when I found him after, he was alone, looking at a picture of you." She smiles sadly. "You were dancing in your ballet attire. It was … a beautiful photo."

"Do you want to marry Walker?" I mutter, keeping my face like stone.

"No," she says, quickly shaking her head. "I'm in love with someone else. But my father and his uncle only see what they want and what can give them an advantage." She sighs. "Trust me, even if I didn't have a boyfriend, I'd never want a man who is in love with another person the way he's in love with you."

I stare at her for a long beat, searching for any signs of bullshit. But much to my surprise, my bullshit alarm never goes off.

"I need to go to Walker," I whisper, looking behind her at the clock. Luckily, that boy is always extremely early to practice, leaving me over fifteen minutes to talk to him. "Apparently, Beckett has blocked my number. Walker's probably still getting changed. Can you call him and ask him to go to the film room?"

Quickly pulling her phone out, she puts it to her ear. After a few words, she looks at me and nods. "He's on his way."

"Thank you," I utter and look at Hudson. "I'll be right back."

He bobs his head up and down once. "I'll be right here."

And then I bolt toward the film room. Because, as always, the clock is ticking, and I can't waste another second.

WALKER

I have no clue why Gia needs me to come see her, but given how fucking weird this day has been, I hurry to get there.

I push the door open, and my breath dies in my lungs when I spot Poppy standing in the center of the dim room. Her eyes are filled with sadness, excitement, and even some anger.

"Hi," I say, closing the door and locking it behind me.

"I need to say some things." She fiddles with her hands. "What I want to say is, how the hell did you sleep with Gia and God knows who else while we were apart?" She looks mad, shaking her head. "I waited for you. I didn't even kiss another man because I was waiting for you." Pulling in a deep breath, she slowly lets it out, closing her eyes.

"Poppyseed—"

Opening her eyes, she stops me. "We don't have time for that. So, just listen, and later, once this shitstorm blows over, you can bow at my feet and tell me how fucking sorry you are," she hisses. "From this moment until the ceremony, you need to be calm. You need to go with the flow and get along with Beckett and Gia's parents."

"What?" I scowl. "Why would I do that?"

Walking toward me, she angles her chin up, exposing her neck, begging me to run my tongue down it.

"Because Hudson and I have a plan. And I promise, if you can play it cool until tomorrow, we will take care of the rest. Okay?" Her eyes soften. "Do you trust me?"

"Fuck yes, I do," I whisper. "You're the only person I trust."

"Good." She nods.

My eyes roam her face, working down her body. She's so unbelievably fucking pretty. Even right now, when she's just come from work, she takes the breath right from my lungs.

Reaching down, I graze my thumb along her cheek, swiping it over her bottom lip. "I'll bow at your feet right now, Poppyseed." I swallow thickly when her breath hitches. "I can't take back the times I've fucked up, but let me try to make it up to you."

Slowly, I hook my thumbs under my sweatpants and pull them down enough for my cock to spring free. Backing up to one of the chairs, I pull her along with me before I sit down.

Reaching forward, I slide my hand between her legs until my fingers sink inside her heat, and she moans. Looking up at her, I rake my bottom lip between my teeth.

"You're fucking soaked, baby. After one day, were you already missing my cock?"

"No," she growls. "I'm too mad to miss anything about you right now."

I don't smirk, though I want to. Because, goddamn, she's fucking hot when she's pissed off.

Moving my fingers in and out of her quicker, I glide my free hand under her sweatshirt and grip her breast before pulling her toward me. Shoving her top up and over her breasts, I run my tongue around her nipple, biting gently before releasing.

"Don't worry, baby. When you're riding my dick in a few seconds, while I move in and out of that tight, drenched pussy … you'll forget you're mad."

I pull her onto me, and she slowly drops herself down, taking me inch by inch, making me shiver.

"Put your hands behind the chair," she growls. "And don't move a fucking muscle." Bringing her mouth to mine, she glares down at me. "And don't you dare make a sound. You don't deserve that."

I think my cock hardens even more, if possible, when she commands me before her hips start to move.

"This isn't for you, Walker. This is for me. Do you understand?" She fucks me harder, rocking back and forth and moving up and down, her pussy soaking my cock before sucking me back inside. "You don't deserve to come, but if you're a good boy and let me fuck your cock until I come, I might just let you." She leans down, biting down on my neck—hard. "And that's only because I want to walk past Gia and know that your cum is dripping from my body instead of hers."

Holy. Fucking. Shit. I groan, unable to help myself.

I'm always the one in control. That's how I like it too. At least, I thought I did. But this right here? Poppy taking exactly what she wants, and what she wants is her pussy full of my dick? I like this. No, I fucking love it.

She throws her head back, and her legs curl behind her as she rides me. I feel her begin to clench around my length, making my balls tingle and my vision grow dark. A few soft moans escape her lips, and her movements slow just as my seed spills inside of her, filling every fucking part of her tight pussy.

She grows still, and she looks down at me, sucking in air. "I'm still mad at you."

"If that's your punishment, I think I'm okay with that," I say, and she swats me.

"You're an asshole," she grumbles.

"Yeah, I know." I lean up, kissing her. "I swear, I'm going to make it up to you. All of it."

Nodding slowly, she smiles. "I know."

WALKER

Even though I know everything is under control, my fingers tremble as I straighten my tie. Beckett isn't a dumb man. Things don't just … slide by him. So, right now, I'm fucking terrified. But Poppy asked me to trust her, so I'm doing what I can to do just that.

"Good Lord, you suck at that," Briar says as she walks into the room. "Let me fix it, would ya?"

"Go ahead," I mutter, turning toward her.

For my entire life, Briar and I were close. So close. But now, she goes along so easily with Beckett's plans. Never so much as putting up a fight. I can't trust her right now, and that really sucks because I could use her in my corner. Poppy and I both could.

"When's your big, happy, not-forced wedding day anyway, B?" I drawl slowly. "Not sure how I ended up in this situation before you did."

Her body stiffens for a split second before she relaxes, as if she's coaching herself to keep calm and not set off any alarms.

"Well, I'm not sure yet. We're securing the venue and all that. It's absolutely gorgeous and in Paris." She speaks as if she's trying to talk herself into it. "You'll be there, right?"

When she finishes my tie, she steps back, nervously looking up at me when I don't answer. "Walker?" she whispers. "You'll be there, right?"

"I don't know." I shrug. "To be honest, watching my sister marry someone she hardly knows—someone our uncle is forcing her to marry just to build more connections and get richer and more powerful—is not really high on my list of shit to do."

Her eyes drop to the ground, and her shoulders slump. Briar has always been incredibly kind and much more approachable than Poppy. But even so, my sister has always been tough and held her own. Apparently not anymore though.

"We're both going to be fine," she says softly. "We aren't at Sunset Drive. No one can hurt us anymore. We made it out safely." She reaches for my hand, giving it a squeeze. "I can learn to love Enzo, Walker. And I know you can learn to love Gia too."

"No," I snap. "I will never love Gia, and you know it." I step away from my sister, pulling from her hold just as my uncle enters the room.

"Looking good," Beckett drawls. "Briar, I just got word that the cake and the rest of the liquor have arrived. Can you go down and get that situated?"

"Sure," she whispers. "Where's Natasha?"

"She's still getting ready," he says in a dismissive tone before waving his hand toward the door like the dickface that he is. "Go along now."

Briar gives me one last look before she makes her exit. I know she hates to leave the room, thinking I'm upset. But the truth is, I am upset. She's a pawn in Beckett's game. And the worst thing is, she's letting it happen. No, she's fucking stringing up banners and welcoming it like it's a fucking promotion.

"Y'all are going to make a damn good-looking couple. And I know she's got a good rack for you to play with because I installed it."

I hold back the things I want to say and keep them inside. Poppy and Hudson need me to play it cool, so I'm doing my fucking best to do just that.

"Hey there, nice hickey." He laughs, pointing to my neck. "Guess y'all hit it off just fine after practice last night, huh?"

I can't stop the grin that spreads across my lips, knowing exactly where that hickey came from. "Yep, I guess so."

I nod, and he seems even more pleased.

"Good, good." He claps his hands together. "I know this whole situation isn't ideal, but look, my sister chose a fucking loser for a partner, and now, she's dead."

My heart stings when he mentions my parents. And although I understand my father wasn't the best husband, my mom had her own demons too. It wasn't all my dad's fault that she went down such a bad road. As far as I can see, they chose that road together.

"So, I guess what I'm trying to say is, I know you and Briar probably wish things were different, but they are a hell of a lot better than they would be if you were still living on that godforsaken street." He pauses. "Marrying into the Romano family will ensure that you have respect and wealth. Even if things don't work out with hockey."

I don't bother telling him that things with hockey will be just fine. He doesn't need to know about my deal with the Bay Sharks. The last thing I'm about to do is let him know anything about the New England Bay Sharks offer.

So, instead, I just nod. "Yep, guess so."

Clapping his hand on my back, he heads toward the door. "It's almost showtime. So, hurry up and head out back to the gardens."

When he leaves, I take one last look at myself in the mirror and pray that everything will be okay.

POPPY

"This is so stupid," I whisper to Hudson. Who, of course, gets to wear his everyday security outfit, making all of the servers here swoon when they pass by. "Why do you get to look like James Bond, and I'm over here, looking like I just stepped out of the *Cake Boss* show?"

His stoic, unimpressed expression hardly cracks, but the corner of his lips lifts slightly when I point to my hat.

"A baker's hat? Really?" I shake my head, looking down at myself. "Here I am, supposed to be looking like hot shit to remind Walker he's not marrying that incredibly sexy Monica Bellucci look-alike. Only from, like, thirty years earlier. And you got me showing up here, looking like the Pillsbury Doughboy." I shake my head. "You are so not allowed to be in charge of our disguises anymore."

"First off, why are we suddenly tied into having disguises together?" He simply shrugs, completely unfazed. "Second, I'm friends with the lady who owns the bakery that Beckett ordered this annoyingly huge cake from. So, getting her to let us deliver it was an easy in." He points to my black wig and glasses. "Besides, Beckett will never notice you behind the cake when you look so different."

"Yeah, unless he notices my chest looks a little too flat in this white jacket. Then, Dr. Boobs will suddenly be using his nephew's wedding day to drum up some business," I huff out. "Come on. Let's get this over with. Run through the plan one more time."

"Once we're in, I guarantee it won't take Walker long to spot you. But he's going to play it cool. Once it's time for the ceremony, it will only be the Romanos, Walker, Briar, Natasha, and Beckett. He's hired me to be on standby to make sure nothing goes south. You'll be hiding behind the ginormous, stupid fucking cake that I can't stand the sight of—"

"Do you have something against cake?" I ask, cutting him off. "Twice, you've talked about this cake in a negative way." I point to it. "It's cake. A huge, beautiful, likely delicious cake. What's to hate?"

"There's hardly anyone coming to this. Why the fuck do they need a cake this big?" he grumbles.

I shrug, looking it over. "I have no idea, but is it weird that I want to take some home?" I tap my finger on my chin. "Yeah, okay, it's weird. Do I care? Hell no. I'm taking it home. My roommates will love it."

Hudson gives me a look that I can't really read, though I'm pretty sure he thinks I'm insane. But that's okay. Maybe he didn't grow up poor. The most exciting thing I got to eat on birthdays was a damn Twinkie. So, yeah, this cake is sort of the bomb in my eyes.

My eyes fix on who's walking behind him, and I feel my heart drop, not just out of fear of being recognized, but also for Hudson's heart.

I mean, the dude's lock screen is this chick.

I look at Hudson, signaling for him to turn around. Slowly, when he does, their body language is undeniable. They both tense up, and he awkwardly clears his throat.

"Hudson," she says, not nearly as sweet as she typically sounds.

"Briar." He gives her a curt nod, but doesn't seem to look directly at her.

"Didn't realize you were working today," she mutters before glancing around him to get a better look at me.

Feeling her eyes zeroing in, I quickly turn and act like I'm going to get something out of the delivery van that the bakery loaned us, but her voice stops me.

"Poppy?" she whispers, and I feel her stepping closer to me. "Holy shit, is that you?"

I slowly turn around to face her, looking at her through my fake glasses and thick black bangs of my wig. "It's me," I utter. "Please, don't say anything."

"I would never," she says, taking my hands in hers as her eyes fill with tears. "I can't believe it's you. You're here."

Swallowing the lump that's suddenly lodged itself into my throat, I bob my head up and down slowly. "I can't let him marry her, B. Your brother deserves to decide who he wants in his life and what he wants, too." I peer down at her. "So do you."

That only makes her more emotional, but Hudson's deep voice speaks before she has a chance to respond.

"We need to get this cake inside. It's the last thing they are waiting for."

Briar turns to look at him, and I watch the giant, hard, kind-of-scary dude that I've gotten to know—but barely—melt into a puddle. His breath hitches, and his eyes soften.

He loves her so much.

When Hudson comes beside me to help with the cake, Briar's eyes search his. "Whatever you're planning, he won't let you get away with it. You know Beckett."

Lifting the cake, he brushes past her. "Walker doesn't want to marry into the Romano family. We're here to stop that because Poppy actually gives a flying fuck about him." He stops walking, keeping his head straight forward, purposely not looking directly at Briar. "You go on and get married, Dove. I won't be there to save you; don't worry."

And then he marches on, and as much as I want to stop and make sure she's okay, I can't. Because today, Walker is the only person who matters.

Never mind whatever the hell is going on between Briar and Hudson.

WALKER

I shouldn't laugh. It's not funny. I mean, for fuck's sake, here I am, under an archway of some smelly flowers that have about thirty bees buzzing around them—which, by the way, I hate bees. They are scary as hell. Tack on, my uncle thinks I'm about to marry Gia, when really, I'm just looking around waiting for Hudson to make his big moment. But even with all of this going on, the image of Poppy, standing behind the biggest wedding cake I have ever seen, in a fucking white jacket and a big, puffy baking hat with some crazy wig under it, will not leave my brain.

Right when I saw her, I burst out laughing, which instantly pissed her off. She scowled, poking her lips out and folding her arms across her chest as she threw a silent hissy fit. It was adorable. So was when she held up her middle finger at me.

She might not have the best etiquette or greatest style. But, goddamn, every part of me loves that girl for who she is.

I guess something doesn't need to glimmer to be gold. Because rough edges and all, that's exactly what Poppy Wilson is. Gold.

I'm glad we convinced Beckett that it would be tacky to invite people at the last minute so we should only have our immediate families. Otherwise, Hudson's plan wouldn't have worked. Because if he ratted out my uncle and Marco Romano in front of a backyard full of people, he'd probably be killed by a hit man the next day. The Romano family is aggressive when it comes to reputation.

The pastor looks between us, seeming uneasy with the entire thing before he sighs. After rattling off a few words, he pauses.

"Is there anyone here who has reason to believe that Gia and Walker should not be wed?"

He swallows nervously when his eyes land on Beckett's. I'm sure he didn't like that the pastor included that part.

"Actually, yeah. Yeah, there is," Hudson's deep voice drawls slowly. "These two are barely adults. They don't know each other, oh, and they aren't getting married by choice either." He steps closer, glaring at Beckett. "As a matter of fact, both are in love with other people."

"Jesus Christ," Beckett growls through gritted teeth, earning a glare from the dude standing with the Bible in his hands.

"Consider yourself fired, Hercules," Beckett says to Hudson, venom dripping from each word. "And see yourself out."

"Nah, think I'll stay." He smirks. "My friend here isn't leaving without cake." He waves to Poppy, who slowly pops out from behind the cake. "After all, we went through all the trouble of toting the fucking thing here."

"Motherfucker," Beckett huffs out, glancing nervously at Marco. "Sorry about this. I'll get him sorted out. Nothing to worry about."

"Nah, I don't think you will though." Hudson's voice is deep and calculated. He's completely unfazed as he holds out his phone to Beckett's face. "See, Dr. Boobie, I have dirt on you. Loads and loads of dirt. So much that I could bury your ass alive right now if I wanted."

He turns toward Marco. "And don't think you're getting off scot-free, my friend." He tsks him, grinning. "I have videos of your business receiving pretty large drug shipments. You know, Mr. Romano, I figured you were smarter than that. Turns out, you're just like this clown." He jerks his thumb toward my uncle.

"Now, here's what's going to happen. This whole insane fucking wedding is called off. Beckett, you're going to leave your nephew and your niece alone. If that's what she wants." He looks at Briar for a moment, seeming almost lost and leaving me really fucking confused before, finally, he looks at me. "I already know this kid wants to sever all ties with you.

"And, Marco, you're going to let Gia live her life and leave her the fuck alone and keep her out of your twisted little games." His gaze sweeps over everyone standing around him. "And if you don't, then you can kiss everything you've both worked for good-bye because this is just a drop in the bucket of the shit I have on both of you."

Marco sighs, rolling his eyes to the sky. "Fine. Gia, let's go." Jerking his head toward his wife, he looks less than impressed. "What are you standing around for? Let's go."

Reluctantly, she begins to turn, but Hudson's voice stops her.

"Oh, and, Marco? If Mrs. Romano wants away from you, your ass is going to give her a divorce and a big lump sum of money." He winks at her. "It's all in the body language, ma'am. I wouldn't want to be married to a dick like him either. Even if he is filthy rich."

"And has good hair," I add, pointing to Marco's head.

Hudson nods. "Really good fucking hair. So unlike Dr. Boobie."

"Yeah, it's pretty obvious those are hair plugs, Unc." I wave my hand toward him.

"Oh, yes, and that goes for you too, Natasha. If you want to leave his obnoxious, heavy-breathing ass … you go ahead. He won't make it hard for you." Hudson nods toward Beckett. "Right, Boobie Man?"

My uncle has always been a heavy breather, but right now, as pissed off as he is, it's about ten times louder, making my skin crawl. I never gave it a thought that maybe Natasha was in the same boat as my sister and stuck with him because of his power.

Now, we're all free.

She gives Hudson a tiny smile. "Thank you, Mr. Bailey."

Gia's hand touches my arm. "Go get your girl," she whispers, grinning at me.

I smile. "You headed home to get your guy?"

"Damn straight." She hugs me, patting me on the back before moving to Hudson and throwing her arms around him. "Thank you, Hudson. I could never repay you. But I appreciate all you just did so much."

"It's all good," he drawls as she releases him before reaching into his pocket and pulling a card from his wallet. "If your old man tries anything stupid, just give me a call. I'll straighten it out."

She giggles, glancing over his shoulder at her father. "Will do."

"Now, if you'll excuse me, I have a girl to get to," I say, looking at Poppy, who awkwardly stands next to the cake, still in full baker's gear. And then I run to her because there's nothing right now that could keep us apart.

Well, other than the fact that in a few months, I'll be moving across the country.

Poppy

Cupping my cheeks, Walker looks highly amused as the corner of his lips turns up in a crooked grin. "Nice hat, Poppyseed," he utters. "I might have you keep it on for some role-play later. Maybe I can butter your biscuits or something."

I try my best to keep an unimpressed, annoyed look on my face before rolling my eyes. "That's not funny."

"You can cream my Twinkie," he mutters, keeping his voice low. "Or I can frost your pound cake."

"I'm about to crush your éclair if you don't cut it out." I give him my best look of warning. "Or maybe stomp on your cream puffs."

"That second one kind of sounds fun." He winks before tugging on my hat. "Were you planning on, like, baking them to death or what?" he says with a chuckle. "Out of all the disguises, how'd this one become the one you went with?"

My lips form into a flat line before I nod toward Hudson, who is staring Beckett down as he struts away and heads toward the house. "Ask him. He got to be the hot bodyguard, per usual, and I got … this." I look down at myself. "I wanted to be a Charlie's Angel or something."

His expression hardens, his jaw ticcing under his skin. "Did you just call Hudson hot?"

"Uh, no?" I bite my lip. "Well, maybe. But not like … that." I wave toward him. "He is hot." I fix my eyes on Walker again, resting my hands on his abdomen. "But you, Mr. James, are hotter."

"I kind of want to go set him on fire, just so you can't look at him," he grumbles. "Now, I'm annoyed."

I poke my lip out, patting his stomach. "My poor baby. Are your feelings hurt?" I raise a brow. "Need I remind you that I am Betty fucking Crocker right now, and you were just standing up next to a goddamn supermodel-looking creature who had the nerve to *hug* you?" I shake my head, removing one hand and putting it on my hip. "Yeah, that's right. I saw."

"I knew you saw," he teases. "I could see your eyes bugging out and your face turning red."

"Well, of course it was red; she's seen your freaking wiener." I scoff. "What do you want me to do, cartwheels and clap with excitement? No. I want to punch her in the face and maybe pull her extensions out."

Wrapping his arms around me, he pulls me closer, rocking us slowly. "So feisty, baby. So damn feisty."

Looking down at me, he kisses my forehead. "Let's go home, Poppyseed. This has been the longest few days of my life, and I finally feel like I can breathe again."

Pushing my lips to his, I kiss him. Our lips smack together, but before we can get carried away—which always seems so easy to do—I pull back and smirk. "We can go home. But we're taking the cake."

185

WALKER

It's been a week since the Bay Sharks called to offer me a spot on their ice.

That phone call should have been the best call of my life. It should have trumped everything and anything I'd ever accomplished. It should be an easy decision.

Keyword: *should.*

But truthfully, I'm at a fucking loss. Everything in my life finally feels like it's coming together. I've not only gotten out of Sunset Drive, but also out from under the control of my dipshit uncle. I get to stop and see Jake a few times a week, which I always love. The boys on the team respect me and look at me as a true leader. But most of all, Poppy and I have finally worked our shit out and are in a good place. And now, what? I'm going to move to Maine. Start over, all by myself, and leave her here?

I can't do that.

I don't want to do that.

"Earth to James," Watson drawls from the other end of the bench. "You sleeping over there or what?"

"Up too late with his newfound love, I suppose," Hunter chimes in, winking at me. "Happy for you, man. But I'm mostly happy for Poppy. Because before you came along, she was fucking scary."

"She was not scary," I scoff. "She was just … going through some shit."

"He's like a dang ghost these days," Elias says, closing his locker. "Only time we see him is when he sneaks by with her behind him, going to his room."

"Hey, if he's happy, I'm happy." Nixon shrugs. "Who the fuck wants to play video games with us all the time when they could be spending time with a pretty little thing like her?" He gently punches my shoulder. "You do you, buddy."

"Thanks," I mutter, giving him a small grin before I pull my jersey over my head.

I haven't even told my teammates about the offer yet. Mostly because I don't know what the fuck I'm going to say when I call them back. Shit, some of these guys are seniors, just waiting for their call, knowing at this point, it won't happen. I don't want to make them feel worse about that.

After all, I know what it's like to want something so bad that it fucking hurts.

"James," Coach calls, coming into the locker room. "When you're done in here, come to my office."

"Yes, sir." I nod, instantly nervous as hell because it's LaConte. And to be honest, he fucking scares me.

"What'd you do now, rookie?" Link says, tipping his chin up.

"I don't know," I grumble. "I hope nothing."

This is when I wish Cade Huff were here to crack a joke.

I can hear him now; he'd probably say something like, *Maybe LaConte is inviting him in for a tea party or some shit.*

That guy could always lighten the team's spirit. Even when, deep down, he was struggling himself.

Getting up, I head to his office. Every step I take, I'm racking my brain with what on earth he could want.

"You wanted to see me, Coach?"

He's running through some plays on his iPad but glances up and nods. "I did."

He points to the door, and I close it.

"When did you plan on telling me about that phone call you got, boy?"

I take a seat, putting my hands on my knees. "To be honest, I don't know what to say about it."

There's no mistaking the frustration on that man's face as he sits back in his seat, puts his hands on his head, and looks up.

"You don't know what to say about it?" he grumbles. "You … don't know what to say about it?"

I swallow harshly, knowing I'm about to get my ass chewed out. So, instead of trying to pull something out of my ass to say, I just wait for him to say something else. Because with LaConte, just when you think he's done speaking, he adds something else.

"Kid, I don't get it." He sighs, his eyes crinkling as he squints to understand. "This is what you've wanted. What you've worked your entire life for." His voice grows deeper, each word striking me in the chest. "I'm one of the few people who knows where you came from. A shithole a few miles from here, where people overdose weekly." He cringes. "I'm sorry. Considering how you lost your parents, I should choose my words more wisely." He pauses, stiffening. "No, fuck that. I'm not going to be soft with you. You know why? Because I actually give a shit about you, kid. That's why. I care that you don't end up like Cade Huff's drug dealer and your childhood best friend."

When he sees the shock on my face, his eyes narrow. "That's right, James. I know everything. I hear everything." He pinches the bridge of his nose, closing his eyes for a moment. "Tell me, what on God's golly green fucking earth would you have to *think* about when it comes to going to the Bay Sharks? They are an absolutely incredible team. And I can guarantee you, you'll walk on and be a first string."

"Look," I say a little harsher than planned. "There are more things in the equation than just me and hockey. Hockey … well, it's just hockey. I have relationships here, Coach. I have people I can't walk out on. I've already done that once; I don't want to be the guy who always leaves," I blurt out quickly, groaning as I ball my hands up. "And this team … this motherfucking team that I love so much, they're finally—*finally*—treating me like I'm part of the family. We're playing like we're supposed to be playing."

"Tell me about the person you're scared to leave." He speaks softer now, but not by much. "And tell me this: if you stay here and never get another call from the NHL, if you pass this up … where will that leave the pair of you? When you look back, five or ten years from now, you will be resentful."

"No," I say, shaking my head. "I'd never resent Poppy. I couldn't." I grind my back teeth together. "She has given up so much to make sure the people around her get what they need and what they want. I won't just leave her the first call I get."

"Tell her that, son." He nods. "Tell her that you're not leaving her. And I promise you, if she's half the woman you think she is and if she loves you as much as she should, she'll make you go." He inhales sharply. "But if playing as a Wolf for another year is what you want in here"—he points his finger toward my chest—"I'd love to have you. But make sure you're here because it's what you want. Not what you think makes you noble. Because if it's love, you two will make it work. No matter the distance or the obstacles."

He glances up at the clock. "Now, forget it all for now and go out there, play your game, and leave it all on the ice. Okay? Because you say it's only hockey, but we both know … it's never *just* hockey."

Slowly, I push myself to stand. I know he's right, but I also don't know what I truly want right now. And it's going to take more than a minute to figure that out.

"Thank you, Coach," I say, heading toward the door.

"I've enjoyed the hell out of watching you grow as a player, James." His voice has me half turning around. "There are good players, and then there are good players who will do whatever it takes to be great. Those players usually are the ones with grit. Grit happens when things didn't always come easy because the odds were stacked against them, making them give that little bit more than the others." He gives me a small smile. "Those are the players I like coaching most. You're a key example of that."

I smile before heading toward the door, gently slapping my palm against the doorframe as I walk into the hallway.

That's just another reason why leaving Brooks isn't as easy as it seems.

Coach LaConte is the greatest coach and the best man I've ever met in my life. Saying good-bye to him after only one year, it would be really fucking hard.

Poppy

"Look at my husband down there, looking like a snack," Ryann says, scrunching her nose up. "Gosh, I love him."

Rearing my head toward her, I feel her forehead. "You aren't feverish. So, I need to ask you this one thing: who are you, and what have you done with my *guys suck, never trust them, I'm a bad bitch who needs no dick to make me happy* friend?"

"Har-har." She rolls her eyes. "Soooo funny." She waves her hand toward the ice, flashing that band with the black diamond. "Trust me, most guys do suck. But that man down there in front of the goal? He is literally an angel." She snorts. "Guess he'd have to be to put up with my crazy ass, huh?"

"Ummm, yes." I nod quickly. "Yes, he would."

I side-eye her jersey as she proudly wears his last name on the back of her Brooks attire. And I frown when I see Sutton heading down the stairs, wearing hers with Thompson on the back, undoubtedly. I wouldn't mind wearing Walker's. Actually, I'd love it. But, dang, those jerseys are pricey. And I'm, well, broke.

Holding out a plastic bag, Sutton smiles down at me. "Special delivery. A certain someone with the initials W.J. gave this to Hunter for me to deliver to you." Her grin grows. "I could clearly tell it's a jersey in there. So, I know it obviously has James on the back. Which, by the way, Ryann and I talked, and Walker James is hands down *the* hottest hockey player's name ever to exist."

"Hands down. Like, all of the team has hot names, but Walker freaking James just sounds soooo hot and kind of dirty."

Sutton plops down next to Ryann. "Here, put it on over your shirt!"

As if on cue, I look down onto the ice to find that Walker hasn't only stopped warming up, but he's also staring up at me. I hold up the bag toward him, and he gives me a smirk as his eyes grow darker. Not really the response I figured I'd get. And when I take it out, a small note falls out, and I hold it so the girls can't see.

P,

Can't wait to see you in this later with nothing on underneath.

—W

P.S. You know what this means, right? If my name is on your back, you're mine. No going back now.

Slowly, I stand and pull the oversize jersey over my head before doing a little spin for him. He stares in complete awe before he slowly skates backward and turns away.

"Okay, so that was cute." Ryann beams next to me before placing her hand on my arm. "Poppy has officially become thawed. She's no longer a frosty bitch."

"Let's not go that far," Sutton jokes but widens her eyes and laughs.

"Yeah, I mean, a leopard can't really change its spots." I shrug.

Ryann rests her head against me. "I gotta say, I like seeing you happy. I really, really do."

My eyes stay fixed on the ice, and I smile.

Because I really, really like being this happy too.

POPPY

The cold air hits my face, and I blow out a breath, watching it turn to smoke above my head before it disappears. It's freezing here in Maine. I've always heard it was, but I've never been here. A few people have warned me that the spring is gross and wet and that the summer is so short that if you blink, it's over. But they promised that the beauty in the fall and the calmness in the winter make the unpredictable climate much more tolerable. Though I only heard one word in that sentence.

Calmness. That sounds nice.

Turning around, I head back into the stadium, where Walker has spent the past few hours meeting his potential new team. He wouldn't give the New England Bay Sharks an answer over the phone. He felt the need to come to check out the facility, formally meet the coaches and the entire team, and talk over the logistics and what a Bay Shark would mean. And since tomorrow is Christmas Eve and he'll have a few days free of hockey, he insisted I come with him. Of course, it didn't take much convincing, seeing that Jake was ditching me anyway to spend the holidays with his girlfriend and I didn't really want to hang out alone.

We flew here after his early morning practice today and plan to fly back to Georgia on the twenty-sixth. Oh, on a five a.m. flight. Ew.

But I guess it's good that we'll be back at Brooks early because Jake and his girlfriend are coming over to celebrate a late Christmas dinner with us that night. It's a little weird this year that, for the first time in my entire life, I won't be spending the actual holiday with him. But I'm sure he'll have more fun with Bonnie anyway.

I've checked in a few times just to see how he's doing because I always get a little nervous about leaving him, but I need to give him more credit than I do. I can't baby him when he wants to live his life, especially when he is more than able.

As I walk farther into the arena, I gaze at how gorgeous this place is, just as Walker heads toward me. Next to him is a guy with a duffel bag slung over his shoulder, who grins at whatever Walker is saying. He looks familiar, but I can't put my finger on why that would be because I know I've never seen him before.

When he spots me, Walker's face lights up. "What did you think?" he says with a smile, but I can hear the nervousness in his voice.

He's worried that I'll tell him I don't like it here. But let me be honest; even if I didn't, I'd lie and tell him it was great just because it means so much to him, and he deserves this. But truthfully, I like it here—a lot.

"Hate it? Love it?" Before I can answer, he cringes. "Too cold, right? You'd never want to move here. Or even visit." He sighs. "You're right. We were raised in the South. It's like the Arctic here. It would get old fast."

Grabbing his hand, I giggle. "Walker, stop. I actually really love it," I answer honestly. "I walked around downtown, and … yeah, it's cold. But it's beautiful. And kind of cozy."

All of the nerves melt away as he sighs dramatically. But before he answers, the guy walking with him does first.

"Oh, thank fuck. I was worried that she'd hate it, and you'd say hell no to the Bay Sharks, and we'd never hear from you again," he blurts out before holding his hand out. "I'm Logan. Logan Sterns."

Looking down at his hand, I take it and shake it. "Sterns?"

"Yep." He nods. "And, yes, Link Sterns is my brother. No, I'm not as much of an ass as he is." He releases my hand. "I'm the super-cool, extra-chill brother. Who's also wayyyyy more fun."

"I'm Poppy," I say softly, already liking his energy as Walker's teammate.

"Oh, trust me, I know." His grin spreads, and he glances at Walker. "This dude probably said your name twenty times during our tour. I was beginning to get a complex that I was boring him to death." His eyes float to mine again. "He says you're a dancer?"

My face feels hot, and I suddenly wish I were one of those girls who wore makeup more often. If I had, it would have covered the heat of my cheeks right now.

"Y-yes, I do." I clear my throat. "I mean, I am. A dancer."

He seems completely unfazed by my total awkwardness as he nods slowly. "Cool. Just so you know, rumor has it, Casco Bay College—that's about a ten-minute drive from here—has a pretty well-respected dance program." He shrugs. "Just in case you didn't want to travel back and forth to see this fella."

"Rumor has it, huh?" Walker grins. "Sounds to me like you've got some personal experience with dancers who go there."

"What can I say? I like 'em sassy. And dancers—no offense, Poppy— well, they are full of sass." He grins before gently swatting the back of his hand to Walker's shoulder. "I gotta run, man. Got a holiday fundraiser tonight, and I can't be rolling in, looking like this."

He holds his hand out to Walker, and he takes it. They collide their chests, patting each other's back.

"I hope to see you real soon." Turning toward me, he winks. "Good luck, Poppy. I'm sure it'll all work out. Oh, and don't worry about the cold; that's what heated seats are made for, right?"

"Right." I laugh, knowing damn well I can't afford a car. And if I did, it might have a dented door or the exhaust falling off, but it certainly wouldn't have heated freaking seats.

He struts off, and it's clear that man has enough self-confidence to fill this entire building and then probably flood the streets outside. But for whatever reason, I get a good feeling about him.

"Well, he's—" I begin to say to Walker as he wraps his arms around me.

"Nothing like his brother, who could literally suck the fun out of every game?" he guesses with a chuckle. "Yeah, I'll believe it once I see him on the ice. But as overkill as he might be, Link's a hell of a team captain and a damn good teammate."

"Whatcha think anyway?" I ask, looking up at him. "Good vibes and all that?"

"I want to know what you think," he answers, his eyes narrowing. "Are you vibing with Maine? Or is it too fucking cold and too far away from Georgia?"

"First off, aside from Jake, fuck Georgia," I blurt out, not holding anything back. "And, yes, as a matter of fact, I am. But this isn't about me. This is about you and your future." I stand on my tiptoes, pressing my lips to his before stepping away from him, waving around the building. "Could you see yourself starting your NHL career here? And wearing the Bay Sharks colors." I scrunch my nose up. "Which are what exactly? I'm sorry. I should have researched. I don't actually know what they are."

The corner of his lips turns up as he jerks his chin toward the countless jerseys on the walls and the huge-ass Shark painted in the center of it all.

"Dark blue and light blue?" I guess before slowly bobbing my head up and down. "You know what? I like it. I like it a lot."

"Me too," he mutters. "And, yeah, I really could see myself here," he says, looking around at everything. Almost like he's taking it all in, not believing it's real. "But I'm not leaving you behind. Not in a million years."

Despite our time apart, Walker has gone above and beyond to make up for it. It's my turn to be there for him. To be the unwavering support system that he deserves. But I'm scared to leave my brother.

"Maybe you won't have to," I whisper, stepping toward him. "I took an Uber to Casco Bay College while you met the coach and your teammates. And, well, I sort of loved it. It's not huge, which I like—"

"You don't usually get to say that, do you?" He winks, and I roll my eyes before punching him lightly.

"Shut up. As I was saying, I really liked it there. It was so different from Brooks." I tuck my hair behind my ear. "Which I liked."

There's no mistaking the shock on his face as he slides his hand into my hair. "You did?"

I nod once, blinking slowly. "I did. But even if I apply to transfer and get in, there's still a lot to figure out. I need to sort everything out with Jake because I can't just leave him behind. Especially since—" I pause, that familiar dread settling in my gut. "Ron will be out of prison someday. And I bet that it won't be that far from now either." I swallow. "I can't leave Jake behind with Ron on the loose."

"We will figure it all out, Poppyseed." He leans down, pressing his lips to my forehead. "I promise. Every decision from here on out, we'll make together."

I smile as that warming sensation spreads across my chest, heating my body. No one else has ever been able to give me that feeling. Ever.

He is my family. He has been since we were scrawny little kids. And as long as we have each other, it's all going to be all right.

"I love you," I whisper. "I can't wait to watch you take the ice here. In your brand-spanking-new uniform."

His lips find my ear, the stubble of his face tickling my cheek and making me squirm. "And I can't wait to fuck you in my new jersey after every game."

Stepping back, he holds his hand out. "Come on, Poppyseed. Now that I've had the tour, let me show you around."

Georgia might have been where we grew up, and Brooks might have brought us back together. But there's something about Maine that feels like … home.

It also feels like a fresh start. For both of us. And maybe that's exactly what we need.

WALKER

Poppy stares out at the Atlantic, her beanie pulled down to her eyebrows as her long lashes peek out and almost curl around the fabric. It's cold today. But not the cold that chills you to the bone, making it hard to breathe. Though I'm sure we'll experience plenty of those days once we live here full-time. But right now, it's sort of refreshing.

The waves roll in, crashing along the rocky coastline before they get pulled back, only to do it again, over and over. It's a perfect, synchronized motion. I swear I hear the saltwater making a fizzling sound, and when I blow out a breath, it turns to white smoke, drifting into the air.

"It's beautiful, isn't it?" she calls over the sound of the churning waters by Portland Head Light, Maine's oldest lighthouse.

Apparently, everyone in Portland is too busy finishing their Christmas shit for tomorrow because we've got the whole place to ourselves.

"It is," I say, keeping my eyes on her as she closes her eyes, dragging in a deep breath before opening them again.

I could watch her forever like this—content. I've loved her when she's been sad, angry, and hurt. But right now … she's happy.

She's at peace, which isn't something either of us can say has always been the case. But right now, she is.

"Have you ever, like … been somewhere for the first time and you just …" She pauses, her voice growing thick with emotion. "You just know that it's where you're meant to be? Like … it's all completely new, but it feels like you've been here a thousand times before?" Her nose sniffles, and she glances at me. "Maybe it's because you're next to me. Maybe I'd feel this way in, like … freaking Arkansas." She looks at the water again, watching the turning tide as the corner of her lips turns up. "But this place, it just … feels like home." She nuzzles her body against mine.

"It feels like *our* home," I murmur, kissing the top of her beanie. "I think Arkansas, or hell, even Idaho, would feel like home if you were with me. But this place, Poppyseed? This feels right."

"Our first Christmas … actually *together*," she says, peering up at me, "and we get to spend it here."

"We do." I slide my hands down her body, burying my face into her neck. "And we get to spend it in a sweet place that overlooks the harbor and the boats. Oh, with a Jacuzzi, where I plan to have you naked by the end of the night."

She giggles. "Sounds nice, but what if some horny fisherman sees me?"

I narrow my eyes at her before nipping the skin of her neck, which I have to work to get to because she's bundled like we're at the North Pole. "You should know by now that I'd make sure they sure as hell didn't," I growl before bringing her mouth to mine. "Actually, I'm not sure I can wait that long. Our condo is a fifteen-minute drive from here, and my cock is straining against my jeans so hard right now that it hurts."

Her head turns to look at me, eyes wide. "Wait, what? Where?"

Jerking my chin up, I nod toward the lighthouse, and she gasps.

"We couldn't. That would be, like … so bad. You can't even get inside of that thing."

"Who said we needed to?" I growl low before lifting her and tossing her over my shoulder.

POPPY

When he finally sets me down, my back is pressed against the lighthouse's exterior. And even though we're no longer in the sunlight to warm my skin, at least being tucked in this crevice blocks the wind.

"You can't be serious?" I whisper as he gazes down at me like he's about to attack. "What if there are cameras?"

"There aren't," he says quickly, narrowing his eyes. "Do you want my cock inside of your tight, greedy pussy, baby? Or are you going to keep pretending like you aren't a whore for my dick?"

My thighs squeeze together, and despite the temperature, my body warms as he steps closer, sliding his hand to my neck and gripping it gently.

"What's it going to be, Poppyseed?"

I don't give him a verbal answer. Instead, I reach down and slide my hand over his impossibly huge bulge, dragging a hiss from his throat.

"Yeah, that's what I thought," he coos before dropping his mouth to mine. His lips are cold, but his tongue is warm, making all the blood inside my body heat up and between my legs ache.

Sliding his hand inside my leggings, he sinks his fingers into my heat, pumping a few times in and out before bringing them to his mouth and running his tongue over them. "Christ almighty, I love the way your pussy tastes when it's dripping and in need of my cock."

A small moan escapes my lips before he pushes my leggings and panties down to give him better access between my legs, and his fingers plunge inside of me again.

"You're fucking soaked for me, and I've barely touched you."

Using his free hand, he brushes his thumb over my bottom lip. "What I wouldn't give to watch you swallow my cock right now. To feel this hot little mouth take every inch of me and watch your eyes water as you gag, needing air. Or to fuck your ass, that tight little hole of yours." He moves his hand to my neck, gripping slightly. "But we don't have time for everything. That'll come later. Right now, I'm gonna take you hard and fast."

Pushing his jeans and briefs down just enough to set his hard length free, he palms himself, making me envious of his hand, and I push it away, replacing it with my own.

"Jealous of my hand, are you?" he growls against my lips, his eyes squeezing shut for a few seconds as I slide my hand back and forth. "You become such a needy little slut when my cock is out, don't you?"

"Yes," I moan as he grips my neck.

"But only for my cock, right?" he growls low. "Only for me."

"Only … for … you," I choke out, and his eyes light up with satisfaction just before he releases his hold.

Lifting me, he presses my back to the building and pushes his hard length inside of me. I whimper as I take him deeper until his hips begin to work in a quicker motion.

His hand fists my hair, and he gives it a pull as he thrusts in and out. "Always so wet. And so tight."

He grunts, and my legs dangle at his sides, unable to keep them clasped around him as his movements grow harder and faster. Just as promised.

Even through my winter jacket, I can feel my spine pressing into the lighthouse. His lips attack mine, moving to my neck. He nips and licks my flesh, making me wince before both of his hands move to my ass, pushing me down harder on him.

At the very moment that I feel my orgasm get closer, his eyes snap to mine. "Gonna come with you, baby. Eyes on me while I fill you full of my cum."

I keep my eyes open, and my vision blurs as I lose control. My body gives in, putting me over the edge at the same time I feel him pulsating inside of me.

His eyes remain on mine, though he shivers slightly. But I don't think it's from the cold.

Moments later, both of our chests heave deeply as we suck in the cold Maine air. And once we both pull our pants up, he cups my cheeks and kisses my nose.

"I love you, Poppyseed."

"I love you too." I smile. "So much."

He suddenly looks nervous, which isn't something Walker James usually shows.

"I know we just got back together not all that long ago, but … don't you think this would be a cool place to get married? You and me?"

I don't think I fully digest his words as I stare at him with likely a dumb, confused look on my face. "Um … yeah? I guess it would."

"So, what if, like … we did?" He swallows hard. "What if we got married here? Just the two of us." He pauses, releasing my face. "I mean, unless you wanted people here. Then, we could have whoever you wanted."

Most of the time, I know where Walker is going with something. But right now, I have absolutely no idea. A few minutes ago, he was spewing filthy words from his mouth, banging me against a beautiful lighthouse. Now, suddenly, he's talking about marriage.

"I mean, to be honest, I've never really wanted a wedding," I say softly, but when I see a frown instantly form on his face, I take his hand. "I don't mean that I don't want to get married. I just mean weddings. All eyes on us. Spending a fortune to show our love for each other in front of a ton of people, who would probably be thinking in their heads that they have better shit to do that day than watch us tie the knot." I pause, smiling at him. "I might not want a wedding. But someday, I'd love to get married."

His frown slowly disappears, and he grins, looking like a geek. "Yeah," he says nervously. "To who?"

Sliding my hands to his waist, I beam up at him. "Oh, you might know him. He's a big deal. He's also the New England Bay Sharks newest center."

"He sounds … pretty awesome." He bobs his head up and down.

"He's all right, I guess." I shrug playfully before I sigh. "Walker, what's this all about? Why are you bringing up marriage?"

He looks around before pinching the bridge of his nose and grabbing both of my hands. "I don't know. I guess I just feel like we've finally got it figured out. The universe is finally letting us just … be together. And we're here. On the rocky coast of Maine—a place I never imagined I'd live and certainly didn't think you'd want to move to with me. But you said it yourself. It feels like home." He gives me a slight grin, showing off that subtle dimple of his I've always loved. "What if we got married tomorrow? On Christmas Day?"

"For real?" I blurt out. "Are you, like, asking me to marry you?"

"I guess I am." He shrugs before he quickly drops to his knee. "Shit, what was I thinking? I have to do this right." He blows out a long breath, keeping hold of my hands, and looks up at me. "I have no ring for you. And I know the traditional way to get married is to have one. And to have a plan. To ask for permission—but we both know you and I don't need permission from anyone. Because we've already been taking care of each other for as long as I can remember."

I can feel the emotion in his voice, which only makes a lump form in my throat.

"Will you marry me, Poppy? Because for my whole entire life, everyone seems to leave or get taken from me. You're one thing I can't afford to lose. Not again."

I smile down at him through my tear-soaked lashes, which I'm sure are about to turn to lash-icles because the temperature seems to be dropping as snow begins to fall from the sky. "Walker James, I would love to marry you." I nod slowly, pulling him to his feet. "I don't care about a ring. I just care about you."

His lips are on mine, and he scoops me up and twirls me around. I feel as light as a feather, like my soul has officially left my body, and I'm flying freely with no risk of hitting the ground.

"Wait," I say, frowning. "Tomorrow is Christmas Day. Who in the world would marry us on a holiday?"

Kissing me again, he winks. "Don't worry. I'll figure it out."

25

POPPY

I t's snowing. Not the kind that stops your plans, but enough that has me and Walker bundled up, trudging back to the lighthouse.

It's Christmas afternoon. And our morning was spent having sex in every crevice of the condo that the Bay Sharks manager set us up in. My favorite spot we christened was probably in front of the fireplace on the faux fur rug.

Pulling me along with him, Walker gives me a small smile before looking forward. We walk along in comfortable silence, preparing to start the rest of our lives together. Legally.

I have no idea who the person is he found online to marry us. I'm just trying to push the feeling of sadness out of my brain that Jake isn't going to be here.

I didn't want a wedding, but it feels strange to get married without Jake.

"You sure about this, Poppyseed?" Walker says, bringing my hand to his lips. "I mean, if you run now, I'll probably buy a camp somewhere in Maine, go off the deep end, change my name, buy a bunch of dogs, and never wash my ass again." He shrugs. "Not to pressure you or anything."

"Well, now that you've made me feel bad, how can I run away?" I deadpan.

When his eyes narrow and his gaze snaps to mine, I pat his stomach. "Relax. I'm kidding. Although the fact that you'd stop washing your ass over me is quite flattering."

"Who would it need to be clean for?" He shrugs as we stop along the water's edge. "My dogs wouldn't care if I smelled like ass. Right?"

"I guess so." I laugh. "Whoever this mystery officiant is should be here anytime now."

Looking over the top of my head, he tilts his chin up. "I see him now actually."

I spin around slowly, and my eyes must bug out of my head when I see Jake is walking toward me. Next to him is his girlfriend's mom.

Unable to stop myself, I bolt toward him and throw my arms around him. "Jake! What are you doing here? I thought you were spending the day with Bonnie."

He squeezes me so hard that it almost takes my breath away. Jake always gives the best hugs to those he loves—something I'll never take for granted.

"I am. She is back at the hotel with her dad," he answers, nodding as he releases me. "Bonnie's mom can marry people. So, she's going to help me."

My eyes find Bonnie's mom, Barbara, and I beam.

"You're an officiant? And you brought him here so that he could marry us?"

She nods, looking from Jake to me before she points at Walker. "This guy is the one who made it happen though. I think he knew how much it would mean to both of you for Jake to be here and to have the honor of doing this." She looks at Jake, smiling at him. "So, we got online, and Jake here is now ordained and can tie the knot for y'all." She pats his arm. "Isn't that right?"

His cheeks are rosy red, and he nods his head up and down. "Yes, it is. I can marry people now."

"Oh boy." I laugh as a shiver runs down my body. "Let's get started. Before we all turn to ice sculptures."

"Mine would probably be worth the most." Walker winks. "You know, NHL center and all."

"Your head is getting bigger by the second," I tease him, putting my palm on his forehead. "Ready?"

"Baby, I've been ready for this since we did that pretend wedding in the woods when we were nine." He kisses the top of my head. "Let's do it."

WALKER

Is it crazy that months ago, I was still trying to convince myself I hated this girl? And now, we're hitched? Maybe. No, it is. But the thing is, we've been attached since we were kids. I've loved her for most of my life. And when I didn't know her, I think I was waiting just for her to come along.

So, crazy or not, I don't really care. Because this thing we have? It's forever. And I want forever to start now.

Yesterday, we were lucky enough to find a thrift shop open, and we each picked out a tacky ring for each other. We decided that traditional rings weren't what we wanted. We want to get tattoos instead. That's how sure I am about her. I'm willing to put something permanent on myself for her.

Taking the ring I picked from my pocket, I hold it out. It's not ugly by any means, but it's plain and simple. Yet still stunning.

"I love you the most, P—more than anything in this whole entire world. You are my reason for waking up every day. And my biggest push to be the best and to try harder. You have been since the first time I saw you." He squeezes my hands. "I know to the rest of the world, this probably seems crazy. Two freshmen in college just finally figured their shit out weeks ago, and now, they're getting hitched. But I don't care. Because I've known since the first time I saw you that you were it for me." I chuckle. "I had to literally collect change from everywhere I found to buy you Warheads to get you to talk to me, but that's okay. Because eventually, you knew you could trust me."

A tear falls from my eye, freezing on the way down as I fight to speak through the lump in my throat.

"There has never been a greater feeling than when you look at me and I know you trust me. Doing that is the best gift you could or will ever give me. And I promise you, with everything I have, I will never break that trust." I pause. "I might piss you off some days—that's the truth. But I swear you will always know where I stand. And that's next to you."

She's crying now, looking up at me through her thick, dark, tear-soaked lashes. I know her body, her face, every part of her. I've studied her for years, wanting to absorb it all. But at this moment, right now, I see something I haven't seen before.

I see my wife.

"I'm not an easy person to love," she barely croaks out. "I'm not a fan favorite. I'm not warm and soft. Sometimes, I swear I don't belong in any room I enter. And I usually don't know the right thing to say or when to say it." She gives me a crooked smile. "But you've never cared. You've seen me at my very worst. And you've seen me at my best. There's no hiding from you because you already know everything." She blinks, and a stream of tears glides down her cheek. "You've loved me since far before I ever loved myself.

You saw me when I didn't want to be seen. And, Walker James, I promise that for the rest of our lives, I will make sure that you are seen. That you are loved. And that you are cherished. Because that's what you deserve. We were already family, but I am honored to have your last name now." She sniffles. "I can't believe I get to be your wife. I am so lucky," she whispers. "This life has been good to me. Because it's given me you."

Jake says a few more things, but all I can do is stare into her big green eyes and melt. My heart is thundering in my ears because I know that in a few seconds, he's going to say the words I've been waiting my whole life to hear.

Poppy Wilson is mine. Only she's not Poppy Wilson. She's finally Poppy James.

WALKER
TWO MONTHS LATER

I take my phone out of my pocket and make sure it's silenced just as a message comes through from Poppy. With the show starting in a few minutes, I wasn't expecting any contact from her till after.

Poppy: I put a note in your pocket. Can you please give it to Cade?

I frown at the message. Cade's been home for a week, and Poppy insisted he come to this show, though I'm not sure why.

Poppy: Don't be a jealous butthole. Give him the note.

Me: I wasn't.

Me: I didn't get a note though.

Poppy: Don't be a whiny ass. Love you.

Me: You can make it up to me later. Love you. Good luck.

Reaching into my pocket, I pull out a tiny piece of paper and wonder how in the fuck she got it into my pocket without me noticing. Or without me getting the wrong idea and getting hard.

"Yo, Huff." I nod toward him before waving him over.

Slowly, he stands and squeezes himself past Watson and Ryann. "Yeah?"

Holding the paper out, I scowl. "This is from Poppy. If it's a love letter, you'd better start running right now because I'll beat you senseless and shove that note straight up your ass."

He gives me his usual charming Cade Huff grin. The season truly wasn't the same without this fucking guy.

"Bro, I'm fresh out of rehab. I've been talking about my feelings and crying into my pillow for the last three months. I'm not equipped to fight tonight," he answers, putting his mouth in a flat line before holding his hand out and snatching the letter from me. "Besides, James, I'm a dad now. Poppy knows any crush she could have possibly had on me now means nothing." He shrugs, I glare harder, and he laughs, swatting my stomach. "Relax. I'm joking. I'm joking."

As he heads back to his seat with the note firmly in his hand, I try not to stare to gauge his reaction, but, holy fuck, it's hard.

POPPY

I shake my arms, letting all the tension in my body release from my hands. Or at least, that's the goal. I'm not sure it works.

The performance I'm about to give means more to me than any other dance I've ever done because I'm dedicating my solo to a dear friend—a person I found an unlikely connection with during the worst day of my life.

Cade Huff.

A man who, months ago, was at my brother's, buying drugs while lying to everyone in his life and hiding that he had a problem. A man who could have continued to go down the same path Van did, but got help instead. And now, fresh out of rehab and expecting his first child, he deserves this.

When I heard the song I chose, I knew it was made for people like me, Cade, Van, and Walker—all of us who just feel like we don't belong here, like we're not good enough, like our lives are a circus and we're the opening acts.

And what I've figured out is, that's okay. Because all these experiences, heartaches, and struggles make us stronger; it makes us damn near bulletproof.

When I took that scrap of paper and grabbed a pen, I wanted to keep it simple while also letting Cade know that he had made an impact on my life just by being himself. And by showing me that even the most lost souls can be found.

I close my eyes, trying to imagine Cade right now while he reads the words. I hope it doesn't trigger him in any way or make him feel uncomfortable. But it's just something I needed to say.

Cade,

I know you're not the most serious guy I know. And you know damn well that I'm not one to get all touchy-feely and shit. But, Huff, I want you to know, from the bottom of my heart, I'm so proud of you for getting help before you put your parents through what Jake and I went through with losing Van.

This song and this dance are for you. Because, Cade, sometimes … being human is hard. And sometimes, it feels like it'd be easier to give up. But just know that your baby will be so happy that his dad chose not to do that.

Love,

Princess Poppy

The tears fell from my eyes as I wrote the letter to Cade. When I found out he was going to be a dad, I was a bit worried because that's a lot of pressure, especially for someone fresh from rehab and trying to stay sober. But I know in my heart he will be the best dad.

When the dancer before me ends her performance and the curtain closes, I make my way to the center of the stage. Moments later, Shinedown's "A Symptom of Being Human" begins to play, and the curtain opens.

Every lyric in this song hits me so deep in my core that it physically hurts. But at the same time, it's almost as though I can feel the pain melting away, lifting from my body and floating into the air in dark, thick clouds. I feel lighter than I ever have, my eyes filling with tears as I do what I was born to do. Dance. Let the music take me where it wants to.

I don't always feel like I belong in a room. Or that I'm wanted in a place. And I've been burned, and I've burned bridges—lots of them. I've been hurt, and I've hurt others. I've stared at myself in a mirror and cursed my own existence. I've looked at someone else and wished that we could trade places. Even if that wouldn't be fair to them. And I've taken out the pity card more times than I can count and asked myself, *Why me?*

But the truth is, if it wasn't me, it would be someone else. Maybe someone who would have given up long ago. So, I've kept going. And fought back. And as corny as it is ... I think the little girl who was curled up, scared, and crying when I was younger would be proud of the woman I am right now.

I didn't need a man to define me or make me who I am now. But Walker James isn't just a man. He's a best friend. A protective shield. An ally. A constant reminder that I'm not in this life alone.

And I can say that without him, I'm not so sure I would have made it out of my childhood alive. And if I had, I sure as hell would have been a lot more jaded than I am.

So, I let myself let go. I let go of everything holding me back, and I vow that from here on out, I won't focus on the bad parts of me or my life. Even on the days when the darkness creeps back in—because it will. It never goes away completely. And maybe that's a good thing. Maybe it's there to remind me that we don't have to be just our sad stories. We can be both.

We can be whatever we want.

The song slowly fades out, and I look out at the crowd. My eyes land on Cade, and I give him a small smile and nod. Because people like Cade, Van, Walker, Ryann, and heck, even Sutton Savage ... they've all felt pain. And yet they fight on.

We fight on.

"I don't think I've ever cried to a dang lyrical routine, bitch," Ryann sobs, pulling me against her as I walk backstage. "Damn you."

I sniffle, giggling at the same time, and hug her back. "Sorry. Good thing you already performed. Otherwise, that perfect makeup of yours would have been ruined. And you know I couldn't help you."

Releasing me, she laughs. "Yeah, that's an understatement. You'd make me look like Bozo the Clown or probably poke my eye out on accident." She puts her hands on my shoulders and sighs. "That was beautiful, Pop. I've seen you dance many, many times. But that was by far my favorite. It was almost like that song was meant for you to dance to. You were stunning."

"Thank you," I say with a smile. "I just wanted to take something sad and turn it into something ... I don't know."

"Beautiful?" she answers, raising her brows. "Because, baby girl, that's exactly what that was." Her eyes narrow a little. "Was it for anyone in particular?"

"It was for a friend," I whisper. "It was for him. And Van. You, me. Hell, even Sutton." I chew my bottom lip. "We're all human."

"Okay, you are not about to make me cry again. Why am I so freaking emotional today?!" she groans and grabs my hand. "Let's go see our husbands, shall we? I got a glimpse of mine from the stage, and yummy. I'm going to climb that man like a tree."

"Too much info." I shake my head, holding my hand up. "I do not need to know any details about you and Watson Gentry."

"Your loss." She shrugs before pulling me along.

When we enter the hallway, I immediately spot Walker standing next to Hunter and Sutton. Next to her is Cade's soon-to-be baby mama, Haley, and Cade himself. Ryann spots Watson immediately, leaping into his arms, and somehow, he catches her in time, and they start making out, giving absolutely no fucks that we're all watching.

Walker sees me right away, but when Cade approaches me first, he stays back. He might joke around about being jealous of Cade, but I know that deep down, he's kidding. He knows that Cade and I just have a weird bond through my brother and his death.

"Princess Poppy," he drawls slowly. "You know I'm not much of a crier. But that shit had me all choked up."

My lips turn up in the smallest smile as I take in my friend, looking at him almost as if he's someone else. Because he sort of is now that he's clean and sober.

"Felt like it was an appropriate song choice." I pause. "For both of us."

He pulls me in for a hug, and I breathe him in. Because this is the first time since Cade left for rehab that I've seen him, and he looks so good. And healthy. And for reasons I don't understand, hugging him makes me feel like … just for a second, Van is here, even if that makes no sense.

Life sometimes doesn't make sense. Van didn't get a second chance to be better. He's just … gone. Meanwhile, Ron has done some unthinkable things, and he's still alive to tell the tale of each of them. And, yeah, Cade Huff will be an addict for the rest of his life. Even after he's been clean for years, he'll wear that title. But unlike Ron—who got out of jail months ago for a total of two weeks before he was caught dealing drugs again, and this time, he'll be in there for a long, *long* time—Cade Huff is a good person. A great man. And he will be a wonderful father.

Keeping his arms around me, he squeezes. "Something one of the counselors told me in there is that we don't have to be the person we were yesterday. We can be whoever we want." His voice grows thicker. "I've chosen to get my life together and be the man my baby and Haley deserve. And you, Princess Poppy, you've chosen to let go of all that anger inside you." He releases me, stepping back. "It's written all over your face, you know? You look like you feel lighter now." He smiles. "And I'm so fucking happy to see it. You're too good of a person for people to think otherwise."

I cringe. "I was sort of an asshole for a while, huh?"

Holding his fingers up, he pinches them together. "Maybe just a tad. But it's all right. You and me? We're going to be better now." He glances over at Haley, who stands next to Walker. "And I think, deep down, we both know that even if it's us putting in the work to make sure of that, we should be thanking them. For giving us a reason to want to be better in the first place."

Walker's eyes find mine, and my vision blurs with tears.

"One thousand percent," I whisper.

Because he's right.

WALKER

"Can't believe this is our last game together," Elias sighs. "Best not fucking lose. That wouldn't be a way to go out."

"No shit, Sherlock," Nixon mutters before looking up at me. "Gonna suck without you, my dude."

"You'll both be getting that call soon." I nod sharply. "I know it."

"Yeah, once Gentry's gone, I will actually get to play," Nixon mutters, only half joking.

Link walks into the room, gazing around at his team. As the team captain, he's led his team here tonight. To this Frozen Four.

"This is really it." He sighs. "This is the last time a lot of us will be sharing the ice together. Because after four years of proudly wearing the colors gray and blue as a Wolf, this is my last season."

He nods toward Hunter. "Thompson's headed to the NHL, and I have no doubt he's going to kill it."

His eyes find mine, and his lips turn up the slightest bit. "Our rookie turned out to not be so much of a rookie after all. And I wish so much that y'all, whose career here at Brooks isn't over, had him coming back next year." He nods. "James, I know I was tough on you, but it's because I knew you could take it. I knew the second you stepped onto our ice that you were the real deal." He shrugs, shaking his head. "Cam Hardy's skates are some fucking ginormous ones to fill. But you did it. You did it with grace too." Walking toward me, he claps my shoulder. "Good luck with my pain-in-the-ass brother though, my man."

Stepping toward Watson, he smiles. "Like me, you've decided to be a Wolf for all four years even though that spot with the pros was secured. It's not an easy choice to make, but you did it so that your mom could see you graduate. You've made Brooks proud, Gentry. It's been an honor to skate with you."

He goes around to each player in the room, saying a few things about them all. Things he noticed that maybe the rest of us didn't. The way a real team captain does.

He stops at Cade Huff, who decided when he returned from rehab that his spot on the team wasn't in skates, laced up. But on the sidelines, coaching.

"Broke my heart, Huff. The day you told me you weren't coming back. Because, hell, don't I love sharing the ice with you. Watching you Tasmanian devil your way through players twice your size." He pauses, and there's no missing the emotion in his voice. "But I think you found your place. A place that lets you still be a Wolf on your own terms. And this program is so fucking lucky to have you." He pulls him in for a hug, slapping his back. "You're the strongest person I know, Huff. Proud of you."

Maybe hockey players aren't supposed to tear up or get emotional. But as I watch two of the best players ever to play college hockey both wipe their eyes, I say fuck that. Crying means they are human. And Sterns is right. Cade Huff is the toughest, most resilient man I know too.

Last for Sterns to talk to is Coach LaConte, who is barely keeping it together as it is.

"I think I speak for every other dumbass in this room when I say that you are the best coach any of us could have asked for. Truly." He waves his hand toward the room. "We are family. All of us. Do we work on the ice well? Hell yeah, we do. Do other teams fear meeting us in the arena? Fucking right, they do. But it's not just about that. It's about this, right here." His eyes move to the rest of our team. "It's about the bond we have. As Wolves." He looks at LaConte. "And that's because of you. For you believing in us. Pushing us. Treating us like family and giving us tough love when we need it. So, thank you, Coach. I've had a hell of a good time playing on your team."

Coach quickly wipes his eyes and pulls Link in for a hug, pounding his back a few times and muttering something in his ear before he releases him.

He quickly looks around at his team, doing his best to hold it together. "I'm very proud of each and every one of you. Some of you I'll see next season, and others I won't." He smiles sadly. "But every one of you will have a great hockey career. Whether it's on the ice or coaching." He inhales, pausing for a moment. "All right, enough with this touchy-feely shit. Let's go out there and win this thing."

We all begin tapping our sticks against the floor, chanting, "Wolves, Wolves, Wolves."

The energy in this locker room is palpable. We all want this win for different reasons, but equally as fiercely.

I've had a great year at Brooks. But winning tonight would be a pretty great way to end my career as a Wolf.

Just as we begin chanting, Cam Hardy and Brody O'Brien walk into the room, and the entire place goes crazy as they both give their signature grins, throwing their arm around players as they walk by.

"I thought I got rid of you two pains in the ass," LaConte says, but we all know he's full of shit.

Even if Cam was a pain in the ass, he's his son-in-law now. So, he'll never get rid of the guy. And O'Brien was the dude whose charity event we had to pair up with the dancers for. If LaConte hadn't had a soft spot for that guy, he sure as hell wouldn't have signed his team up for that. Besides, I'm not really sure anyone could truly not like either one of them, to be honest.

And that's coming from a dude who got compared to Hardy all season.

Cam approaches me first, giving me a head nod. "Been catching a few of your games online, James. I'm not sure why those reporters spent so many weeks busting your balls about filling my skates." He widens his eyes. "I think you had them fuckers filled up in week one."

I'm a pretty chill dude. Not much gets me overly excited, and I'm definitely not one to grin like a fourteen-year-old who just felt his first boobie. But right now, that's probably exactly what I look like.

Because if a player like Hardy thinks you're good, you can fucking quit now. You're finished. All has been achieved.

"Comin' from you, that means a whole fucking lot." I pat his shoulder. "For real. You're, uh … someone I look up to more than I could ever explain."

"I hear you're headed to the Bay Sharks," he says, smirking. "You know, that's not too far from Boston. We'll have to meet up and shoot around a bit."

"For sure." I nod, probably far too eagerly, so I try to remind myself to play it cool and not look like Cam Hardy's next stalker.

Which I'm not. Even though he's pretty fucking awesome.

"Well, we'll let y'all get to it," he says smoothly just as Brody comes beside him, grinning like an absolute fool.

"For as many times as I watched your interviews and heard Cam Hardy Junior, you don't look a whole lot like my friend Cam," he jokes, jerking his thumb toward my face and looking at his friend. "Walker James is handsomer." He winks. "Younger too."

"Well, that's just rude." Cam frowns, looking me over. "My wife thinks I'm the handsomest man in the world. So, I guess it's fine." He pouts a little, and Brody throws his arm around his shoulders.

"And Isla, my dude. Can't forget our main girl. She thinks you're handsome too. Because that's a daughter's job. To tell her dad he's handsome."

"I am handsome," Cam utters, looking at me again. "James just has, like … really nice hair."

Brody nods in agreement. "That he does." Reaching forward, he holds his fist out, and I bump mine to it. "Good luck tonight, James. Go light them up."

"I'll try my best." I nod just before they turn and head out of the locker room. But not before fist-bumping every player in the room once again.

The two of them left behind a legacy. I can only hope I can do the same tonight. Because after the clock runs out, it's time to say good-bye to Brooks. And to this team and Coach LaConte. But before I do that, I need to play my heart out and make them all proud. Because being a Wolf has been one of the greatest achievements of my life.

And I'm sure going to miss it.

Poppy

It's crazy when you love someone so much that their happiness becomes yours. And when their dreams come true, it feels like it was your dream all along.

That's exactly how I feel right now, watching Walker and his team all crash against each other. Champions. That's what they are.

A few days ago, I found out I was accepted into Casco Bay College for the fall semester to study dance. And even though I'll miss my friends here at Brooks, I'm more than ready for the move, especially now that I know that Bonnie's parents are going to check in on Jake and Bonnie, who are sharing an apartment.

Out of all of this, one of the things I'm most thankful for is that Jake is happy. And all his dreams are coming true too.

I don't think people who had childhoods like Walker and I did are ever healed. We just sort of … find a way to push through the pain and find our happiness. Those feelings of abandonment, grief, loss, and painful memories will always stay with us. And some days, they feel extra heavy. But I guess they make the bright days seem brighter.

Because when you've lived in the dark, the light … reminds you that the pain won't last forever. I've started to trust that after the rain, that's when the sun comes. Eventually.

Walker beams up at me, grinning from ear to ear, and I can't help but bounce on my feet. So excited for him and his team in this moment.

I love you, I mouth.

Ryann bumps her hip against mine when he does it back. "Look at you, being all sweet and sticky. Like a marshmallow."

"Ooh, she is a marshmallow." Sutton nods in agreement. "I never thought I'd see the day."

Next to Sutton sits Haley, who pays no attention to our conversation, but instead watches Cade as he celebrates with the other coaches.

Cade and she aren't together romantically, but I know he'll do the right thing and be a good dad for his baby. I also know that he loves Haley more than anything, and one day, they'll figure it all out.

"How are you feeling, Haley?" I ask, leaning forward to look at her.

"Fat," she says, her lip forming a flat line before, eventually, she smiles. "But I'm so happy for Cade and the guys. They all deserve this."

I look from her to Cade and nod. "Yeah. They sure do."

In just a few months, we'll be in a brand-new state with a fresh start. And I know my husband is going to keep reaching his dreams when we get there.

And I can't wait to watch.

WALKER
SEVEN MONTHS LATER

Patting a towel to my forehead, I toss it in the hamper before unlacing my skates. Being a college hockey player was hard. *Really, really* fucking hard. But playing in the pros? It's a whole other level of hard. But I welcome it because the team I'm on is a great one. And I'm proud to be here, wearing their colors.

Maine has this deep sense of community. Something Poppy and I have really enjoyed doing since we got here is going around to schools, recreational centers, and even homeless shelters. We take boxes and boxes of food and even sometimes clothing and sports gear, and we listen to people's stories. We talk to kids about their dreams. We sit with a homeless man who tells us about his life's best and worst days. It's not all happy. A lot of times, we go home feeling like we're not doing enough. But somehow, when I step onto the ice here in Maine and the crowd cheers so loud that it fills the entire arena, waving their signs … it reminds me how fortunate I am that I get to do what I love for a living.

It could have easily been either of us in the homeless shelters we've visited. And the kids we've seen in the schools with the long, dirty, shaggy hair and the worn-out clothes? We were those kids. We walked in those footsteps.

They aren't easy footsteps to trudge along in. And only the strongest will make it. And I guess we just want to do what we can to help more of them make it. To be like Poppy, who's chasing her dreams and attending a dance program and running a nonprofit to fight to get the number of yearly overdoses down. Or to be like me. Even though I sometimes still feel like that kid playing hockey on Sunset Drive, I'm now getting asked for autographs, and people pay to see me play.

Tossing my skates in my bag, I look up to find Logan in a deep conversation with our coach. Logan's face is pale, and he rests his back on the wall and stares off into the distance. After a moment or two, the coach pats his shoulder, and Logan heads toward me, sitting down on the end of the bench.

"You good, man?" I ask, not wanting to push too hard for information, but just letting him know I'm here.

He's quiet for a few seconds, focusing solely on the ground before him.

"No," he whispers. "Coach just got a call from someone." He pauses, his hands shaking. "A girl I hooked up with a while back just died in a car accident."

"Oh shit, man," I say quickly. "I'm sorry."

"No, that isn't all." He finally looks at me, and I can see the fear in his eyes. I can't predict what's going to come out of his mouth. "She was pregnant. And they were able to get the baby out safely somehow." He swallows. "Her parents … they are saying the baby is mine."

I stare at him in complete shock, not knowing what to say or how to say it because I can't imagine the thoughts going through this man's head.

He drags his hand over his head and squeezes his eyes shut. "I could be a dad, James. To a kid whose mother I can hardly remember sleeping with."

Holy. Fuck. Logan Sterns is about to be a single father.

THE END

Are hot, single dads your thing? Preorder Logan Sterns's book now!

Need a change from hockey? Preorder Hudson and Briar's book, a bodyguard/Mafia story, now!

Want more Puck Boys? Binge the entire series now!

Read on for a sneak peek into Logan Sterns's book, *Tell Me Lies*.

This is book one in the New England Bay Sharks series. And I promise, you won't want to miss this single-daddy romance.

LOGAN

I stare through the glass window as a nurse walks around from baby to baby, doing some sort of exam. I feel like I'm in a dream. Or maybe a nightmare. The faint sound of machines beeping in the hallway and the smell of hospital cleaner usually bother me. Right now, my brain is too numb to even think about it all.

"She was on her phone and …" The brunette sniffles, wiping her eyes. "I guess she wasn't paying attention and pulled right in front of oncoming traffic."

I hear her talking. The girl who is the best friend of the woman I now have a child with. A woman who … is dead. I hear her voice, sort of. But nothing makes sense.

I'm nobody's dad. I'm Logan Sterns. Right winger for the New England Bay Sharks. I was on the cover of *Sports Illustrated* last year in a briefs campaign. A photo shoot that got me more ass than an airport toilet seat. I'm fierce on the ice. Feared even. But I'm a good time off of it.

I can't be a father. I wouldn't know the first fucking thing about it.

"Are you going to, you know …" she begins to say but pauses. "Be able to care for her?"

Her.

As in my baby. A baby I didn't even know existed until an hour ago.

The nurse gets to *her*. My daughter, apparently.

And after a few moments of examining her, she glances up at me nervously. When she looks me in the eyes, I can read the pity all over her face. She feels bad for me because she thinks I lost someone today. Judging by the way she's looking at me, she's hurting for me.

But I'm so much of a piece of shit that I can hardly remember hooking up with this woman.

A woman who is dead.

I look at the baby again, watching her mouth open before she brings her fist to her lips.

I don't deserve to be her dad. When she's older and she asks me about her mom, I won't even know what the hell to tell her.

She sucks on her tiny fist before she scrunches her face up in a look of pure disgust, and tears fill my eyes out of absolutely nowhere.

My phone buzzes in my pocket, but I can't pull myself away from watching her.

The nurse pokes her head out the door. "Mr. Sterns? Would you like to hold your daughter?"

Putting my palm on the glass, I lean closer. "I … I don't know how. I … I might drop her. I've never—"

Taking a few steps toward me, she gives my arm a pat. "You're going to do fine." Turning around, she points to a vacant room with a bed and a recliner in it that is right next to a large picture window. "Go on and sit in there. I'll bring her to you."

For a moment, I freeze. My feet stay in place, and I can't move. But when I see her walking back into the nursery and slowly lifting her up, my feet take me toward the other room, and I sit down in the recliner just as she brings her in.

The nurse makes it look so easy. Then again, she's in her late fifties, I'd say, and she's likely done this for a long time. Looking at her name tag, I take note that her name is Judy.

"Just relax, love," she whispers with a smile before slowly setting the bundled-up baby in my arms. "Support her neck. You're doing just fine."

I look down at her, and I feel … everything. Her eyes are closed, but she squirms slightly, trying to get her fist back into her mouth.

"She's hungry, it seems." Judy chuckles. "I'll go get you a bottle. And before you panic, don't. I'll give you a feeding and burping lesson." She pauses. "She still needs a name, you know."

My heart races, and I feel panic soar through my body. But when Judy leaves and the baby's eyes slowly open, even though it's clear she can't look directly at me, I dip my head down closer.

"It's all going to be okay, baby girl. I promise." I kiss the top of her head, feeling tears spill from my eyes and down my cheeks. "I don't know the first thing about taking care of a baby, but I promise … I'm going to protect you with all that I am." I breathe her in before looking at her again. "Amelia," I whisper. "That's your name."

I study her more before giving her another kiss, this time on her cheek. "It's just you and me, Amelia. You and me."

OTHER BOOKS BY HANNAH GRAY

NE UNIVERSITY SERIES

Chasing Sunshine
Seeing Red
Losing Memphis

READ IT NOW!

BROOKS UNIVERSITY SERIES

Love, Ally
Forget Me, Sloane
Hate You, Henley

HEAD TO THE BROOKS UNIVERSITY FOOTBALL-VERSE!

FLORIDA EAST UNIVERSITY

Playing Dane
Stealing Bama
Catching Kye

BINGE THE SERIES TODAY!

THE PUCK BOYS OF BROOKS UNIVERSITY

Puck Boy
Broken Boy
Filthy Boy
Chosen Boy
Lost Boy
Perfect Boy
Last Boy

MEET THE OTHER PUCK BOYS NOW!

acknowledgments

What a ride this series has been. And sadly, this time … it's really over! I know; I know. You all probably expected me to add another surprise puck boy at the end. But all good things must come to an end, I suppose. But I have so much gratitude for the characters in these stories. Not only have they taught me so many lessons and challenged me to dig deeper, to give their stories justice, but they have also found me so many new friends and readers. As most of you know, I often choose topics that might not be shiny and easy to write or read. But every one of my books has a happily ever after. Proving that love really does conquer all.

First, I want to thank my husband and my kids because they are the reason I do this. I love you all so much. You are my whole world.

My mama—I love you so much. Thank you for always being my biggest cheerleader. If I could be half the mom to my girls that you have been to me and my brother, I'll think I've done well.

Thank you to my dad for instilling in me long ago that if you want to see your dreams come true, you have to work for it. And to always remember that nothing happens overnight. I love you lots.

Thank you, Autumn, who has been with me since the beginning of my writing career. You believed in me when I had no works behind me. No one knew my name or my pretty covers. I was just … Hannah Gray, aspiring author. Thanks for sticking by me and holding my hand as I navigate through this ever-changing industry.

My fabulous editor, Jo, at Unforeseen Editing—This is book sixteen, and I have loved working with you on each and every one. Thank you for being patient with me. Especially in the times when I didn't have a clue what I was doing. (Still don't most days!)

Sara Stewart—Thank you for keeping my TikTok from having tumbleweeds blowing through it. Your love and support have meant so much to me!

Candice Butchino—Thank you for listening to my five thousand voice messages each day. And for always cheering me on, but giving me constructive criticism when I need it. I am so thankful I have you on this author journey!

Sarah Grim Sentz—I adore you. I love your work, and I love how beautiful your brain is! I can't wait to work with you in the future!

Amy Queau—Thanks for always being so easy to work with and for making my model covers so sizzling hot!

Amanda Mudgett—Thank you for making some gorgeous edits and helping me create a badass PR box! I love and adore you so much, and I'm so happy the book world brought us together.

Thank you, Jaimie Davidson, for always dropping everything to be an extra set of eyes for me when it's crunch time. I love and appreciate you so much. I can't wait to meet you in Kentucky!

And thank you so much to my readers. Without you all, I wouldn't get to continue doing what I love. I have met so many incredible souls in the book world, and I am forever thankful to each of you. And I am so excited for all that's to come!

about the author

Hannah Gray spends her days in vacationland, living in a small, quaint town on the coast of Maine. She is an avid reader of contemporary romance and is always in competition with herself to read more books every year.

During the day, she loves on her three perfect-to-her daughters and tries to be the best mom she can be. But once she tucks them in at night—okay, scratch that. Once they fall asleep next to her in her bed—because their bedrooms apparently have monsters in them—she dives into her own fantasy world, staying awake well into the late-night hours, typing away stories about her characters. As much as she loves being a wife and mom—and she certainly does love it—reading and writing are her outlet, giving her a place to travel far away while still physically being with her family.

She married her better half in 2013, and he's been putting up with her craziness every day since. As her anchor, he's her one constant in this insane, forever-changing world.